FALL FOR ME

FALL FOR ME

BOOK 1: THE TATE CHRONICLES

K. A. LAST

www.kalastbooks.com.au

K. A. Last
kalast@kalastbooks.com.au
www.kalastbooks.com.au

ISBN: 9780994217585

Book and cover design by KILA Designs | www.kiladesigns.com.au

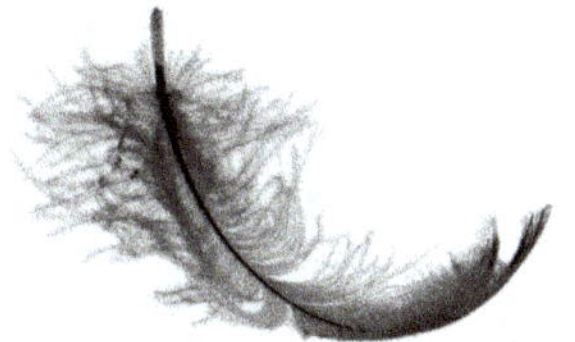

For Katrina, because you were there from the start.

My only love sprung from my only hate!
Too early seen unknown, and known too late!
Prodigious birth of love it is to me,
That I must love a loathed enemy.
William Shakespeare – *Romeo & Juliet, Act I, Scene V*

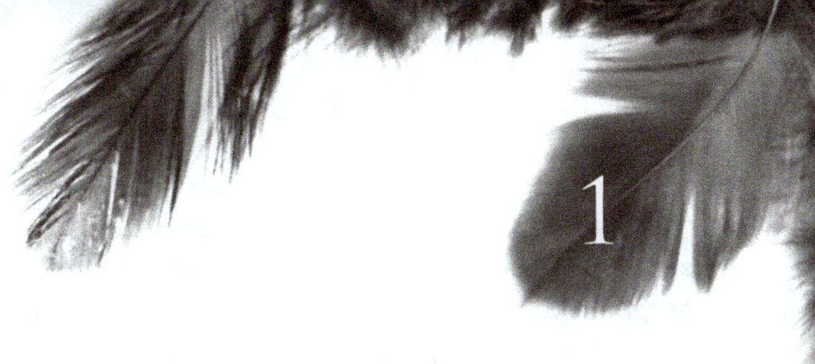

1

England, 1642

The stars twinkled above as we raced through the castle. We were not permitted to stay long—only until our task was complete.

On Earth everything was tangible and unique, but back home the realm was an endless white void where everyone existed in unison. We loved our home, but once the magnificence of this world had been experienced, it was hard to go back.

Over the years, Grace and I had been sent on many missions, but I was sad because this would be our last. In Heaven, falling in love was forbidden, and coming to Earth was the only way I could be close to her.

The sound of Grace's giggle as she ran ahead brought a smile to my face. It was like a beautiful melodic bell chiming inside my head. I followed close behind, taking note of the way her dark hair flicked out behind her and caressed the nape of her neck. I imprinted in my memory every line, and every curve of her body, because I wasn't sure if I'd ever see her again. Grace turned to glance over her shoulder, and I caught a glimpse of her radiant face, her sparkling sapphire blue eyes and perfect porcelain skin. She was beautiful and heavenly, and I loved her.

Keeping my feelings from her was the hardest thing I'd ever had to do, but making the decision to leave was harder still. She couldn't know my intentions. She'd want to come with me and I wouldn't allow it; I couldn't let her make that sacrifice. We were best friends, and I was closer to her than I had been to any angel I'd known. But where I was going there was no turning back, and she didn't deserve that life. It would be better to live without her than to stay and live with her just beyond my reach. I couldn't do it anymore. I couldn't risk Grace's existence to satisfy my own.

She grabbed my hand and pulled me into a small stone alcove. Her touch was warm and spread happiness through me, consuming me like a burning fire. Touching her always made me feel like I was home.

"We have to go back now," she said.

Yes, we did, but I didn't want to leave. Not yet. This would be the last time I saw her this way, possibly the last time I would see her at all, and I wanted the moment to stretch on forever.

"A few more minutes," I said. "I'm sure they won't mind."

"They see everything. We should be back already."

Grace was right; she was always right. For a moment we stood gazing into each other's eyes, and I wanted what I couldn't have, wanted it so much it hurt. I almost told her there and then exactly how I felt, but instead I hardened my heart.

"Fly with me first?" I said.

Grace hesitated, then smiled and nodded.

I slid my hands around her waist, and she rested her head on my chest. Closing my eyes, I sent my orbs of light around us. The tiny glowing spheres swirled until they joined together and we left Earth, bound for the Outer Realm. There we could fly freely without the risk of being seen.

We flew side by side, twisting and turning in unison, so in tune with each other that no words were needed. I knew exactly what Grace would do before she did it.

A gentle breeze made by the flutter of her wings caressed my arm and sent a shiver through me. She was magnificent, and even more so with wings spread wide. Grace shimmered in the night sky, beautiful and silvery white. It took all my strength not to kiss her. I longed to feel the silky smoothness of her feathers beneath my fingertips, to hold her close, and it broke my heart knowing that when she arrived home, I would not be there.

We danced and twirled. Grace's giggle floated amongst the stars which twinkled brighter as she passed. I wished we could stay like that for eternity, happy and free, but I'd made my decision, and the time had come to let her go.

We should have been back already, so I reached for Grace and took her into my arms. For a moment I savoured her touch, drew in the fresh scent of her hair, which smelt like summer rain, and relished the way her body seemed to fit perfectly with mine.

We were together for the last time. Grace lifted her

head, and I looked deep into her eyes. She pulled back and I could tell she was about to ask what was wrong; she always knew when something wasn't quite right. Struggling to hold it in, struggling to hide my emotion, I lost the battle, and a tear trickled down my cheek. Grace reached up and caught it in the palm of her hand where it sat glistening, then solidified into a diamond. Before she could speak, I said the words I'd been waiting a long time to say.

"I renounce you and all your ways."

The expression Grace held was one that would haunt me for the rest of my life, and I hated that I'd made her look that way. She shook her head and tried to grab for me, but I was already slipping away. I had no way of telling what was in store for me, or what my fall would be like.

Grace's angelic face faded into the distance. She became a blur at the end of a long, black tunnel, and I could see her lips move as she called my name but I couldn't hear her. Before long Grace was a distant memory, and I was surrounded by a cold, heavy blanket of darkness.

2

GRACE

Present day, late Sunday night

Crouched in the scrub, with rocks digging into my knees and bracken fern tickling my nose, I could think of much better ways to spend my Sunday night. Then again, it was how we spent most nights.

"Archer, get your head down," I said. "Have you forgotten everything Pa taught you?"

"Chill out, Grace. This one's not too bright."

I rolled my eyes in the darkness, knowing he could see me. Excellent eye sight was a genetic inheritance and came with the job description.

Our target stood with his back to us about twenty metres away, striking a defensive pose. He was alone—they usually travelled in pairs or more—which was why my brother was being so careless.

"Easy, Arch. He'll find us if you're not careful." I put

my hand on his arm.

Our subject knew we were there but couldn't quite pinpoint our location. He'd be able to hear Archer's heartbeat and smell him, too, but not enough to accurately follow his trail. In-built defences also came with the job description.

"Come out, come out, wherever you are," he said. "I can hear your little hearts beating; there's no use trying to hide."

Archer scoffed under his breath. I parted the ferns and looked at the figure through the darkness. The moon was bright, but the dense canopy above blocked most of its light. The guy we were up against hunched over, ready to strike. He flicked around in one swift motion and I stared into a pair of deep black eyes, as black as death itself.

"I think he's seen us, Arch," I said.

"Really? You don't say."

The man sped towards us, his dark figure a blur between the trees, and in less than a second he closed the gap. I used my gift and orbed us to where the guy had stood a second before. Travelling via a ball of light was pretty cool, and the ability to do so came in quite handy.

Our target growled, angry he'd been outsmarted.

Archer and I stood side by side, smiling in the darkness. A breeze wafted through the tallowwoods and rustled their branches, allowing a little more moonlight to shine through.

"You," he said, snarling.

"Yes, us." Archer laughed.

"There were rumours your lineage died out. I didn't

think it was true."

"Yep. Unfortunately for you, we're still here."

In a flash, the man came at us again. I gave him top marks for bravery, or was it stupidity? Archer spun on his heel, and I smiled as he drew his weapon from his belt, stabbing our victim in the chest. Archer was right; this one wasn't too bright, pretty much running straight into the stake. He turned to dust and fell to the ground in a heap.

"Fancy that, thinking he could take us on." Archer shook his head.

"You're getting too big for your boots, you know?" I turned to walk back towards the shed. "Dad would've been proud of you, though." I playfully punched Archer's arm as we walked. "Maybe not the attitude, but your skill is second to none."

Archer smiled slyly and pushed me hard. Before I hit the ground I orbed and came round to land in front of him. I shoved him in the chest with both hands and sent him flying backwards.

"You don't take compliments very well, do you?" I put my hands on my hips. "And you know I'd kick your butt in a fight."

Archer laughed, jumped to his feet and brushed himself off. But the smile on his face faded quickly.

"Do you miss them?" he asked.

"Who? Mum and Dad?" I frowned. "Every day."

"I just thought … I don't remember much about them. And you've been doing this for so long. Aren't you used to it?"

"I'll never get used to watching my family die."

7

Archer pressed his lips into a tight smile. "Good thing we have a few more years then, before it's my turn."

I sighed, not wanting to think about how my mission worked. Every generation of the Tate family bore a son, the Hunter, and a daughter, the Protection Angel. That meant Archer was human and could get himself killed. I helped train and protect each generation before I was born into the next, usually a short time before my brother and I hit twenty-five, and the cycle went on … and on. More than a hundred and fifty years later it gets a little repetitive, but I knew what I'd signed up for, so I couldn't complain.

"Are you looking forward to tomorrow?" I asked, changing the subject. Archer fell into step beside me as we walked down the rocky path towards home.

"Let me see, school. That would be a no." Archer rubbed his chin.

"Come on. It's our final year, then we're out in the big wide world."

"In case you haven't noticed, Gracie, we're already in the big wide world."

That was true, and I hated being called Gracie.

I stopped in my tracks and grabbed Archer's wrist. Something was wrong; I could feel it. To avoid making a sound, I spoke in his head.

Truck, now, I thought.

He nodded and we scurried over to the old Bedford farm truck that was rusting away in our carport. The rickety structure sat on the edge of a clearing that made up the centre of our property. The carport had enough space for five cars, but only three were in use. The far spot was occupied with various pieces of farm junk that had accumulated over the years; another housed our black Defender. The big truck in the end space hid us in its shadow.

Moonlight streamed into the clearing. Three figures on the far side stood on the edge of the darkness, and their voices travelled to us easily on the breeze. I listened carefully but couldn't hear any names floating around in their thoughts. I didn't know who they were; I did, however, know what they were talking about.

"She's close," one voice said.

"Good, I'm getting sick of chasing her. Is she really worth all this?" said another.

"Of course she is," the third one said. "She's the key to everything. Just think how powerful we'll be."

Key? Archer thought.

I shrugged. *They're after a pretty blonde girl.* Her face flashed through their thoughts and I showed Archer with my mind.

The three figures sped away in a blur of motion.

"More vamps." I got to my feet. "I haven't seen them around before."

"Well, they won't last long." Archer stood as well. "We'll take care of them."

I wasn't in a hurry to chase them. We'd catch up with them sooner or later. Besides, we'd done enough hunting for one night, and we needed some rest.

After I took a few steps, the hairs on the back of my neck stood on end. Archer froze, sensing something, too. I whipped around to face the way we'd come, then flung my right hand in front of my chest and caught a wooden stake before it could pierce through my skin and reach my heart. Its sharp point tore a hole in my black top, but the cut it made on my skin healed almost instantly. There went another top, though; I was getting tired of having to replace my clothes.

Crouching just off the path, shielded by the ferns and undergrowth, was a slender figure dressed in black. Her face was perfectly pale and surrounded by wavy strawberry gold hair. The girl's black eyes glistened in the moonlight, and I gasped at what they revealed. Before I could gather my thoughts and even think about delving into hers, she was gone, another blur through the trees.

"What was that about?" Archer said, letting out a long breath.

I frowned. "She threw a stake at me. Does she think I'm a vampire?"

Archer shrugged.

I let my arm fall to my side. "She's the one those vamps are after." I stared into the forest.

"If she's a vamp, and she thought you were a vamp, why was she trying to stake you? I didn't think they killed their own kind."

"They don't." I turned towards home. "It's like an unwritten law."

What I didn't tell Archer was what I'd read in her eyes. She was different, and in all my years I'd never seen a vampire like her.

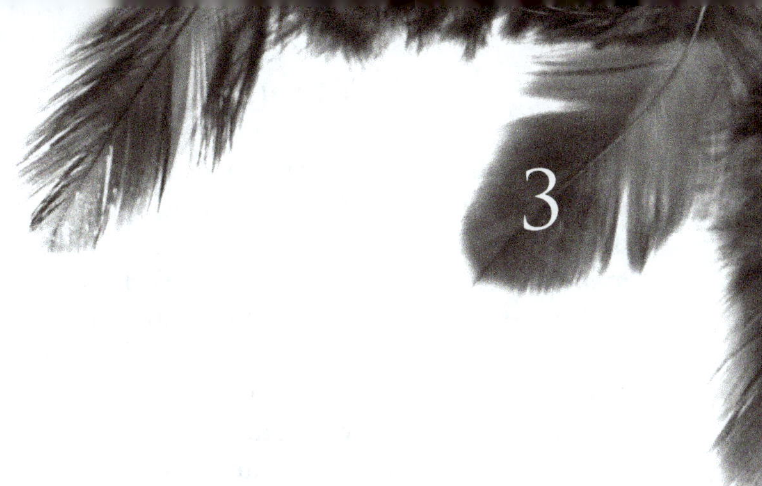

3

GRACE
Monday morning

The feeling was always the same—the elation I felt when the cool breeze brushed my face. My hair trailed behind my head, and my white dress fluttered in the wind, gently flapping against my thighs. I dove elegantly through the air, relishing the faint rustling noise my wings made as I descended, never wanting it to stop. But it would, as it was how most of my dreams ended. If only I was out there flying for real, something I didn't get to do often.

My dreams were a way of consulting with the Council. I never knew when they'd come, but I had them pretty regularly. It was Heaven's way of checking up on me to make sure I was toeing the line. After spending so many years on Earth, I didn't always do everything by the book, but so far I hadn't gotten into too much trouble.

I rubbed the sleep from my eyes and propped myself

up on my elbows. After the fog in my head cleared, I threw my legs over the side of the bed and wrapped my summer dressing gown around my shoulders. I bounded down the stairs from the loft two at a time, hurried across the shed, and burst out the door into the fresh morning air. As I walked briskly across the clearing to the seemingly neglected weatherboard cottage that stood on the other side, I hoped Archer wasn't already in the shower.

I was in luck. The warm water was heaven on my skin, and I let it wash away all the tension in my body. I wished I could stay there all day, but eventually I turned the taps off and stepped out to get dressed. When I walked back into the shed, Archer was not alone.

Wards of the state—that was what we'd technically become after Pa died. I didn't mind as long as we got to stay together and on the property. This was agreed to on the basis that we had a social worker visit every week. This morning was one of those visits.

Our social worker, Annie Sage, was quite an attractive woman with friendly brown eyes, but she wore her chestnut-coloured hair pulled tightly back in a bun, giving her face a sharp, angular look. She was dressed in a smart cream suit and low heels, and had a delicate silver chain around her neck. It sat as if there were something hanging from it, tucked inside her blouse.

Annie sat across from us at the old Formica table which stood on the kitchen side of our shed. I'd lived on the Tate property for well over a hundred years. Originally we'd been in the tiny two-bedroom weatherboard cottage on the other side of the clearing. When the house had gotten to a certain stage of disrepair, the shed had been built in the early 60s. It had never been fitted out properly, comprising of one large room with the loft split into two as our bedrooms, but we loved it.

Archer and I were already in our uniforms—there was nothing like grey and navy to brighten your mood—waiting for Annie to start. Archer had so lovingly left me with the job of answering the usual questions. *Are you eating right? Is there enough money? Are you being responsible? Are you both happy?* Blah, blah, blah. We were two seventeen-year-old kids living with no parents. Did she think we were happy? Happiness would result when we were free of the system, which would be in one week. Our eighteenth birthday couldn't come soon enough as far as I was concerned.

"All seems to be in order, then," Annie said. "Archer, you're doing a great job of looking after Grace. I'll let you two get to school."

I shook my head when she'd left, and Archer hid a grin behind his hand.

"Ha! Looking after me indeed," I said. Archer laughed. "It's me who's looking after you." I pointed my finger at him. "And don't you forget it."

Annie had no idea I could flatten a mob of angry men in less than a second with one swift flick of my wrist.

"Come on, Arch, let's go. I call driving."

"Hey, not fair! You know I can't get to the car as fast as you."

"Not my problem." I smirked.

I orbed into the front seat of the Defender and waited for my slow coach brother to catch up. He slumped into his seat and pretended to ignore me.

"Come on, look on the bright side. It's another week before we have to see Annie again." I turned the key in the ignition. "You can drive home."

No response. *Grow up you big baby,* I thought. That put a small smile on his face.

"You don't play fair," he said.

"Since when is life fair, Arch?"

The Defender bumped down the long dirt driveway towards the road. I turned right, and we headed east to school and the small country town of Hopetown Valley. Dense forest lined the highway, and our driveway could only be seen if you knew it was there. The drive took all of ten minutes from door to door. It wasn't really long enough to have a decent conversation, especially when my brother was being an idiot.

"What's the deal with that girl last night? She was pretty cute, for a vamp," Archer said.

"I'm not sure, but I know we can't kill her."

"What? Cute or not she's still a vampire, Gracie. We kill them. It's what we do, in case you've forgotten."

"It's not that simple, and I really hate it when you call me Gracie."

"What's not simple? Vamp, stake, dust."

"She's different."

"Oh no you don't—do not go all political on me. It's us and them. There is no in between."

"Oh look, we're here. Can we talk about it later?"

"This conversation isn't finished," he said.

I swung the Defender into an empty spot in the student car park at Hopetown Valley High. Before jumping down onto the gravel—I was five-feet two-inches, and a little vertically challenged—I threw my brother a look that said, *it's over for now.* I grabbed my bag from the back seat and flung it over my shoulder, then walked the short distance to the school's main gate. I loved that gate—big wrought-iron arches held up by beautifully carved sandstone pillars. I couldn't say the same for the two Moreton Bay figs that flanked it, though. They gave me the creeps. I never really knew why—there was something about them that sent shivers down my spine.

"Remind me again why we had to be here so early?" Archer said.

I led him across the yard towards the school cafeteria. He wouldn't stay mad at me for long. He was a good fighter and tough on the exterior, but deep down he was a big softie.

"It's the first day of the year. And breakfast."

"You've got to be kidding," he said.

"No. I like the food here."

"Everything tastes like cardboard."

"Yes, but while eating said cardboard the view is great," I said, with a skip in my step.

Archer raised his eyebrows. "You know you can't, Gracie."

"I know. But just because I'm window shopping doesn't mean I'll make a purchase."

He laughed and gave me a playful hug. Archer was very protective and had spent a lot of time through our high school years fending off potential suitors. I'd never really been interested so it wasn't a problem.

I was completely focused on my mission and the task at hand.

At least, I used to be.

Fight the bad guys; keep the good guys safe. Simple, right? Yeah, that was what I'd thought until I'd noticed Joshua Chase. The problem was he had a girlfriend. So not only was I lusting after Josh, but the object of my desire was already in a relationship. *Thou shalt not covet thy neighbour's wife,* or in this case, boyfriend. If my memory served me correctly that was a big no-no for anyone, angel or human.

4

JOSH

Boarding school was the ultimate test. I swear the idea was created by some mad lunatic scientist who wanted to experiment on the cause and effect of teenage life experiences. I was glad to be starting my final year as I didn't think I could take much more. No escape from school was every teenager's nightmare, and I envied the students who got to walk out the front gates at the end of the day. Living in the country was great, but it definitely had its drawbacks.

The drive from our property near the small town of Flats End took a couple of hours. I lived on a cattle farm with my dad and spent most holidays helping him out. We wound along the highway as fast as the old ute would go, and that wasn't very fast. The scenery was breathtaking and had a calming effect. I liked staring out the window and watching the hills roll by.

I needed to be calm because today was the day I planned to break up with my girlfriend. I wanted to let her down gently, and I'd spent the Christmas/New Year break rehearsing what I would say, but running over the words in my head wasn't helping my nerves. She was going to hate me.

Even though Abby lived across the creek, we'd only seen each other twice since school let out last year, and neither of those times seemed right to break it off. I was beginning to think that no time would be right to tell her I didn't want to be with her anymore. I was actually hoping she'd get the message from being ignored.

"You okay, Son?" Dad asked as we rounded another bend. "You seem a little distant."

"Abby," I said. "I'm going to tell her …"

Dad chuckled but smiled at me warmly. "The ups and downs of teenage relationships."

"Three years, Dad. Do you think I'm throwing everything away?"

"That depends. Do you love her?"

"I thought I did, but not anymore."

"Then no," Dad said.

We spent the rest of the trip in silence. The early morning air had been crisp when we'd left home, but when I stepped from the ute onto the school's gravel driveway, heat settled on my skin. It was going to be a hot one.

"Well, another year. Your final year," Dad said as we stood at the big wrought-iron front gates of Hopetown Valley High School.

"Yeah, final year," I said with a tragic half-smile. I

pulled my suitcase from the ute's tray and threw my backpack over my shoulder.

"Hey, come on, Josh. I thought you liked it here."

"I do, Dad. It's just with Abby and ..." I trailed off.

"I know. I miss her, too."

Dad knew that my mum's death still affected me, even though she'd died more than seven years ago. He thought I hated coming to Hopetown Valley because I didn't want to leave the farm and him. That was mostly it, but not the entire reason. Mum was buried in the school's cemetery, and I preferred not to have her so close. It wasn't that I didn't love her. She'd been a great mum; it was just distracting. I wouldn't be able to stay away from her grave again this year and I'd be there more than I should.

"See you at term break," I said, giving him a hug.

Dad drove away and I pulled my case towards the gate. The monotonous drone of the cicadas' song surrounded me and a magpie stood on the gravel with one clutched in its beak. Oh, to have a simple life, like a magpie or a cicada ... but maybe not the cicada, since it was being eaten. I passed through into the school grounds and instantly heard a familiar voice.

"Josh, you're here." My girlfriend, Abigail West, walked quickly towards me. "I've been wondering when you'd show up." A huge smile covered her pretty face. She threw her arms around my neck and gave me a tight hug.

"Here now," I said, giving her a quick half-hearted kiss on the cheek. I prised her off and continued to walk towards the boys' dorm.

"I came in last night," she said, then jabbered on about some new girl and how she thought she was weird and

God knew what else. I blocked her out.

"Joshua Chase, are you listening to me?" Abby stood in my path and put her hands on her hips.

Short of pushing her out of the way I was forced to stop, too. Her platinum blonde hair flowed loosely over her shoulders. She looked more confused than angry, and for a second I wondered why I'd made the decision to break up with her. Then it all came flooding back. Abby may have been beautiful, but she was shallow and we had lost our spark. I was an accessory to her—something she could show off to her friends. There was no love in our relationship, and it had taken three years for me to notice.

"Abby, I want to get to my room and unpack."

"But I didn't see you much over the break. Josh?"

Oh boy, this was going to be harder than I'd thought. But how did you tell your first love, the girl you'd spent the last three years with, the girl that you first ... that it was over? The way she looked made me wonder if I should go through with it, but I needed to stay focused. Now was probably as good a time as any to say what I'd rehearsed.

"See, here's the thing," I said.

Her face fell and her beautiful features contorted into a crumpled mess. "You're breaking up with me, aren't you?"

My prepared speech flew out the window. I had absolutely no idea what words I should be using. What could I say? Nothing was going to change the way I felt, or how much she was going to hate me.

"I can't believe we're breaking up," Abby said.

Her hands shook and tears spilled down her cheeks making her mascara run. I hadn't even said anything and she was already crying. The good guy in me wanted to take her in my arms and hold her until she stopped, but it would only make it worse. These things had to be done like ripping off a Band-Aid—quick and in one smooth motion.

"I'm sorry, Abby. I just … don't think we should be together anymore."

I left her standing on the path to the dorms, angry with myself for being an arse to her. But how did you break up with someone nicely? I walked past a few other students and I was pretty sure they could hear the sobbing. It was loud. Claudia Spencer, Abby's best friend, came down the girls' dorm steps staring at me. She glanced from me to Abby, and back again, then frowned.

My jaw ached from clenching my teeth. I climbed the front stairs to the boys' dorm. The housemaster, Mr Bruner—who also happened to be my soccer coach and P.E. teacher—looked up from behind the front desk. We had the usual 'How was your break?' conversation while I signed in. He also proceeded to remind me of the rules, the same way he did every year. I nodded in all the right places, then trudged off down the hall to the stairs. As long as I signed in and out and got ticked off the class roll, no one would bother me too much.

My case bumped up the stairs. Room twenty-nine sat on the top floor, and as a senior I was lucky enough to have it to myself. The juniors were the ones that had to share, and I was glad my sharing days were over.

Everything was the way I'd left it the year before. The bed was freshly made, but the walls were still plastered with posters of Maradona, Harry Kewell, and Kelly Slater. There was a big difference between soccer and surfing, but I loved them both. Obviously living in the country put a slight limitation on the surfing.

Mr Bruner had left my timetable on the bed. I picked it up, had a quick glance, and noticed my first weekly chore was to empty the common room bins. There were worse things; I could have been given bathroom duty.

After dumping my case in the corner, I sat on the edge of the bed and put my face in my hands. What had I done? How was I supposed to go back outside and face Abby? To stop myself from punching something, I stood back up and paced the room. Training was what I really needed. Kicking a soccer ball was a fantastic stress reliever, especially when I pictured someone's face on it, but training didn't start for a few days. I stopped in front of the mirror and stared at my reflection for a moment, running my hand through my messy dark brown hair.

The dorm rooms at Hopetown Valley High were like shoe boxes, but I was amazed at what they managed to fit into them. Each room was identical and consisted of a small cupboard, a sink with a mirror, a single bed, and a desk. I went to the window and watched the movement in the yard. Students on their way to breakfast—cafeteria food was another great joy of boarding school life.

Then I spotted her. She was with her twin brother.

Grace Tate.

There was something about the way she moved that mesmerised me. I'd just broken up with my girlfriend of three years, but the truth was I'd been watching Grace for a while. We'd been at school together since the seventh grade, although she probably didn't even know I existed. Our conversations never really consisted of more than saying hello in the halls.

Grace was beautiful but in a completely different way to Abby. She had an ethereal presence. I loved the way her short black hair stuck out oddly all over her head, and her eyes were two perfect pools of blue. As far as I knew, she never dated, even though she could take her pick. Eventually, the guys at school had stopped trying. The answer would always be no, and I wondered if she knew I'd had a crush on her all those years ago. Maybe now she'd start to take notice since we were all a little older.

She was attached at the hip to her twin brother, Archer, who sometimes seemed a bit over-protective. He was kind of intense, and Grace didn't strike me as a girl who needed protecting. Plus, they didn't even look like twins; they were different in so many ways it wasn't funny. He was tanned with sandy brown hair and hazel eyes; she was blue-eyed and perfectly pale, like porcelain. Grace wasn't a boarder either, and I wondered why she was here so early. I wouldn't be if I lived only ten minutes from school. I'd probably be late every day.

Eventually I tore my eyes from the window, threw my suitcase open and dug out my grey pants and white school shirt. They were a little creased, but after a few good shakes they'd do. I shrugged out of my T-shirt and jeans and got dressed. Then, after attempting several times to knot my school tie, I gave up. I still hadn't mastered it after the first five years of high school so I probably wasn't going to be able to now. I left it hanging around my neck, flipped the lid to my case closed, grabbed my back pack and left for the cafeteria.

Hopefully I'd run into Grace.

5

GRACE

The cafeteria sat on the far side of the yard. It was modern, tacked onto the sandstone wall of the school's main building. The interior was open and bright, thanks to the big windows and high ceiling. It wasn't too busy. There were just enough students inside to emit the low hum of conversation through the room.

Archer and I stood in line for our food. Only two students were in front of us—some guy I didn't know and Abigail West, Hopetown Valley High's popularity queen. Oh yeah, and she was Josh's girlfriend. Abby was slim and athletic with a perfect cheerleader's body. It was nauseating. She was nice enough, but we didn't have anything in common. I was about to say hi, then thought I'd skip the risk of a conversation involving high heels and lipstick.

Instead, I turned to Archer and said, "What are you having?"

24

"Just an apple."

"An apple? You could've grabbed one at home."

"It's probably the only thing that doesn't taste like cardboard," he said.

We took our food, and I followed Archer to our usual seats in the far corner next to the window. The cafeteria gradually filled with more students, and the noise level lifted. Archer and I ate in silence while I scanned the room. Most of the time I didn't listen to people's thoughts, but since it was the first day of school I couldn't help being interested. Everyone was at various stages of peril in their young lives, but no one had anything to really worry about. An eight-grader stood in line saying a quick prayer, hoping she didn't look fat in her uniform. I shook my head and chuckled. If only looking fat was all I had on my mind.

"Are you going to share?" Archer frowned. "Or is it a private joke?"

"Oh, that's right. I forgot you can't hear *everything* that's going on."

"No. Some of us aren't freaks like you."

"So I'm a freak now?" I leaned into him and gave his shoulder a nudge.

"Yeah, but I still love you," he said.

I took a bite from my toast and scanned the room again, smiling at the odd person here and there before settling my eyes on Abby. She sat close to Josh, and his best friend, Ryan, was on his other side. Ryan fell into the 'guy you'd date due to genuine niceness' category. His skin was tanned and his light brown hair fell across his friendly chocolate-coloured eyes. He had a crush on my best friend, Emma, but was too scared to ask her out. It all came down to the different-social-group thing.

Abby talked to Josh in hushed tones, leaning in close to him. I got a slight shock from the way it made me feel. I didn't like seeing them together, and then I took a closer look. Abby was crying, and Josh stared off into space. I focused harder.

Neither of them were vocalising what they were actually thinking. Abby was asking him not to break up with her, but thinking about what she would do without a good-looking guy on her arm. Josh was saying he was sorry when really he wasn't. He couldn't wait to be free of her. Then I heard something else. Did he just say my name? For a moment, my heart froze in my chest then skipped and kept on beating, faster than before. My hands broke out in a sweat and I wiped my palms on my skirt.

Joshua Chase was thinking about me.

I had to plant both my feet firmly on the floor to stop myself tumbling off the chair. Josh was thinking about me; I couldn't believe it. What did this mean? Confusion burst through my head and I had to shake it to clear the fog. Josh raised his eyes and I stared at him, drowning in their blue perfection. I couldn't have torn my gaze away if I'd tried. His messy dark brown hair fell to one side of his sun-kissed face. Heat rose inside me and rushed to my cheeks.

Archer asked me what was wrong, but I ignored him. I stared at Josh, and his expression changed. He locked onto my gaze and a smile spread across his face, reaching his eyes. I couldn't help returning it. Then I heard it again in his head.

Grace.

My heart skipped another beat, or two.

26

6

JOSH

Ryan followed me out of the dorm, drilling me about the break-up. I didn't really want to talk about it, but he insisted. He didn't like Abby and was relishing the good news.

The cafeteria buzzed when we entered. A few groups of students milled around, catching up, I suspected, on what everyone had done over the break. Ryan and I grabbed our food then made our way to our table left of the counter. I'd spotted Grace in her usual seat, next to her brother, when we'd first walked in, but I was attempting to restrain myself from looking in her direction. From the corner of my eye I saw her chuckle and I smiled, wishing I knew what had made her laugh.

No sooner had we sat down than Abby turned up. My guess was she'd already been inside the cafeteria and was waiting to pounce on me.

"Hey, Abby," Ryan said. "What did you do over the holiday *break?*"

"Shut up, Ryan." She pulled out a chair and sat close to me. First she started berating me, telling me off for even thinking about dumping her. Then she moved on to crying, with a few theatrical sobs thrown in for good measure. I tuned her out and Ryan threw me an unsympathetic look that said, *I told you so.*

All I could think about was Grace.

She sat straight across the room but I was too nervous to look up. What if she caught me staring at her? It was torture. With my arms folded on the table and my head slightly bowed, I dared a peek at Grace.

She was looking.

My heart leapt to my throat.

Slowly, I raised my head and met her gaze. I became lost in her eyes. Everything else around me no longer mattered and all I could see was her. Her black hair framed her pale angelic face, and her cheeks glowed. *Grace,* I thought as a smile spread across my face.

What I saw next was the defining moment in my mind—the thing that helped me to make the decision I did. She smiled back, and it was like the light from a thousand suns illuminating her. Not just her face but her, all of her. I'd found my reason for breathing, for existing. It sounded clichéd, but she was the one.

"Ouch!" I said, turning to Abby. "What was that for?" I rubbed my arm where she'd just pinched it.

"You aren't listening to me."

"I'm not either," Ryan said.

Abby scowled. "What were you smiling at? I'm trying

to have a conversation with you." Her eyes followed where my gaze had been and a funny noise came from her throat. Did Abby just growl at me? Next she'd be hissing like a cat and scratching my eyes out, or maybe Grace's.

I leaned back in my chair and rubbed my face then quickly stood up. I'd had enough.

Loud enough so pretty much everyone could hear, I said, "It's over, Abby. We're done. I don't have anything else to say to you. Please, leave me alone." As I walked to the door and out into the yard, I realised how much she'd actually gotten under my skin. I wanted to punch something again.

"Hey, Josh, wait up." Ryan came up behind me. "You really gave it to her in there. Everyone's buzzing. This will go down in Hopetown Valley High history as the public break-up of the year."

"Thought you'd be happy," I said.

"No, seriously, dude. I just want *you* to be happy, and you weren't with her."

7

Our locked gaze broke when Abby pinched Josh's arm. I watched and listened as Josh very publicly stood and told her it was over. I may have appeared just as surprised as everyone else on the outside, but inside I was jumping for joy. His relationship with Abby was over, and he'd been thinking about me!

Josh left the cafeteria with Ryan in his wake. Then my gaze fell on Seth Brone. He sat with his cronies near the door, his handsome face plastered with a sly smile that didn't touch his dark eyes. He'd been listening in. Not to me—he couldn't do that without me knowing—but to Josh. Seth leaned forward onto the table and I stared at the intricate pattern of the Celtic cross tattooed to his inner left forearm.

Seth was my polar opposite. We'd been close friends a long time ago, before his fall, but that had changed, and I still didn't know what had happened. He'd made a choice I didn't understand, and I hated him for it. I worked hard to block the memories we shared, which was difficult since he'd been following me almost the entire time I'd been on Earth.

It looks like you'll be joining me soon, Seth thought.

Not a chance.

Oh come on, Grace, you can't fool me. Admit it—we're too much alike.

I am nothing like you, and I would never join you.

We'll see. Seth's laughter rang through my mind. *You know you can't stay away. That's the beauty of us, Grace. We have forever.*

Archer spotted Seth across the room and predicted our exchange. He could see I was a little rattled and put his hand on my arm.

"Ignore him. We're better than he is."

I gave my brother a tentative smile. "I know. He just gets under my skin sometimes."

Around us everyone talked about the recent break-up. Josh and Abby were both popular people, and what was high school without gossip?

"Okay, Arch, as much as I love you and want to spend every moment with you, I'm going to find Emma before class starts."

"Are you okay?" he asked as I pushed my chair back.

"Seth is nothing, you know that."

"No, I mean Josh."

I didn't know what to tell him on that subject. We both knew the rules.

"I saw the way you two were looking at each other

before," he said.

"Nothing could possibly come of it, so why think about it?"

"Just don't do anything stupid."

I chuckled and shook my head as I walked towards the cafeteria doors. If anyone was going to do anything stupid in the Tate family, it would be Archer.

When I reached the door, Seth and his two creepy sidekicks stared at me again. Ivan and Blake were also fallen angels, but there was something different about them I couldn't quite put my finger on. The only difference between them I could see was that Seth wore a ring on his right hand, like all angels did, but Ivan and Blake had no rings, and I was yet to work out why.

With no regard for school rules they all wore ripped black jeans, black T-shirts, and the white school shirt unbuttoned over the top. I guess actually wearing the school shirt was a step in the right direction, if those boys could even go there. We'd all been at Hopetown Valley High since the seventh grade, and I was actually surprised they hadn't been expelled for one reason or another. They'd earned their bad boy label at an early stage, and most students steered clear of them for obvious reasons. They were plain creepy.

I wouldn't let Ivan and Blake intimidate me, though, or Seth for that matter. They weren't as tough as they made themselves out to be. I walked out the door and cringed, not because they scared me, but because they disgusted me.

My knuckles rapped on the door to room number nine in the girls' dorm, and I waited for Emma to answer. The first bell for the day rang and the hallway went from silence to mayhem instantly. I raised my hand to knock again, but before my knuckles connected Emma's door swung open.

"Hey, Grace, how's your morning been?" Emma rushed out, slamming the door behind her.

"Just great. We had a visit from Annie."

"Ugghh." Emma shuddered.

"Then Josh and Abby broke up."

"Oh … well that's interesting. What's it been, like three years?"

I nodded, but didn't say anything further. I definitely was not a gossip girl.

We didn't waste time talking about the Christmas break. I'd taken the two-and-a-half hour drive to Emma's place at least twice a week, and she'd come to the shed a couple of times as well. Instead, as we crossed the yard to class, she told me about the new girl in the dorm. Emma was in the middle of a detailed description when something hit me on the shoulder and sent my bag flying. A normal person would've been rattled, but I'd copped worse. It was really only a tap. I turned to tell the person nicely to watch where they were going, but faltered when I saw who it was. Heat rushed to my cheeks as I looked at the very person who could be my undoing.

8

JOSH

Ryan and I walked in silence the rest of the way back to the dorm. The first bell for the day rang, causing a flurry of movement. The next bell would ring ten minutes later, so I got a move on with everyone else and headed back to the yard. The place was alive with activity—students hurrying here and there, attempting to get to class on time. I had my head down with my nose in my timetable, so I didn't see her until it was too late. I clipped Grace on the shoulder and sent her bag flying. She didn't seem too rattled, which was kind of odd. Our eyes connected. A brilliant smile unfolded across her face, and her cheeks flushed a radiant rose colour on her pale skin.

"I'm sorry, Grace. I wasn't watching where I was going." I picked up her bag.

She reached out to take it. "It's okay."

Our fingers brushed, spreading warmth up my arm

that made me tingle all over. Why did this girl have such a hold over me? I was vaguely aware that Grace's friend, Emma, stood beside her, but my eyes were fixed on Grace and I couldn't pull them away even if I'd wanted to. She was mesmerising.

"What have you got first up?" she asked.

I almost forgot how to talk. This was more than the usual 'Hi Josh'.

"English, I think." I consulted my timetable again.

"Great. Us, too."

"I wonder what Mr Martin will have in store for us this year," I said, and then kicked myself for not finding something better to say.

"Only good things, I hope." Grace chuckled.

I couldn't help smiling and laughing as well; her radiance was infectious. Emma cleared her throat loudly, and Grace and I both looked at her.

"In case you haven't noticed, that was the second bell and we are now late."

I glanced around the empty yard. We all turned and hurried towards the main building. We climbed the big stone steps and entered through the large double wooden doors. When we got to our English classroom, Mr Martin was already at the front of the class and had begun the lesson. He watched us disapprovingly as we came through the door.

"Nice of you three to join us." He squinted through his large wire-framed glasses.

Mr Martin was the classic image of an English teacher with his slightly balding head, bushy beard, and tweed jacket. I didn't get his reason for wearing it when it was at least twenty-seven degrees Celsius outside.

We walked quickly to our seats in the dreary, musty-smelling classroom, and Grace and Emma took their places in the back next to Archer. I sat in the only seat left, which was roughly in the middle.

"Now that we're all here," Mr Martin began, "we can discuss our first assignment. I trust you are all familiar with the works of Shakespeare."

Most of the class let out a unified groan. This was the twenty-first century, and although I didn't personally have anything against Shakespeare, I didn't particularly like his work either, probably because I didn't understand it.

Mr Martin dropped a copy of a brick-like book on every desk. This book was big enough to be covered in fabric and used as a substantial doorstop. He passed me, and I risked a glance at Grace who looked at her copy with sheer admiration. She smiled as she held the book in her hands, treating it as if it were made of gold. Obviously she liked Shakespeare.

"Your task," Mr Martin said, as he returned to the front of the room, "is to study two of Shakespeare's tragedies—"

More groaning reverberated around the class.

"Which ones?" a voice said from the front. "Didn't he write, like, heaps of plays?"

"Yes, he did, but if you had let me finish you would have heard me say that I will narrow it down for you. We will be watching renditions of *Macbeth* and *Romeo and Juliet* over the next week or so."

The class erupted into chatter, with a few more protests thrown in for good measure. *That's just great. Boredom*

101, coming up. I put my face in my hands then waited for Mr Martin to continue.

"Your task," he said again, over the noise, "will be to write an essay on the differences in character relationships."

Essay? Differences? Boy was I in trouble. How could I possibly write about something I had absolutely no hope of understanding? I played soccer. Ask me to explain a two-touch pass, or how to narrow the angle, and I was your man. Ask me to decipher Shakespeare and I'd offer you a brainless, blank expression. On the plus side, I'd broken up with Abby and didn't die in the process, and Grace had talked to me. Maybe the rest of the day wouldn't be so bad.

9

GRACE

Shakespeare, I could hardly contain my excitement. Mr Martin dropped a copy of *Shakespeare's Complete Works* on my desk and I held it in both hands, marvelling at its beauty. So much was written on those pages. Through my lashes I noticed Josh stealing a glance at me, and it made my heart skip. I heard him thinking he didn't like Shakespeare, or rather, he didn't understand it.

"We will start with *Macbeth*," Mr Martin said as he put the DVD in the player. "This movie is a modern representation and runs for almost two hours. We will watch as much as we can today. You may think this is a nice relaxing start to the new school year, but please pay attention." He dimmed the lights.

The credits for the 2007 Australian version of *Macbeth* danced across the screen. I sighed and made myself comfortable, making sure I had an unobstructed view of Josh. He rested his chin on his hands and already looked a bit baffled.

I let my mind wander, imagining what it would be like to have Josh hold me, running his hands through my hair and down my back, caressing my soft lips with his. A shiver shot down my spine, and I shook in my seat. Of course this could never happen, and I quickly snapped out of my fantasy.

With one eye on Josh and the other on the screen, I rested my chin on my hands as well and went back to watching the movie. I knew it by heart but still loved it, and when I heard Archer stifle a yawn I looked at him disapprovingly.

What? he thought at me.

Pay attention. You're supposed to be able to understand this version!

He rolled his eyes. *I don't care how modernised it is; it's still Shakespeare.*

What was it with boys? Could they not appreciate good literature? I shook my head. Emma doodled on her note pad and paid no attention either.

When the bell signalled the end of class, I picked up my bag and walked with Archer and Emma across the yard. The school hummed around us with a pleasant vibe, and the heat of the summer sun shone down on us. We entered the cafeteria for morning break while having a heated discussion about the movie so far, and I was losing, two against one. I must have been naïve to think Emma and Archer would enjoy the contemporary version with guns blazing. It seemed the old-fashioned dialogue was lost on them.

"The only thing I give it credit for is Sam Worthington and his hair," Emma said, laughing.

"And the witches," Archer said. "Hot."

I groaned and gave up, accepting defeat. Today's world was just too far removed, so I decided to change the subject. "Who's this new girl everyone's talking about?"

"There's a new girl?" Archer asked, putting his arm around my shoulders.

"Yeah, I saw her this morning," Emma said. "Blonde, tall, and gorgeous. Just what we need—another good-looking sort to put the rest of us to shame."

Emma was a little touchy about her looks. I couldn't see the problem; she was pretty. She wore her mouse brown hair in a straight bob, and her hazel eyes always had a nice sparkle. I tried not to listen to her thoughts too often, but she was self-conscious about her glasses, and the bit of extra weight she carried. I didn't care. I thought she was beautiful anyway.

I didn't continue with the new girl questions because I didn't want to upset Emma. Instead, I quickly looked in her head, just for a glimpse of this girl. What I saw almost stopped me in my tracks, but I pulled myself together in time as a ripple of shock surged through me. Archer felt it and tightened his arm around my shoulders. The familiar dark eyes and strawberry gold hair, that perfectly pale face, floated into my head. It was the girl Archer and I had seen at the property. Now I was really confused.

"You guys better get to class." I ducked out of Archer's embrace. "I've got a free. I'll see you at lunch."

I stopped at the cafeteria counter and grabbed a muffin,

picking at it as I headed out the door. Archer would have more questions now, and I didn't have the answers yet.

The students were mostly expected to spend their free time studying, but few of us did. There was a special place I liked to go to think, or just exist, without any interruptions. I strolled across the school grounds to the sandstone outer wall and followed it until it finished in the far corner. No one really went down there much. It was too out of the way, which was exactly what I wanted.

I skirted the edge of the trees, found the path I was looking for, and ambled down the narrow, worn trail. It opened out to my favourite spot and I dumped my bag, taking a seat on the rock ledge. I gazed across the valley at the contrast of the blue summer sky against the browns and greens of the landscape. The school sat on a beautiful country hillside on the outskirts of Hopetown Valley, with the coastal town of Macquarie Cove about an hour's drive to the east.

I twirled a twig between my fingers and recalled the image of the blonde girl. I wasn't exactly sure how she could be at the school. She was a vampire, and the vamps in my world didn't come out during the day, but I had a theory. Archer was not going to be happy when I told him why we couldn't kill her. He was so focused on ridding the world of as many vamps as possible.

With my attention back on the beautiful view, I decided to change the course of my thoughts. At the outcrop, I could forget about my problems. An image of Josh formed in my mind and I sighed, closing my eyes. Imagining his touch on my face, how warm it would be, sent a quiver through my body. But the realisation that my desire could never be fulfilled saddened me. I was marred with the curse of an angel on Earth, able to offer unconditional love, but forbidden to receive a deep, passionate love in return. My purpose was to protect, not get involved with trivial human experiences. I needed to pull myself together and look at the big picture, continue the fight. But I was sick of fighting.

The sound of a twig snapping sliced through the silence, and my eyes flew open. If I could have died, I would have done so on the spot. Josh stood at the mouth of the path. I inhaled sharply, scrambled to my feet and took a step away from him. What was I supposed to do? There was no security of having other students around. I felt exposed and vulnerable. We were completely alone, and I didn't know if I could control myself, but I guessed there was only one way to find out.

10

JOSH

English had passed in a blur. I'd attempted to pay attention to the movie, but I didn't try too hard. It was so boring. The contemporary Melbourne setting didn't fit with what came from the actors' mouths, and with no solid understanding of Shakespeare, I was lost. There was that, and the fact I couldn't stop thinking about Grace.

By the time class had ended, I was out of sorts and very thankful I had a free next period. Back home I loved to go walking in the paddocks to clear my head, and fortunately Hopetown Valley High had its very own beautiful landscape. After ditching my backpack, I ambled out into the grounds. The walk to the outcrop took less than ten minutes, but I made my way there slowly.

The countryside was glorious at this time of year. I loved the heat of summer and the way the sunlight glinted off everything. With my hands in my pockets, I found the first path that led to the outcrop. Lost in my own world, I walked the trail until I came to its end.

I heard a little gasping sound and looked up to see Grace sitting on the outcrop. She hastily got to her feet, tucked her hair behind her ear and knotted her fingers together.

"I'm sorry," I said. "We seem to keep bumping into each other. I didn't think anyone would be here." I didn't want to intrude, so I smiled then turned to leave.

Secretly, I wished she would call me back. I wanted to spend some time with her. I walked as slowly as I could without making it obvious I wanted to stay, and waited for her to say something.

I'd nearly given up hope when she spoke.

"Wait, Josh."

My heartbeat quickened and I turned to face her. I tried to move my mouth to say something, but no words would come. Instead, I stared, completely and utterly spellbound.

"Do you come here often?" I finally asked, taking a few steps towards her.

"Yeah, I love it. It's peaceful." Her shoulders relaxed.

"It's a beautiful spot." I took another step closer. Her eyes were a little red. "You've been crying?"

"It's nothing." She shook her head and looked down, fiddling with a delicate silver ring on her right hand. Flowing curves surrounded a sapphire as blue as her eyes. The curves looked like wings.

Not knowing why she'd been crying troubled me. I hated to think someone had hurt her, but who was I to demand such information in the first place? Grace didn't know me well enough to confide in me, and yet I was drawn to her.

My heart pounded in my chest. For a split second it occurred to me that Abby had never made me feel this way, and I felt guilty for how I'd treated her.

"You know, you shouldn't beat yourself up about it," Grace said.

What on earth is she talking about?

"I saw what happened with Abby this morning," she said quickly.

"Oh, that. Yeah, I probably should have been nicer."

"Sometimes we think with our head, not our heart."

I chuckled. "Why have we never had a conversation before?"

"Different circles I guess."

We stood in silence for what felt like an eternity.

"I really like you, Grace." I closed the gap between us.

We were as close as we could be without actually touching. I sensed that Grace was a little nervous and it excited me, having that effect on her. At least we felt the same about each other, or I thought we did. The warmth emanating from her was amazing. Little sparks of electricity flew between us. She took my breath away, and all I could think about was her.

"I like you, too," she said.

"Remind me again why we've never really spoken?"

"Um … Abby. You know, your ex-girlfriend."

"Who?" I asked with a smile.

Grace looked up at me—she was almost an entire head shorter—and for a brief moment I thought I saw apprehension in her expression.

"What is it?" I raised my hand to tuck a lock of hair behind her ear. She closed her eyes and pushed her cheek into my palm, and her warmth spread through me.

"I shouldn't be here with you," she said, her eyes still closed.

I put my other hand on her back and pulled her close. "Why? Why not?"

She put her palms on my chest and I gazed into her eyes. Behind their beautiful sparkle was a hint of sadness. "I can't explain it to you, Josh. I just can't."

I didn't think either of us knew what to say. I bowed my head and pressed my forehead to hers, wishing I could hear what she was thinking.

What I did next was probably the single most stupid thing I'd done in a long time. I should have let the moment be, but instead I ruined it. The glorious kiss I'd imagined in my mind never eventuated. When I leaned in to gently brush her lips with mine, she quickly turned away and stepped out of my embrace.

"I'm so sorry," she said. Her hand flew to her mouth. "I can't." Tears welled in the corners of her eyes and she blinked them away.

I was pretty sure my expression displayed exactly how hurt I was, and all I could do was watch her run to the path, taking the broken pieces of my heart with her.

11

GRACE
Monday, lunchtime

I couldn't believe I'd called out to Josh. What was I, crazy? This guy had me trembling with emotion and it wasn't allowed, so I'd called him back. Way to go, Grace. What a good way to dig your own grave.

Josh was like an open book as he walked towards me. I could hear the thoughts bouncing around in his gorgeous head. I had to admit I liked them, but he was wondering why I was upset. How was I supposed to explain that? *I'm crying because I'm an angel, and if I fall in love with you I could be damned forever.* Maybe not the answer he'd be expecting.

He held me close, our foreheads touching, and we stood on the rock ledge with the valley spread out before us. Josh's breath was warm on my face, like a thousand tiny kisses caressing my cheek. I knew what he was about to do before he did it, and I also knew I couldn't let him. Josh leaned down, intending to kiss me, and I turned my head away.

I didn't want to hurt him, but a sickening, falling feeling overcame me and I quickly took a step back. Dread pooled in the pit of my stomach, and I had a theory why. I was about to break the rules. It was a warning.

My hand flew to my mouth. "I'm so sorry. I can't."

The hurt and confusion in Josh's eyes tore my heart in two, and I had to muster all my strength to pick up my bag and run towards the path. My shoulder lightly brushed his arm on my way past, and I felt the warmth his touch left behind. Tears blurred my vision and I fell, cutting my knee on a rock. I picked myself up and continued on. The wound healed, and by the time I reached the sandstone wall, only a small trace of blood was left.

I could have orbed myself anywhere—home, the cemetery, China—but running made me feel more alive. When I reached the yard, I slowed to a walk and stopped under a big gum tree that stood on the edge of the lawn. No students were out yet as the lunch bell hadn't rung so I sat in the shade. I faced the open, grassed grounds, and took a deep breath to calm myself. The tree was ours. Archer, Emma, and I sat under that tree every day. I opened my bag, took out my water and had a sip. With a deep breath I closed my eyes and leaned against the rough trunk, waiting for the others to show up.

Archer was the first to arrive. He gave me a good once-over with a concerned look. "Okay, so spill. What's up?"

"I'm fine, Arch, really."

"Then why is there blood on your knee, and why have

you been crying?"

Scowling, I licked my finger and wiped the blood away. Was it that obvious I'd been crying? Sometimes I hated being so in tune with my brother. It was hard to hide things.

"It's nothing, Arch. I had a bit of an encounter with Josh."

"Encounter? If you don't tell me, I'll get inside your head and make you."

"No, you won't. I'm way stronger than you."

"True. But I can always catch you off guard."

"Then I'll just push you back out again," I said.

We stared each other down, but I wasn't giving in.

"Seriously, Gracie, what happened?" he asked.

"I'll tell when I'm ready."

"Like what you saw in that vamp girl last night?"

"That's different ..." I trailed off as Emma plopped down beside me. There was a moment of awkward silence as she looked from me to Archer.

"What did I interrupt? Or is it secret family business?" Emma laughed.

She wasn't far off.

"How was Chemistry?" I asked, in a hopeful attempt at changing the subject.

Emma cringed. "It's only the first day and I already wish I'd chosen something else."

"Come on, Emma. Chemistry is fun. It's really cool putting stuff in test tubes and watching it bubble," Archer said.

Realising I hadn't been to the cafeteria to get lunch, I snatched half of Archer's sandwich when he wasn't looking. He went to say something, but I smiled with my mouth full and he laughed.

The yard was alive with activity. Josh's group sat on the grass in the far corner, but he wasn't with them. Seth, Ivan, and Blake sprawled on the front steps of the main building, and I peaked at their thoughts. They were annoying anyone who came too close.

"Excuse me, Emma?" a tentative female voice said.

I looked over my shoulder and met the gaze of a strikingly beautiful girl. I hoped I didn't look as surprised as I felt. Actually, surprised didn't quite cut it. Shocked, was more like it. She was the girl we'd seen at the property, and the one I'd plucked from Emma's thoughts. Up this close she seemed taller, probably because I was sitting on the ground, and she was sleek and indescribably gorgeous.

Don't, Arch. He stiffened beside me and I could see his hostility rising. *She's different.*

I don't care. She's a vamp.

Just let it go for now, please, I thought.

Emma was oblivious to our silent exchange and invited the girl to join us.

"I'm Charlotte Fallon," she said as she sat down in one swift, elegant motion.

The new girl met my stare with her black eyes, and recognition dawned on her face. She went perfectly still. She was so pale out in the sunshine that her skin almost glowed. The grey and navy check skirt of the school uniform fitted her in all the right places, and the white button-up blouse showed off her near-perfect figure. If I was a guy, I'd have drool running down my chin.

This was not good. Archer gave me a sideways glance,

not even attempting to hide his annoyance.

Trust me, I thought. *Besides, you can't exactly stake her out in the open.*

Archer took another long, hard look at Charlotte.

"I hate being around crowds," Charlotte said.

"This is the girl I was telling you about this morning, Grace," Emma said.

I nudged her foot, hoping she'd stop frowning. She didn't like how pretty Charlotte was, and I wished Emma would stop comparing herself to other people. Archer pulled big clumps of grass from the ground in front of him, his lips puckered into a scowl. And I freaked out at the fact this vamp was sitting with us *in the sunshine.*

"Welcome to Hopetown Valley," I said in my nice-as-pie voice. "I'm Grace. This is Archer, my brother."

"Really?" Charlotte said. "You look nothing alike."

"We get that a lot. Are you in the dorm?" I asked, trying to continue the conversation.

"Yes, room thirteen. You?"

Very fitting. "Arch and I don't board. We have a place about ten minutes west of here." *But you already know that.*

Charlotte seemed a little uncomfortable with us. I caught her thinking she should probably apologise for throwing a stake at me.

Emma tried unsuccessfully to stop scowling when Charlotte asked her a few questions about dorm living. I took the opportunity to grab my dumbstruck brother's attention.

Arch. Archer, look at me, I thought.

He tore his gaze away from Charlotte. Sometimes, I wished he could read people the way I could; it would

51

make things so much easier.

Wipe your chin. A minute ago you wanted to kill her; now you're ogling her?

Huh?

Oh, snap out of it! I looked at him with wide eyes.

Archer struggled between the urge to kill this girl and ask her out on a date. Give me a break. *Boys!* Emma chatted away and Charlotte responded in all the right places, but she was also watching Archer and me. I snuck into her head and caught a thought. She knew who we were and had been searching for us, looking for protection. It seemed like the three of us had a few things to talk about, and Archer was not going to be happy.

12

GRACE
Monday night

Moonlight glinted in Archer's eyes as he pulled his arm back. He released the stake and it flew past my ear, embedding itself into the tree behind me.

"She has a what?" Archer said from where he stood in the middle of the clearing. "I don't even know what that is."

"I didn't tell you because I knew you'd be angry."

Besides, I hadn't had the chance. We'd had no classes together that afternoon, and I'd thought it would be safer to talk at home. Not in public with lots of witnesses.

"That's great, Grace, but in case you've forgotten, we're supposed to kill vampires, not play nice and have lunch with them."

Even though Charlotte was a vampire she could walk around in the sunlight like any normal person. She went against all vampire lore as we knew it. I was just as ruffled around the edges as Archer, but someone had to be calm. That someone would be me, the protector, and the brains of this outfit.

"So you would have risked exposing our world? You would have staked her right there in the yard, in front of everyone? In front of Emma?"

Archer grunted and jogged over to me. He wrapped his hand around the stake he'd thrown minutes before and pulled it from the tree.

"No ... So what do we do?" he asked.

"Charlotte is no ordinary vampire."

"I think I've already noticed that."

"But you can't see what I can," I said. "She's been looking for us and wants our protection."

"What?"

"She has what we call a white soul, Arch."

He stared at me and furrowed his brow. "Again, not really sure what that is."

I motioned for him to follow me along the path away from the clearing. "Come on. We need to start hunting for the night. I'll explain on the way."

The moonlight broke through the canopy here and there, casting dappled shadows on the ground. The summer heat hung in the air, and it was warm enough for shorts and a T-shirt. We were both dressed entirely in black, for obvious reasons.

"All creatures have a soul," I said. "Even the damned. It's the colour of your soul that counts."

"I thought vampires were soulless." Archer scanned the forest as we walked.

"Most people who know of their existence do think that. Vampires have a soul; it's just usually so dark it's as if it isn't there, and it's mostly in tatters like there are holes in it. Charlotte is a unique exception. I've never met another like her. Take me for instance. If you could see my soul, it would be a pure white, blinding light, because I'm an angel. Then there's yours. You're almost as white as me, but you're human so your soul has a nice blue hue."

"Are you serious?"

"Yes." I chuckled. "No human can have a perfectly white soul, but they can be tainted with darkness. Usually the dark ones end up in Hell."

We turned off the path and headed deeper into the forest. I hadn't heard any conspicuous sounds yet, but I was sure they would come. Archer and I usually dusted one or two vamps a night—sometimes up to ten if they were travelling in big groups. Tonight, there had been no sign of the three we saw on the weekend though, which made me a little nervous. I wanted to know why they were after Charlotte.

"We can't kill her, Arch. Regardless of the fact she's a vampire, she also has a soul almost as pure as mine. Whoever Charlotte was before she was turned, she was good, and she is *still* good."

"Then I'll ask you again, Gracie. What do we do?"

"I say we wait and see how it pans out. Maybe get to know her a bit."

"And protect her? You've got to be kidding."

"Just have an open mind, please. I really don't think she's a threat."

"Okay, Sis, if you say so."

Something rustled, and we both froze where we stood. I dropped to a crouch and scooted to a nearby tallowwood, pressing my back against its trunk. Archer did the same.

On your right, I thought. *Three of them, and …*

Oh great, Seth was there. What did he want? Before Archer could protest I orbed around to the other side of the tree, landing in front of the four figures. At first I didn't recognise the three vamps, but soon I realised they were the ones we'd seen at the shed. When I picked a few thoughts from their minds, I discovered they'd been discussing Charlotte with Seth.

"Fancy meeting you here, Grace." Seth chuckled, and the sound chilled me.

"You know if I could, I'd kill you. What do you want?"

"What do I always want? I'm protecting my reason for existing. Annoying you is a bonus."

"As long as we're here we'll keep killing your reason to exist, even if we can't kill you," Archer said.

He whipped a stake from his belt and ran at the vamps, ready to drive it home. The three vamps spread in a flash and Seth misted, moving to block Archer, sending him flying backwards. Misting was the fallen angel version of orbing, but not as pretty. Archer landed with a thud against a tree and fell flat on his face. I laughed; it looked pretty funny.

"Tell us what you want with Charlotte," I said, as Archer picked himself up.

"You can't make me," Seth said.

I shook my head. He could be so childish.

"That's true, but I can pull it from their heads." I

nodded towards the other three who were snarling and baring their fangs.

Seth scowled. "Not if I keep you occupied."

"Oh Seth, don't you know girls can do more than two things at once?"

I orbed to another section of the path and Seth followed. To the others we would have looked like balls of white light and black mist, flying around each other. But Seth was right; I couldn't hear anything about Charlotte in the vamps' heads as they were too preoccupied watching us.

Seth misted again and landed behind me, but he wasn't quick enough. I spun and orbed at the same time, then thrust my arm out and grabbed him by the throat, putting all my force behind it and knocking him to the ground. Straddling him, I pinned him down—I loved being freakishly strong—and asked him the question again. "What do you want with Charlotte?"

"Kinky. Do you always play rough with your enemies?" Seth said. "I like it rough."

"You disgust me." I let go and jumped to my feet.

"Well, you won't be getting any info from me." Seth clenched his teeth.

It was right about then I noticed Archer was in trouble. I'd left him to fight three against one, and Seth wasn't going to give me what I wanted, so there was no point wasting the energy. I orbed away from him and came down next to one of the vamps fighting Archer.

"Hey there, good-looking," I said.

The vampire threw a sloppy punch, and I ducked before it connected with my face. I swung my leg in an arc, taking his feet out from under him, and he hit the ground with a thud. I pressed my knee hard into his back and pulled his arms around behind him.

"Thanks." Archer punched one of the other vamps in the face before grabbing his throat and shoving him into a tree.

I smiled, scanning the forest. "Where did vamp number three go? Where's Seth?"

"I don't know, but this one is dust." Archer pulled his arm back.

"Don't!" I said. "We need to find out what they know."

My brother faltered then let the hand holding his stake fall to his side, but it didn't stop him from clamping down harder on the vamp's throat.

"Tell us what you want with Charlotte." I pressed down on my knee and the vamp I'd caught trembled underneath me. He squeezed his eyes shut, concentrating hard on not letting his thoughts betray him. Seth had obviously told them about my ability. I wondered if he'd shared the fact that he could do the same. One word floated to the front of the vamp's mind.

Blood.

"Blood?" I asked. "Well that was easy. I was hoping for a harder fight; you just took the fun out of it."

Seth appeared in his black mist. "You idiot. What have you told her?" He misted again and landed between Archer and me. He grabbed the arm of the vamp Archer held captive.

"Arch, let go," I said.

No sooner had the words left my lips than Seth and his filth disappeared. If Archer hadn't let go he'd have ended up going with them. It sent shivers down my spine even thinking about it.

The vamp beneath me growled and rolled, throwing me off him. I landed on the forest floor with a thud, and the vampire ran through the trees in a blur. My momentary lapse in concentration had let him get away.

"Damn!" I got to my feet and brushed the dirt from my hands.

"Well," Archer said, with his hands on his hips. "That was fun; let's do it again sometime."

I laughed, and shook my head, but it wasn't very funny.

"Did you get anything?" he asked.

"My knee in that guy's back did persuade him to think about wanting Charlotte's blood."

A vampire wanted blood? That wasn't new, but as far as I was aware they didn't usually want the blood of their own kind.

"Yeah, I heard that part. I mean did you get anything else from him?"

"No, Seth has taught them well. All I got from their minds was a whole lot of la-la-la, la-di-dah etcetera."

It was Archer's turn to laugh.

We ambled back towards the shed, inspecting all the superficial cuts and scrapes we'd acquired in the fight. Mine were pretty much healed by the time we reached the clearing, but Archer had one cut on his right forearm that looked a little deep. Usually he was against me healing him, but this time I wasn't going to take no for an answer. I didn't want it getting infected. I wrapped my hand around his and channelled my energy into him. My body glowed, and the glow spread up Archer's arm to heal it. He was good as new before we even reached the door to go inside.

Why these vamps wanted Charlotte's blood baffled me. It didn't seem like that big a deal, but I guessed if they were fighting this hard it had to be for a reason. We were both curious to find out what that reason might be. It also meant that for now Archer wasn't arguing with me, and Charlotte was safe from a stake through her heart.

13

GRACE
Tuesday, lunchtime

The next day, Charlotte asked if I wanted to take a walk with her to the vineyard. Nestled in the far back corner of the school grounds, the vineyard's entrance was framed by a beautiful rose garden complete with a heart-shaped arbour.

We walked through and stopped at the fountain which sat in the centre of a cobblestone circle. Water cascaded out of the top of a low-lying urn with three cherubs in the middle. I listened to the crash of the water and waited, assuming Charlotte had asked me there because she had something she wanted to talk about.

"You know what I am?" she finally said.

I nodded. "And you know what I am."

Charlotte sighed and stared at the vines in the vineyard which hadn't borne fruit in years. They were a bit creepy, but Charlotte seemed to like them and she meandered off down the rows to have a look. I didn't want to push her to talk to me, so I waited for her to come back.

"She's really something, isn't she?" a voice asked from behind.

I spun around and Seth stood under the arbour, the last of his black mist dissipating.

"What do you want, Seth?"

"Oh, nothing much. Just thought I'd come and annoy you again." He walked over and leaned against the edge of the fountain. "Working, is it?"

"Didn't you get the hint last night?" I said. "I don't like you. There is nothing left between us, and you don't scare me. But I'm going to find out why you're after Charlotte."

"You're always so sure of yourself, aren't you?"

I didn't answer; instead, I took the high road and ignored him, hoping he'd go away. Seth was always itching for a fight every time we met, but it was pointless, since we couldn't actually kill each other. At least with vamps there was the satisfaction of the kill. Fighting Seth the night before had been a rare occurrence, and although pointless, I had to admit it had felt good.

"Why are you still here?" I asked. "Don't you have some demon friends to go play with?"

"Most of them are hiding this time of day," he said.

Watching him closely I couldn't help but think, *why is he like this?* "What made you fall, Seth? Where's the fun in being evil? I just don't get it."

"If you were on this side you would."

"See, I think you're wrong, and I also think you're not

as bad as you make yourself out to be. Your soul isn't completely black."

"That's a shame, really. I was aiming for a nice shade of ebony."

"It's more like a smoky grey. So come on, why the fall?" I asked again.

Seth hesitated. "It's not so much that being evil is *fun,* it's more to do with not having to answer to anyone but myself. I mean, look at you. You've spent your entire existence doing what someone else has told you. That's not for me. I remember what it was like, and I much prefer this life." Seth smiled, but his eyes darkened. There was something he wasn't telling me.

"Really? You can honestly say this is better? After—"

"You don't know what you're talking about, Grace."

Then he left, just like that, disappearing behind a thick cloud of his black mist.

What he'd said was definitely food for thought, but I pushed it to the back of my mind. Even though Charlotte was a way off, I was pretty sure she'd been able to hear what we were saying. Not that it really mattered—she knew who and what Seth was. I closed my eyes and rubbed my temples with my fingertips.

A moment later, Charlotte stood beside me. She gave me a questioning but kind look as she pulled herself up and sat on the lip of the fountain.

"Seth likes to stir the pot." I climbed up next to her.

"Yes, I've noticed that."

Because I was still feeling my way with Charlotte, I wasn't sure how much I could trust her. I'd met her less than three days ago. She had tried to stake me and she was my sworn enemy, the very thing I had been incarnated on Earth to kill. I waited to see if she would speak first.

"I've been searching for you for a while, you know," she said. "You and Archer are part of our legend."

"Vampire legend?"

"Something like that." Charlotte nodded.

Smiling, I wondered if I should be worried or flattered. I'd been a bit naïve to think no one would know about us. Of course they would; vampires had mouths, the same as humans. The thought had just never entered my mind.

"Is this where I'm supposed to ask you what you want?" I said. "Why have you been searching for us?"

"I've always felt lost," she said. "From the day I was made I was different. When I found out how different it was quite a shock, and they've been chasing me ever since."

We fell into a comfortable silence. The hot February sun shone down on our surroundings. Magpies swooped through the trees, and the cicadas hummed their monotonous song.

"Who are *they?*" I finally asked.

"The vamps that know my secret. Matthew and his crew, Cain and Tyler, are the most recent to try and get to me. Seth hooked up with them shortly after I came to Hopetown Valley."

"So that's who I met last night. Those vamps?"

"Oh, you've had the pleasure then?" Charlotte chuckled. "I chose Hopetown Valley because I'd finally figured out you and Archer lived here, and I'm sorry, I didn't know who you were the first time I saw you. I was frantically trying to get away; I guess I would have staked anything that moved.”

“No hard feelings,” I said.

“I heard about you, the Protection Angel and the Hunter, through my creator. He seemed to think you would help me.”

I may have been able to hear Charlotte’s thoughts, but I could only read what she was thinking at that moment. There was something odd about her, though. She seemed to have a dull spot in her mind, like a box with a lock on it. I didn’t think much of it; she was a bit of a jumbled mess, so it was hard to piece things together. All I could do was wait for her to tell me.

“Arch isn’t too happy about the whole idea.” I offered her a weak smile.

“I understand that, but you need to hear me out.”

Nodding, I shifted on the lip of the fountain and made myself more comfortable.

Charlotte took a deep breath and launched into her story. “Vampires of my kind are rare. I’m not the first, but right now, I think I’m the only one.”

Charlotte told me about how she had come to be what she was today. She’d been sixteen and had snuck out with friends to meet up with a group of boys. There was one who’d caught her attention. His name was Lucas, and he became her creator.

“Lucas was so charming, and very hard to resist. He was handsome and polite, and had me under his spell. I know now that he had good intentions.” Charlotte sighed. “He promised me a life I couldn’t resist, one that would count for something, one that would make a difference, so I agreed to go with him. He drank my blood until I was almost dry, and then fed me with his own. I can still remember the sweetness of it, so much richer than any blood I've ever tasted. He stayed with me throughout the transformation. I don't recall much of it, and I couldn't tell you how long the change took."

As I listened to Charlotte, my heart went out to her. Here was a girl who'd never asked for this life, coerced into a situation she could do nothing about. Once turned, Lucas had taken her to his home in the city and trained her to fight.

"We fought other vampires on a regular basis, like you," Charlotte said. "Lucas and I believed our purpose was to fight the dark vamps. Someone has to, right?"

I nodded. The world would be a sad and sorry place if no one was there to keep the balance. "And what's more perfect than fighting fire with fire?" I said. "Have you ever wanted to, you know, eat someone, or turn someone?"

"I have never fed from a human; it's not part of who we are, but the feeling of thirst is indescribable. Your throat burns beyond belief. There were times I wanted to, when things were not so good, but I wouldn't intentionally inflict this life upon anyone. I didn't know the full extent of what I was getting myself into, and I would never willingly take someone's humanity from them."

By that statement alone, I loved my new friend. I could never harm her, even if she was technically my enemy.

"Do you know how white your soul is?" I said.

"Soul? Vampires don't have souls."

"Trust me, they do. All creatures, even the damned, have a soul." I watched as Charlotte's eyes widened. "Creatures of the night have a black soul, except you.

You are the exception, although you aren't actually a creature of the night for obvious reasons." I pointed to the sky. "You're damned for eternity but your soul is completely intact."

Charlotte shook her head in disbelief and looked at me, waiting for me to continue.

"It's almost as white as mine," I said.

"I didn't think I had one anymore. You can see it?"

"All angels can. We see other things, too, and hear thoughts. I think your soul is the reason you can be outside in daylight hours."

Charlotte Laughed. "And I thought I was a freak. The first of my kind was created long ago by an angel that had some sort of beef with God, so I guess we're distantly related somehow, but that's a story for another day. What's unique about us, and the one thing everyone wants, is our blood."

"Yeah, I learned last night that's why those vamps are after you," I said. "But you're a vampire? What would other vampires want with your blood?"

We sat in silence for a few minutes. I had so many questions, but I wanted to let Charlotte answer the first one in her own time. Besides, I couldn't quite get my head around an angel and a vampire being related. That piece of information deserved a little silence.

The sharp trill of the bell rang in the distance, signalling the end of lunch. Charlotte jumped down from the fountain and walked under the arbour. She seemed deep in thought. I followed her and we headed back towards the school.

"Vampires disgust me, the way they kill innocent people," she said. "Sometimes I'm ashamed to be one, and since I don't sleep, why not rid the world of them one at a time? Makes me feel better, and it's fun."

"I know. It gives Arch and me our kicks."

"I've heard so much about the Tate family. You don't seem so scary."

"That's because we don't have fangs," I said, teasing her. "Arch wanted to kill you yesterday when you sat with us at lunch."

"What stopped him?"

"Me, and the fact that dusting you probably wouldn't have gone down too well in broad daylight." We smiled at each other. "Why do those vamps want your blood?"

The look on Charlotte's face was the saddest I'd seen in a long time. Blood tears trickled from the corners of her eyes and it took me a moment to understand that she was crying.

"Lucas died because of our blood," she said. "He staked himself because he was captured. He died protecting me."

"I won't let you die, Charlotte."

"Sometimes I think it would be better if I was dead."

"But why is it so special?" I asked.

Charlotte looked at her hands before staring into my eyes. "Because those who drink from my veins, even a drop, would have access to an immense power ... Vampires would become stronger and faster, and be able to walk in the sunlight."

I froze, too shocked to reply.

If what Charlotte said was true, forces of evil could be created like nothing we'd ever seen before, and that was definitely not good.

14

JOSH
Tuesday afternoon

One and a half days down and way too many to go. I couldn't believe how slowly the first week of school was passing. Friday seemed so far off, and I was feeling a little dejected after my knock-back from Grace. I noticed she was spending a lot of time with the strange new girl.

Charlotte was different, but not in a bad way. She was gorgeous, a little creepy, and carried herself differently to the rest of the students. Kind of like a rose amongst thorns. When I thought about it, Grace was much the same, less the creepy part.

I sat with my group at the far end of the yard. The sun was shining and the girls were making the most of it. Abby, Claudia, and a handful of others lay on the grass, their uniforms hiked up as high as they dared, sunning their legs. Abby had pretty much left me alone since I'd publicly humiliated her. I didn't expect forgiveness any time soon, which was fine by me if it kept her off my back.

Ryan drilled me for details about Grace. I'd only made a pass at her the day before, and I hadn't told him much. It's embarrassing telling your best friend you got sidelined by a girl.

"I'm sure she has a good reason," he said. "Like maybe she doesn't want to be the re-bound girl, or she's just not into you, or she's got a secret third leg."

I laughed. "I very much got the feeling she's into me. She pulled away at the last second, like something made her. It was weird. And she is definitely not a re-bound."

We sat watching the movement in the yard. A lot of the guys took precious minutes out of their day to stop and stare at Abby and the girls. I must admit the view was nice, but been there done that and sorry, not really interested.

I glanced in the direction of the main gate at the tree where Grace and her friends usually sat. Archer and Emma were deep in conversation, but Grace and Charlotte weren't there.

"When are you going to ask Emma out?" I said.

"Am I that transparent?" Ryan raised his eyebrows.

"I think we both are."

Emma was Grace's oldest friend. Besides Archer, she was the only one who was always with her, and I could never remember a time at school when they were apart. I suddenly had an idea.

"Come on, let's go talk to them." I got to my feet.

"Are you serious? What's our excuse going to be?"

"Do we need one? Can't we just be nice?"

Ryan scrambled to his feet and followed. From the corner of my eye I saw Abby turn her head to watch. It dawned on me that over my entire high school life I'd never once gotten up and gone to sit with another group. It felt good.

"Hey guys, can we sit with you?" I said.

"Grace isn't here," Archer mumbled through a mouthful of food.

"I can see that. Can we sit with you?"

Ryan gave Emma a warm smile, and she blushed.

"Sure," she said.

We plonked down and formed a loose circle. Archer looked at me with a quizzical expression, but I'd expected him to be wary. I would have been if someone was infatuated with my twin sister, and I was sure Grace would have told him about me.

"So ... where are Grace and Charlotte?" I asked.

"If you're going to try and get me to tell Grace that you like her, you're wasting your time," Archer said.

"Arch!" Emma swatted him. "Be nice."

"She already knows that," I said. "We just wanted a break from the boring fake people over there."

"I don't know, the view looks pretty good." Archer leaned around me.

"The view is better here." Ryan smiled at Emma.

She blushed again and looked at her hands.

An uncomfortable silence settled over us. Archer possessed so much pent up anger, it made me wonder what the reason behind it was. He and Grace had lost their parents at a young age and their grandfather had died last year, but I knew what family loss was like, and this wasn't it. The death of their grandfather was big news for a while, leaving them both parent-less. A lot of the kids at school were jealous the Tate twins got to live on their own. I'd take keeping my loved ones over living alone any day. Archer's anger seemed to be fuelled by something else, and I made a note to ask Grace what that was if I ever had the chance.

"You should join the soccer team, Archer," I said. "We could use a new player."

"Why would I want to do that?"

"Looks like you could handle a bit of rough and tumble. Plus, it's a good energy release."

"I get plenty of that in my spare time, so no thanks," he said.

Okay, it looked like I was going to have to try a different angle. The 'talking sports' routine didn't seem to be working; he was a tough nut to crack.

"To answer your question," Emma said softly, "about where the girls are, they're off doing their thing." She sounded a bit jealous. "Grace is trying to make Charlotte welcome by showing her around. If you ask me, the school isn't that big."

"You're just upset she's ditched you," Archer said.

"Am not." She threw a crust of bread at him.

From a distance you would think they were an item, the way they played and joked around, but they'd known each other for too long. Archer looked at Emma like a second sister, and I got the feeling he'd do anything for her.

The end of lunch bell rang. Ryan jumped. He'd been staring at Emma as she talked, and we all laughed. I think it was the first time throughout the entire conversation when we'd all felt comfortable with one another.

"We'd better get to P.E. ... Mr Bruner will go spare at us if we're late," I said.

"I'll walk with you. See you later, Emma," Archer said, giving her a wink.

The two of us headed towards the school hall/basketball court/gym while Ryan hung back. When I glanced over my shoulder, I caught a glimpse of Emma's smile. Way to go Ryan. At least it looked like romance was working for one of us. A few minutes later, Ryan ran to catch up. He threw me a high five, unable to contain his excitement.

"Date tonight. Starting in the common room, then maybe a nice walk and a nightcap in my—"

"You hurt her and I'll break you." Archer stopped and got in Ryan's face.

"Hey, I would never do that."

"Easy, Archer." I touched his arm. "Ryan's a good guy. He won't cause any trouble."

Archer wasn't exactly big but I wouldn't call him small either. He looked as if he could hold his own, and I definitely didn't want to get on the wrong side of him.

We walked the rest of the way to class in silence. I couldn't help wondering how I would fare if and when I actually did start dating Grace.

We changed quickly then took our seats on the stage at the far end of the basketball court just as the ten-minute bell rang. The class chattered noisily until Mr Bruner walked in. He raved about the fitness obstacle course set out in front of us, and I paid absolutely no attention. My eyes scanned the other students' faces, trying to find Grace. She was in my class but I couldn't see her.

"Where's your sister?" I whispered to Archer.

He didn't reply, pointing to the big timber-framed glass doors at the entrance to the hall. Grace ran across the school grounds. Even at a run she looked elegant, like she was flying, and I wished I could be the one to catch her if she fell.

15

GRACE

The doors burst open, and I came to a screeching halt. Charlotte wasn't with me and I looked around, wondering where she'd gone. The entire class stared at me. I mouthed *sorry,* and gave Mr Bruner a sheepish look, then hurried across the basketball court and quietly sat down next to Archer. He shook his head. Suddenly, I was very aware of who he was sitting next to. Being so close to Josh made my heart flutter.

"As I was saying," Mr Bruner said, "teams of two, one full circuit around the court. Complete each station before you move to the next." Then he blew his whistle. The class sprang to its feet and spilled onto the court, sneakers squeaking on the polished wooden floor.

"Grace, could I see you for a moment please?" Mr Bruner asked.

I approached my gym teacher with a little trepidation.

"I trust you have a reason for being late?" He towered over me, crossing his thick arms over his broad chest.

"We lost track of time, sir," Charlotte said.

Mr Bruner spun around, his eyebrows raised. She must have snuck in. She flashed him her beautiful smile. Mr Bruner blinked, his face blank for a moment, then shook his head.

"Very well. Please don't let it happen again."

Mr Bruner seemed to forget she'd also been late, and he waved us both away. Charlotte had just used her glamour on our P.E. teacher and I shot her a thank you smile as we ran to the change rooms.

We changed into our sports uniforms—consisting of navy shorts and a gold polo top, they were quite unflattering. Somehow, Charlotte made it look good. I didn't feel the need to hide from her since she knew what I was. Normally I would have gone into one of the toilets to change.

I caught her standing motionless, her head tilted to one side, staring at me. I stood so she could see most of my back, and I knew what she was looking at.

"They're beautiful," Charlotte said.

My back was smooth with no blemishes, besides the rose-coloured lines that ran next to my shoulder blades. Each one was about six inches long and the two lines almost joined in the middle, forming a V-shape. I didn't really know what to say; no one had commented on my scars before.

"Thanks," I said.

"You have wings in there?"

"Yeah, but they haven't been out for a while. It's a bit risky, and with orbing it just isn't very practical."

"Don't they get cramped?"

"Like you would not believe," I said. "Sometimes in a fight I unfurl them. Makes me look bigger."

Laughing, Charlotte and I went back to the court. Archer waited by the rope ladder.

"You first," he said to me.

"No one else wants to buddy with you?" I smirked.

"Odd one out I guess." Archer shrugged. "Now climb like I'm hot on your tail."

I heaved myself onto the bottom rung.

"I want you all the way to the top, Grace," Mr Bruner yelled from the other side of the hall.

Great, now everyone was looking at me again. I did as my P.E. teacher said, climbing the rope rungs with ease. I glanced down at the bottom of the ladder where Archer and Charlotte stood staring up at me. Archer shook the ladder, a wide smile on his face, and I shimmied down to let him start his turn. He climbed to the top almost as fast as I had.

Archer dropped back to the floor. "Why were you two late?"

"Talking and lost track of time," I said.

Charlotte grabbed the rungs and climbed the ladder.

Josh came and sat with us today. He was asking where you were. Archer craned his neck to look at Charlotte.

I grabbed his arm. *Really?*

Archer sighed and stared back at me. *Gracie, you need to get your head out of the clouds and stop dreaming about something that can never, ever happen.*

I hated it when he used his big brother scolding voice. Who did he think he was? He was only a couple of minutes

older than me anyway.

Why? It's nice up there. You should visit sometime, I thought.

Archer shook his head. I looked to the ceiling and Charlotte smiled at me before sliding back down the ladder.

"Everything okay?" she asked.

I nodded. "Sure."

"Ryan asked Emma out," Archer said.

"Wow, that's great ... or not?"

Archer gripped the rope ladder and frowned. "Is it?"

"Emma will be fine, Arch, she's a big girl. You can't wrap her in cotton wool."

"Ryan seems like a nice guy," Charlotte said.

Archer clenched his jaw and stared at me. *Since Emma's out tonight I thought we could case the cemetery.* Archer glanced sideways at Charlotte. *Maybe see what we can find. A change of scenery will be nice.*

"Great idea. Charlotte can come with us," I said so she could hear. Somehow I didn't think that was the response Archer was hoping for.

"Where are we going?" Charlotte asked.

"Cemetery. Tonight," I said. "See if we can ..." I made a stabbing motion with my hand and she laughed.

"I'm up for that."

"Great." Archer moved to the next obstacle and we followed.

We fell silent for a while. It was kind of hard to talk while running at a spring board, jumping, then vaulting over a horse. We still had the balance beam, trampoline, and parallel bars to go. Of course the three of us could complete each station with ease, and I caught Josh watching us several times.

The balance beam was a cinch. Why Mr Bruner included it in the line-up was beyond me. By the time we'd moved on again to the trampoline I understood. I hadn't really been watching any of the other students, and I took a couple of minutes to glance around the hall. It amazed me how bad some people were with this stuff. I guess I took being coordinated for granted.

Archer showed off, doing somersaults on the tramp. I shook my head, with my hands on my hips. Charlotte smiled, her head moving up and down as Archer twisted and turned through his routine.

"You going to get up there with him, give him a run for his money?" Josh said.

He'd wandered over while Ryan was mucking around on the parallel bars. Blood rushed to my face, and my heartbeat quickened. Josh stood close enough for our arms to lightly touch. He was trying to imagine what I'd look like on the trampoline, then his mind wandered to other thoughts of what I'd look like and I quickly closed him off, blushing even more. The heat from his skin against mine was too much, and it took all my strength not to lean into him.

To be safe, I took a small step away and concentrated on my exhibitionist of a brother. Everyone knew Archer and I were great on the tramp—I just didn't like showing off as much as he did.

He came to a graceful stop in the middle of the mat. "Come on Sis, tandem somersault? Or a double twist if you're game?"

79

"I could out twist you any day, Arch."

I flicked myself up onto the mat and stood facing him. My head was a little clearer now I wasn't standing next to Josh. Archer stepped back until we were both towards the edge, then we began to jump in unison. We mostly used our connection hunting, or if we wanted to annoy one another, but it was also immensely helpful for things like this.

I'd forgotten how much I loved the trampoline, not having been on one since last year. The feeling of weightlessness and gliding through the air was magic. It almost compared to flying, but not quite. The entire class had stopped to watch.

We should put one of these in the clearing, I thought as Archer and I came out of a twist in perfect time.

It would be great for training, Archer thought.

The bell sounded, scattering the class in the direction of the change rooms—Mr Bruner didn't even get the chance to dismiss us.

"You know, it's a shame Hopetown Valley High doesn't have a gymnastics team," Josh said as I jumped from the tramp. "You two are really good."

"We do it for fun, don't we?" I elbowed Archer.

He grinned. "Yep, just for fun."

16

JOSH
Early Tuesday night

After P.E. all I'd been able to think about was Grace. She was amazing, and I was totally smitten. The way she moved through the air jumping on the trampoline was beautiful. I kept finding more and more reasons to wonder why I had wasted so much time with Abby.

By the time we got back to the dorm at the end of the day, I thought Ryan was sick of hearing Grace's name. I probably would've been, too, if I were him. When we reached the front gates, I had an idea.

"I'll catch up. I just want to talk to someone first."

"Let me guess—Grace," he said. "See you in a bit."

I leaned against the big sandstone pillar and waited. Grace and Archer hadn't left yet; their black Defender was still in the school's car park. After a few minutes, I spotted them walking across the yard. With a huge grin plastered on my face, I must have looked like a bit of an idiot. Archer glanced at me angrily as he walked past.

"I'll wait in the car," he said without breaking stride.

With raised eyebrows, I watched as he walked to the car and got in the driver's side. "Is he always so intense?"

"Just around you," Grace said.

"Great. That makes me feel just … great."

The way Grace looked at me made my heart beat faster, and for a moment I was lost for words. I wanted to tuck a stray strand of hair behind her ear, and I had to stuff my hands in my pockets to stop myself. She smiled, and her cheeks glowed.

"I was wondering what you were doing tonight?" I said. "Can we … can I see you?"

Grace tensed as soon as I asked the question, and I immediately wanted to take it back. She wrung her fingers. A pained expression crossed her face and I took her hands in mine. She relaxed a little, opening her fingers so our palms fitted together.

"Sorry, I can't tonight. We have plans." She glanced at the car where Archer frowned at us. "Besides, it's a school night."

We laughed, and still holding her hands I stepped closer, leaning down until my forehead almost touched the top of her head. "Why do I feel so drawn to you, Grace? I can feel you pulling me in, like a magnet."

She closed her eyes and took a deep breath, holding it for a second. When she exhaled, a tremble coursed through her body and flowed into me, making me shiver. Her hair smelled like rain, fresh and sweet.

"Because … I'm sorry, I have to go." Grace pulled her

hands free and ran to the car.

She didn't look at me until they were driving out of the car park. The expression in her eyes stirred something deep inside me. She felt the attraction between us, but I couldn't understand why she was fighting it. Girls, why were they so complicated?

On my way back to the dorm I didn't see the figure flying down the steps. It took me by surprise, and I almost fell between two large roots of the Moreton Bay fig that stood across from the girls' dorm.

"You don't waste any time, do you?" Abby said, planting herself in front of me.

Great, just what I needed. And here I was thinking I'd gotten through the worst of it since she hadn't spoken to me all day. I looked at her with a blank expression and waited for her to continue, not wanting to add any fuel to the fire.

"Well? What do you have to say for yourself?"

"I don't have to explain myself to you," I said. "It's over; you need to accept that."

Abby's face crumpled. "I don't know what I did wrong, Josh," she said.

My heart twinged with a little sympathy but I wasn't going to fall for it. Sure, I felt bad after breaking it off with her, but she could be manipulative, and I was tired of being one of her pawns.

"Like I said, Abby, it's over."

I turned away before she could respond. My feet felt heavy, and I wished things didn't have to be so hard.

"Wow, dude, who died?" Ryan said. He sat on the steps outside the boys' dorm, watching everyone come and go.

"Did things not go too well with Grace?"

"I can't figure out why she's holding back." I sat beside him. "I can see in her eyes how she feels, but then her face clouds over and she runs away."

"Maybe you're losing your touch." Ryan punched my arm. "What did Abby want? She looked intense."

"Just trying to get under my skin, or win me back, or I don't know, make my life even more miserable."

"Girls can do that. Come on, let's grab dinner. I'm meeting Emma during free time."

"That's right, the big date. You excited?"

"Just a little." Ryan smiled.

"You know Archer will kill you if you do anything wrong by her."

"It's cool. Why would I do that anyway? She's great."

"Just … be careful," I said. "Something tells me Archer is the kind of guy you'd rather have as your friend than your enemy."

We headed towards the cafeteria, which was already full of students. I had no plans after dinner and study hour, and lights out wasn't until ten so maybe I'd visit my mum.

Back in the common room, Ryan and I took a seat on one of the couches and waited for Emma. The girls' and boys' dorms were the same inside, but a mirror image. They each had three floors with thirty-four rooms, ten on the first, and twelve on the other two levels. There was a shared bathroom on each floor and a large common room on the first. It actually joined the two buildings together and could be accessed from the hallway of both dorms. There was also a main entrance to the common room from the outside for all students to use, because the boys weren't allowed inside the girls' dorm, and vice versa.

The space was comfortable with a few small tables and chairs scattered here and there. A kitchenette with a sink, fridge, and microwave sat on the back wall. There was a large pool table, a TV, and two three-seater couches. Abby and Claudia had their heads together at a table in the far corner, and about ten other people milled around the room.

Ryan's face lit up when Emma walked through the main glass swinging door. It was nice to see such an expression of happiness in his eyes.

"Hey," she said. She looked great in her skinny jeans and a yellow tank top, but I got the impression she didn't quite know what to do.

"Here, take my seat." I jumped to my feet. "I'll leave you to it. Think I might take a walk."

"Catch up with you later?" Ryan asked. "Thought we might head over to the hall for the movie."

"Maybe," I said as I walked out the door. I already knew I'd be giving the Tuesday night movie a miss.

The night was pleasant with the heat of the day lingering in the air. On my way to the cemetery I passed a few groups of students out enjoying the weather and eating their dinner on the grass. I stuffed my hands in my pockets and walked around the cafeteria, then along the back of the main building, past the library and the hall. The big doors were open and I heard the scraping of chairs on the floor inside, as eager viewers got ready for the movie.

As I rounded the back of the library, the school's church came into view. In the dusky light cast by the rising moon you'd have been forgiven for thinking it looked like a haunted house. Holy Trinity Cathedral was a beautiful and majestic building with grounds large enough for it to be a separate property. It had its own gate on the main road, an enormous circular gravel driveway and a front garden. Built from the same ageing sandstone as the school's main building, it had matching wooden doors with ornate cast-iron hinges. The two spires reached out to the heavens and there were seven stained-glass windows down each side, beautifully depicting the fourteen Stations of the Cross. I could appreciate the building's beauty, even though I'd never really been one for attending church, especially since Mum had died.

The old and rundown cemetery sprawled out behind the cathedral. The low sandstone wall surrounding it was dirty with algae and moss, and the wrought-iron pickets were mostly brown with rust. I pushed the gate open, walked through, and went straight to the third row. Mum's grave was about halfway down, next to my grandparents'. Their headstone was a large cross nearly twice my height, and the intricate floral pattern was stained with algae. Mum's stone was simple and modest. Made from a slab of black marble, the gold lettering of the inscription sparkled in the moonlight.

Marion Patricia Chase 1963–2005
Wife of David, mother of Joshua
She lives on in our hearts

Reading those words pulled at my heart, but after more than seven years I was beyond crying. I sat cross-legged

in front of her grave then told her all about Grace and the last two days. It felt good getting it out even if it seemed I was talking to myself.

When I'd said all I needed to say and was almost ready to leave, I resigned myself to the fact that I had nothing else to do. There was a big fat doorstop of a book sitting on the desk in my room that needed reading, but that wasn't a very exciting prospect.

When I got to my feet the night was lighter than it should have been. The back of the cemetery housed a thick row of trees with another giant Moreton Bay fig in one corner. A ball of pure white light appeared, seeping into the shadows of the enormous tree. My mouth dropped open, and I leaned against the cross of my grandparents' grave to stop from falling over. The light spun, casting smaller balls of light into its orbit. Then the light shifted and expanded until it became the shape of a person.

I wrestled with the image of someone appearing from nowhere in a ball of light. How was that even possible?

Another person emerged from the light. They spoke but I couldn't hear them, and my brain attempted to figure out where they'd come from. It was all very weird.

Then the hairs on the back of my neck rose.

Something in my gut told me I was being watched.

With my heart thumping in my chest loud enough so I could hear it, I turned and looked into the darkest, most menacing pair of eyes I'd ever seen.

Then I think I passed out.

17

Archer had reprimanded me when we'd left school. "You know nothing can come of it," he'd said.

"Don't remind me," I'd mumbled back to him.

I couldn't wait to stab something with a stake. Dust on my boots was exactly what I needed.

After a light dinner, Archer and I headed to the cottage. I walked up the steps onto the concrete veranda and looked at the door, which hung askew on its hinges. Using my shoulder, I shoved it open, wondering why we hadn't fixed it when we did the renovations. I added its repair to my mental list of other highly important things to do.

The old veranda, which now served as the foyer, was sparsely furnished with a bookshelf on the left wall and a small table across from the door. Archer pushed the door closed with his foot, and we walked through the open-plan dining room to what used to be the main living area.

At first glance it looked like any other room—white walls, a timber floor, and a couch and coffee table at one end. Along the far wall, we'd built a second wall about two metres in. I walked over and pushed a section of the panel. A small square flipped down to reveal a silver keypad. The buttons beeped softly as I entered the code, then part of the wall slid sideways revealing a hidden doorway.

I reached around and flicked the light on. Our entire arsenal was in this room. Stakes, knives, swords, axes, even a couple of whips, were all hung up in rows on the wall. You name it, we probably had it. The really heavy-duty stuff was housed in a cabinet at the far end.

Archer went back and forth loading himself up with weapons—his stake belt, a small dagger strapped to his ankle, and a tiny arrow gun that could fire with the flick of a wrist. I strapped my dagger to my upper arm and put my stake belt on.

Outside, the night was still, and the stars twinkled in the dark summer sky. Dressed in our usual black T-shirts, jeans, and boots, we'd be perfectly hidden in the shadows. Before we left, we practiced some manoeuvres in the clearing. Archer was a pretty good fighter, but still no match for me. While we were sparring, I decided to bring up the subject of our birthday. It was less than a week away, and I thought we could have a little party on the weekend.

"A party? Here?"

"Yes," I said to my unenthusiastic brother. "You know, with friends, and music, and some drinks?"

"I don't know if that's a good idea, Gracie, what with the kind of people we attract to this place. It could end up turning into a big feeding frenzy."

"Oh, come on. Even the vamps of Hopetown Valley aren't that stupid." I flicked my leg around and knocked him on his butt. "Everyone knows they hunt inconspicuously so they don't risk exposure."

"Everyone?" He jumped up.

"You know what I mean. Plenty of parties happen around here; why shouldn't we have one?"

"We'll talk about it later," Archer said.

"Fine." I stomped off across the clearing, determined to have a party whether he liked it or not.

We'd agreed to meet Charlotte at the school cemetery. Archer wanted a change of scenery but wasn't too keen on her tagging along. I thought it was a fantastic idea. Matthew and his boys were after her, so we were bound to run into them, which meant we could do our job and dust them. After one final check of our weaponry, I orbed us to the back of the cemetery. We landed in front of the big Moreton Bay fig that stood in the far corner. Charlotte hadn't arrived, so we waited on the edge of the shadows.

Archer toed the dirt with his boot, his face twisted into a scowl.

"Are you going to snap out of this mood you're in?" I said.

"That depends." He folded his arms. "You haven't been thinking all that straight the past couple of days, Gracie."

"I'm thinking perfectly fine, thank you."

"Then how come every time Josh is around you go all girly and mushy?"

"I do not," I said. "What brought this on?" Archer had obviously been thinking about it since we'd left school.

I tried to read him but he pushed me out.

A gentle puff of wind brushed my arm and Charlotte stood next to me. She cocked her head to one side and pressed her lips together. It took me a second before I figured out she was trying to read our expressions.

"Don't worry; it's nothing," I said.

Before Archer could protest, Charlotte put a finger to her lips and stood perfectly still. *Listen,* she mouthed. I could hear four separate sets of thoughts around the middle of the cemetery. I sifted through them, trying to work out whose they were.

"Josh!" I said.

"Oh, great, just what we need," Archer said.

Without thinking, I orbed to Josh. When I got there he lay crumpled on the ground unconscious, blood running down his temple. Before I could blink twice Charlotte was at my side, and we faced Matthew, Cain, and Tyler. Archer arrived just as Matthew lunged at Charlotte. He sent her flying across the cemetery, and she landed hard against a headstone. I formed two orbs in my palms and threw one each at Cain and Tyler, hitting both vamps in their chests. They landed about twenty metres away; it wouldn't hold them off for long.

I spun towards Charlotte and everything seemed to happen in slow motion, like we were wading through mud. She sprung back to her feet in a defensive crouch, a guttural sound coming from her throat. Matthew crouched as well, edging around her, his fangs bared and growling. They both lunged simultaneously and Charlotte came out on top, throwing him across to the next row of graves.

Then Seth showed up. I was beginning to wonder where he was. It was unlike him to miss the action.

"I didn't think you'd be too far away," I said, guarding Josh.

I threw another orb at Cain, and it sent him flying. He landed with a thud then rolled into a crouch, his dark hair hanging like a curtain around his chiselled face. Archer had a stake in each hand and was busy fighting Tyler who unfortunately had the upper hand.

"Just came to watch the fun," Seth said.

"Well, I have a question for you. If Charlotte's blood is so precious, why is Matthew trying to kill her?"

"Not kill, capture."

Oh. That wasn't good.

Archer looked like he needed help. I orbed to his side, spun around, and connected a flying kick with Tyler's head. He momentarily lost his bearings then whipped around to face me. Blood ran from his nose, and he licked it from his top lip before snarling at me.

"Oh please, you are so not scary," I said.

He bared his fangs, and I chuckled. I orbed again, came down behind him, and drove a stake into his back. Excellent, some dust on my boots. Just what I wanted.

A deafening roar echoed across the cemetery. Matthew did not look impressed. He came towards me and I tried to see what he was thinking, but losing Tyler had clouded his thoughts. All he wanted was me dead. I found this a little amusing; he could pound me into the ground for eternity and I still wouldn't die. I laughed again and Matthew pulled up short. He towered over me, our faces only a few inches apart.

"You can't kill me, no matter how hard you try."

"I'd still enjoy making you bleed," Matthew said.

This time I laughed right in his face. "Careful. You'll end up like your friend here." I shook the dust from my feet. He snarled.

Charlotte came to stand on my right. Seth watched with a very amused look on his face, the corners of his mouth turning up into a smirk.

"Call off your boys, Seth," I said, my gaze still fixed firmly on Matthew's. "I may not be able to rid the world of your filth, but these two are laughable." Cain attempted to voice his opinion with more snarling, and I glanced at him. "Like I said, you don't scare me."

"You don't scare any of us," Archer said from behind me. He stood guard over Josh who was still out cold, blood covering his temple.

Archer told me his leg was badly hurt, but he was going to have to wait. As far as I could tell, he wasn't going to die in the next few minutes, and there were more pressing issues, like the two vamps still trying to kill us. I concentrated on Matthew, attempting to listen again. Seth had his guard up so he was no help. With Matthew only inches from me, I decided to just come straight out and ask him.

"What do you really want with Charlotte?"

Something in his eyes changed, and his thoughts came flooding to the front of his mind—strength, power, and an image of the sun. Matthew had already experienced light walking, and he wanted more, but his next thought was the one that nearly knocked me off my feet.

I saw Seth's expression shift. He knew what I'd learned,

and his growl echoed across the cemetery. He lunged forward, grabbing Matthew with one hand and Cain with the other. All three of them disappeared in seconds, leaving Seth's black mist in their wake. All I could do was stand there for a moment, numb.

"What was it?" Charlotte asked. "What did you see?"

"We can't let them capture you, Charlotte."

"Well, we wouldn't let them do that anyway, duh," Archer said.

Was my sceptic brother having a sudden change of heart? I went to him and put my hand on his arm, channelling my healing power through him. We watched as the gash on his leg closed over, leaving no trace of a wound behind.

"You don't understand. Under no circumstances can Charlotte ever go with them," I said.

Josh groaned and tried to move his head. He hadn't opened his eyes, which was a good thing, but there wasn't much time before he came around. I orbed Josh to his room, healed his wounds, and made sure he was comfortable before he had a chance to know what was happening. I didn't think he'd remember anything, but a part of me wanted him to know. It saddened me that the first time I'd set foot in his room was under such circumstances, but I couldn't think about that. I needed to tell Archer and Charlotte what I'd learned.

Back at the cemetery, I told them that with Charlotte's blood Matthew intended to create an army of vampires who were stronger, faster, and more powerful than any we'd ever seen.

That was not good. Not good at all.

18

GRACE
Early Wednesday morning

Bright light completely surrounded me. My long white dress flapped in the gentle breeze, tickling my legs. My hair softly whipped the back of my neck with the occasional strands caressing my cheek. I was bathed in a soft pure whiteness, and surrounded by warmth. The elegant curves that flowed from my shoulder blades glowed against the light. I was ethereal and angelically beautiful.

Under any other circumstances I would have loved being right where I was at that moment. I never thought about how much I missed home until I was back there, but something wasn't right; there was a feeling in my gut that things were about to get complicated.

"What are we to do with you, Grace?" an angry voice said, echoing around me.

I didn't answer. Instead, I waited for them to continue.

Facing the Council could sometimes be a little unnerving. They seemed to speak with one voice, but also with many, and their sound was all encompassing.

"You do know the rules, do you not?" they asked.

"Yes, but I haven't broken any."

"You revealed your secret to a human," the voice thundered, and it resonated through me.

"Oh, that. In all fairness, he was unconscious."

"You are only permitted to reveal your power to those in the immediate Tate family."

"Well, there aren't many of those around anymore, are there?" I said.

"You seem to be getting a bit lazy after all this time."

"Lazy? I'm working my butt off. The human death rate due to vampire has fallen considerably since I've been around."

"That is beside the point—"

"Well, what is the point?" I said.

Silence.

I wanted to scream and never stop. It was impossible for silence to be deafening, but it rang in my ears louder than any noise I'd heard.

"Charlotte is a vampire, Grace. Did you fail to notice that?" the Council asked.

"She is good."

"Her soul must be released and laid to rest."

My breathing quickened as I tried to comprehend what they were asking of me. I liked to think of myself as quite smart, but sometimes the Council could skirt around the issue.

"Released? So basically you're asking me to murder

my friend?"

"Charlotte is not human—"

"She is immortal," I said.

"There are ways to stop immortality," the Council said. "You do it every day."

This was not going at all the way I'd wanted it to. I'd lost the argument before it even began.

"But her soul is pure," I said. "Charlotte never hurt anybody; she's on our side. I will not murder her, I won't—"

"We don't see it as murder, Grace; you will be freeing her," the Council said. "You were created for a purpose. It is not your place to make this decision, and you must carry out your work without question."

"But *she* is the one in danger. Charlotte is the one who needs protecting."

"She is still a vampire, a creature of evil."

Well screw you, I thought, knowing they could hear me. One thing about the Council I'd always found irritating was their immensely strong mental guard. It was impossible to penetrate so I never knew what they were thinking. An unfair advantage, really, since they could hear me loud and clear.

"Might we also remind you to use great discretion when it comes to human relationships? Intense physical contact is forbidden."

"Can you tell me why that is?" I scrunched the fabric of my dress in my fists. "It seems so natural."

"It is natural for humans, but not for us."

That was unfair; why should humans have all the fun? I ran my hands through my hair as I sank downwards. The light around me faded as the voice spoke for the last time.

97

"If you don't bring Charlotte's soul to Heaven you will fall, and another will be sent in your place to do what needs to be done."

This time, the flying feeling as I exited my dream wasn't nearly as nice. I felt like a ball of lead falling from the sky. Yes, Charlotte was a vampire, and yes, I hunted them, but she was good. How could I possibly kill someone I cared about?

The corrugated roof sheets of the shed came into focus as I opened my eyes. I rubbed my face and let out a quiet groan. A feeling of dread hung in the pit of my stomach, and my mouth felt dry. I pulled myself out of bed and went to the small mirror on my wall. The face I saw in the reflection didn't look like me. My skin had lost its lustre, and there were circles under my eyes. I couldn't believe how tired I looked.

The morning sun streamed in through the high window of my simple loft bedroom and threw light across the bed. I didn't have many earthly possessions; I didn't really see the need. My small side table was bare except for a lamp and one photo of me, Archer, and Pa. The bed was covered with a fuss-free white quilt, and a small carpet square lay on the floor.

There was one other piece of furniture in the room—my bookshelf, which stood about three-feet high. It ran the length of one wall and was crammed full of books—the only material things I treasured. Actually, that was a lie; there were two other things I cherished. One was the small silver ring I wore on my right hand. A dark blue sapphire surrounded by angel wings that curved around the band. It had been given to me when I was first brought into creation. All angels had one. We were told it was a symbol of our union with God and to never take it off. The other was a small metal pill box hidden under the mattress. It wasn't the box itself that was important, but what lay inside—a perfect diamond, shaped like a teardrop.

"Damn it!" I said out loud, my thoughts returning to Charlotte. I couldn't do it. I would not let her die, and I'd made this decision pretty much the day I'd met her. I didn't care about the Council. I didn't care that I'd broken the rules and revealed part of myself to Josh, if he even remembered, and I didn't care what they said up there on their fluffy white clouds. What did they know? They weren't down here living it. I truly believed that Charlotte was good and that she belonged right where she was, fighting, and if I had to spend eternity by her side to protect her, I would.

My phone trilled and it made me jump. I grabbed my bag from the floor beside the bed, fumbled around inside until I found the noisy object, and swiped the screen to answer. It was Emma.

"Hey," I said. "How did last night go?"

"Perfect! He's a fantastic kisser."

"That's great. I'm happy for you."

She obviously couldn't wait until I got to school to tell me all about Ryan. Emma babbled on for a few minutes before we hung up, giving me explicit details. It made me smile, hearing her so happy.

I went through the motions of the morning, trying not to think. After showering and having a light breakfast, I sat at the table with Archer. He'd been eyeing me off, and I knew what he was about to ask.

"I'm fine," I said.

"You don't look it. Council?"

I nodded.

"What did they have to say this time?" he said.

"Charlotte has to die, and I have to return her soul to Heaven."

"Are you serious? They want you to kill her?"

"She *is* a vampire. We are supposed to kill them."

"But she's different. Don't they see that?"

"You seem to have had a change of heart." I raised my eyebrows.

Archer blushed and looked away. What was going on? I decided to give him his privacy and not look to find out. He would tell me when he was ready.

I spent a few minutes trying to get the next words straight in my head before I said them. "They gave me an ultimatum." Archer stayed silent and waited for me to continue. "If I don't release her soul and take it to Heaven they'll send someone else to kill her, and I will fall."

"Oh. Well that sucks."

"Big time." We stood and headed to the car. "I get the feeling I'm being tested, Arch. It's like I'm being forced to choose sides."

"No matter what your decision, we know what side you're on." Archer hugged me.

I opened the door of the Defender and climbed in, smiling to myself. He was right. Good always triumphed over evil—or so I thought.

JOSH
Wednesday morning

The warmth of the morning sun came through the window and hit my cheek. I lay in bed for a moment, my arm hanging over the side, attempting to piece together the events of the night before.

I remembered standing at my mum's grave and watching a bright ball of light create people, which sounded crazy. I remembered staring into someone's dark eyes, and then nothing. I must have passed out, and I wondered how I got back to my room. I felt like I had a hangover but was otherwise fine, so I busied myself with getting ready for the day.

The cafeteria was almost full by the time I got there. Emma sat in my usual seat next to Ryan, but I didn't mind. What was the point getting territorial over a chair? I slid my breakfast tray onto the table, sat down on the other side of my best friend, and picked at my toast.

Then Grace and Archer walked in. The room suddenly felt warmer, and my breath caught in my throat when they headed towards us. I had to quickly remind myself it would be because of Emma and not me.

"Morning guys," Grace said, sitting across from me. She put her bag and her copy of Shakespeare on the chair beside her. I offered her what I hoped was a warm, welcoming smile. It was probably more like a big goofy grin.

Archer plonked himself down next to his sister and didn't say anything. I couldn't help noticing a change in his mood when Charlotte joined us as well. When he'd first sat down he'd looked pissed off; now his eyes were filled with sadness. I sure had some weird friends.

My gaze floated back to Grace. I wanted to reach across the table and hold her hand, just to feel her soft skin and make sure she was real.

"What did you end up doing last night after you left us?" Emma asked.

"Not much," I said, dragging my gaze away from Grace. "I visited Mum's grave, then … not much."

Archer exchanged a look with Grace and Charlotte, then Grace jumped in and changed the subject. "Arch and I have been talking about our eighteenth birthday."

"Gracie." Archer's expression clouded over, and he looked pissed again.

"We are having a party," she said.

"Sounds like fun." Emma smiled.

Archer didn't look too happy about it, but I couldn't work out why. A party sounded like a great idea to me.

"This Saturday night. Who's in?" Grace asked. We all

said *me* at the same time. That is, except for Archer. He just looked mad. "Great. Invite some of your friends as well. The more the merrier." Grace grinned.

"Gracie!" Archer sat forward in his seat.

"Chill out, would you? We have plenty of room."

"I'm going to class." Archer pushed his chair back with a loud scrape and got to his feet. He threw his backpack over his shoulder, stuffed his hands in his pockets, and walked off before anyone could respond.

"Should we follow him?" I asked.

"He's just being a drama queen," Grace said.

"I'll go." Charlotte got up gracefully to follow Archer.

"We should go, too." Ryan pulled Emma to her feet.

The bell hadn't even rung and all of a sudden I was sitting there alone with Grace. My palms went sweaty, and I tried to wipe them on my pants without her noticing. I had the overwhelming urge again to reach out and touch her cheek, but instead I started to fidget. I didn't know where to put my hands.

"Stop, Josh," she said. "You don't have to be nervous around me; I won't bite."

"I just don't want you to leave again."

Grace leaned on the table, putting her hands in front of her. Before I knew what I was doing, I leaned in as well and traced the back of her hand with my finger. Little sparks flew between our skin, and she turned her palm upwards so I could place mine on top. In that moment of silence between us I was so happy, just sitting there holding hands in a noisy cafeteria. We could have been the only two people in the room.

"Come on," Grace said in her melodic voice. "We probably

should head to class." She grabbed her bag and hugged her copy of Shakespeare to her chest.

"You really like that stuff, don't you?" I asked. We walked towards the door and all eyes were on us, but I didn't care. "Me though, I can never understand it."

Grace turned towards me and smiled. "You sound like Archer. He loathes Shakespeare. I guess it's like an acquired taste."

"It's not that I don't want to understand it. I just wish …"

"It was more modern?"

"Yeah, I guess," I said.

We took our seats in the classroom, and I wanted to sit closer to Grace. Having my back to her was torture, and no matter how I sat it was really obvious every time I tried to look at her.

We spent the rest of the lesson watching the movie we'd started on Monday, so at least I didn't have to think too much. The only thing I could think about was Grace.

The end of lesson bell made me jump, and I nearly fell off my seat. A little giggle came from the back row and glanced over my shoulder to see Grace smiling. She hadn't moved from her seat, and I heard her tell Archer she'd catch up with him at lunch; she had a free. I hung back and waited until the room was empty, then turned in my seat to face her.

There were no words in my vocabulary to describe this girl. I could not believe how completely and utterly head over heels I was for her, and she knew it.

"Do you have any weird memories from last night?" Grace asked.

I was sure my face reflected many emotions, confusion

probably the highest on the list. Why was she asking me about last night? Grace was going to think I was a nut job if I told her what I'd seen. I wasn't sure if I should continue, but for some reason I trusted her.

"I did see something, but you'll think I'm crazy."

"Try me," she said.

"I'm not sure that's a good idea."

"I can handle it, Josh. Please … I need to know what you remember. And I can guarantee I won't think you're crazy."

I took a breath. What did I have to lose? She'd either, laugh and say nice knowing you, or she'd listen. "Bright lights making people in the cemetery. I can't explain it any other way. There were these balls of light, and then people appeared. And there was a guy with dark, creepy eyes. Then I blacked out."

Grace closed her eyes and rubbed her temples with her fingertips. I rose from my chair and moved into the one next to hers, then I gently pulled her hands from her face, entwining my fingers into hers. The warmth from her touch flowed through me and I felt connected to her, like we were one person. Grace turned in her seat, pulling herself closer to me.

"I'm not supposed to be with you," she said. "I'm different. I have a secret."

"We all have secrets, Grace."

"It's not the same. You're the one who's going to think *I'm* crazy," she said.

"Try me." I chuckled.

"What you saw last night was me and Archer orbing to the cemetery."

"Orbing?"

"Travelling by balls of light," she said.

"You materialised in a ball of light? Like something from *The Twilight Zone?*"

"But not quite as scary."

"I'm not quite sure what to do with that." I tried to continue talking but I didn't know what to say. My mind knew what it had seen; Grace's confirmation just made it that much harder to grasp.

"I can hear and see things, too," she said. Her hands trembled and she blinked a few times. "The eyes are the windows to your soul, Josh."

"And what do my eyes tell you?" I asked. Grace stared at me. Her eyes glistened and her skin glowed.

"That you think you're in love with me," she said. "And not just in a schoolboy crush kind of way. Deep inside, you believe with all your heart that I'm the one. Scared yet?"

"How could someone as beautiful as you be scary?"

"There's a whole lot more to it. Can we get out of here?" Grace gently pulled me up and took me to the back corner of the classroom. "Do you trust me?"

"Too late to turn back now."

"Hold on then." She folded herself into my arms.

Light emanated from Grace's body. It swirled outwards and around us until we were bound together, and then in a flash we were gone.

For a moment I was completely disorientated, and I thought I was going to be sick. Then there was rock beneath my feet. We landed softly on the outcrop at the end of the path. Grace pulled away, and I loosened my hold on her. What had just happened was amazing, and although I'd never felt more alive than I did at that moment, it took all my strength not to vomit on her feet. Grace wouldn't look at me so I gently raised her chin with my hand. She glowed lightly and looked beautiful.

"How do you do that?" I stroked her upturned face.

"It's one of my many talents," she said. "I have a lot to share with you, but only if you won't freak out on me."

"Oh, I'm freaking out. But so far you haven't tried to kill me so, I figure it's all good."

We stood, holding one another and gazing out over the valley. Above us, the mid-morning sun peeked out from behind a fluffy white cloud. Grace rested her head on my chest; the summer breeze gently whipped her hair against my cheek.

"Why haven't you run a mile?" Grace asked, turning to stare into my eyes.

"Like I said, I'm still alive, and I'm curious to see what else you can do. Besides, you haven't actually done anything scary, just mind-blowing, impossible, and a little stomach-churning, but not scary."

"Then there's something else I want to show you." Grace stepped out of my embrace, her eyes never leaving mine. "Ready?"

Before I could answer she unbuttoned her school blouse, revealing a singlet underneath, and threw it to the ground. She stood with her eyes closed; her body glowed like it had in the classroom. Her hands were clasped loosely in front of her, and the blue sapphire in the ring on her right hand pulsed. Tendrils of light reached out from the ring and encircled themselves around her. I watched in amazement as two beautiful pure white shapes formed behind her, reaching up and out as they grew. Her smile was radiant, and her skin shimmered with light. Grace had become her own light source, and she was absolutely glorious.

Gobsmacked, my mouth hung open, and she stretched her wings wide, the gentle breeze ruffling her feathers. The faint rustling noise they made had an entirely different beauty of its own.

I took a step back as Grace opened her eyes, but I didn't scream, or yell, or run.

"You're still here?"

"You're an angel?" I said. "I think I need to sit down." I shook my head, and then blinked a few times. I sat on the rock, put my head between my knees and took a deep breath. All the while Grace didn't move, and I felt like an idiot. "No, on second thought, I think I'll stand." I got back up and paced a little, running my hands through my hair. "You're an angel?"

"You already said that."

"You're … beautiful."

Grace stepped towards me, and I slowly reached out to touch her wings. Faltering, I asked if I could and she nodded. Ever so lightly, I stroked her feathers; they were the softest things I'd ever touched, like liquid silk beneath my fingertips. I couldn't believe this was happening. It was like I was dreaming. Grace reached up and pressed her palm to my cheek. I circled her waist with my arms, then she squeezed her eyes shut and grimaced.

"What is it?" I loosened my hold.

"This is against the rules, Josh. Showing you my true self, getting involved with a human, is forbidden. Every time I get close to you I'm overcome with dread. I guess it's their way"—she pointed to the sky —"of keeping me in check."

"So that's why you keep pulling away?" I asked. Grace nodded, her hands resting on my chest. "What if you push past it? Is that possible?"

"Anything is possible. But there is something else I need to tell you."

I held her close, resting my forehead on hers, our noses almost touching, still feeling like I was dreaming.

"It's about Charlotte, and Archer." Grace launched into an explanation fit for a crazy person living in a fantasy world, but the even crazier thing was I found myself hanging onto every word she said and believing all of it.

"It seems I'm destined to fall no matter what I do. I refuse to kill her. I've vowed to protect her for as long as it takes. Plus, I've fallen for you."

"But that's a good thing, right?"

"I will be committing the ultimate sin. I'll be turning my back on my God and my family, and you have to know it will be dangerous."

"I'm still adjusting to the fact you're an angel, and you tell me you're also a vampire hunter and Archer's protector?"

"Feel like running now?" she asked.

I pulled her closer. "Where would I run to?"

"You can't tell anyone. My world, the people I protect, would all be in danger. Emma doesn't even know."

"Your secret is safe with me."

Grace turned her face up to mine and finally, I felt

the velvet-soft touch of her lips. We both trembled as our bodies intertwined. Grace ran her hands up my neck and curled her fingers into my hair. Nothing else mattered, and we were lost in one another. I moved my hands from her waist around to her back, then traced the line of her spine up to her wings, ever-so-gently caressing them. Grace tilted her head back, and I placed feather-light kisses down her neck to her collarbone then back up the other side.

"You are Heaven in the flesh." I gazed into her sparkling blue eyes.

Grace smiled and tears spilled down her cheeks, shimmering in the sunlight like tiny flecks of quartz. I kissed her again, only this time with a hunger so intense I never wanted it to end.

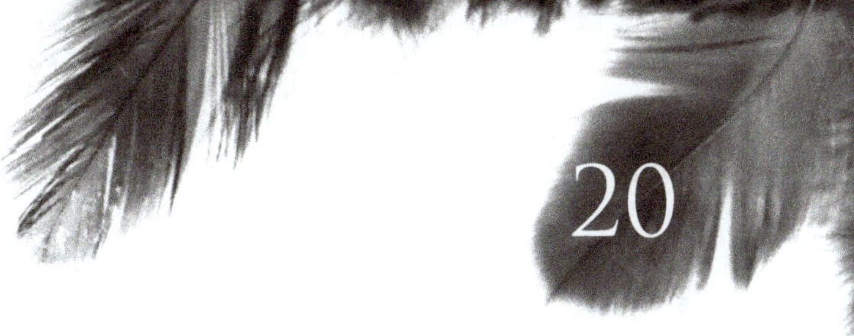

20

GRACE
Wednesday afternoon

Charlotte sat on her bed while I leaned on the desk and looked out her dorm room window. Her room was on the second floor so it had a better view of the yard than Emma's. I'd come to make sure Charlotte would be okay for the night and to borrow some clothes. Archer wouldn't be happy when I told him what I'd done and that I wasn't planning on going home. I wanted to spend a little time with Josh—surprise, surprise.

"You did *what?*" she asked. "How did he take it?"

"A lot better than I expected actually. I think he's a little freaked, but he didn't run. Arch is going to spit chips." I sighed.

I quickly threw on one of Charlotte's singlet tops and a pair of jeans, which I had to roll up considerably, then flopped down onto the bed next to her. When I'd first looked in the wardrobe there were Charlotte's uniforms on one side and an assortment of dark jeans and black tops hanging on the other. She owned one jumper because she didn't feel the cold—it was also black—but I wasn't one to judge. Black was practical.

Charlotte had gone to no effort to liven up the place. She hadn't changed the standard-issue blue bedspread, and the walls were bare. Emma, on the other hand, had posters of her favourite bands everywhere in her room.

"I'm sure he won't be too hard on you," Charlotte said, smiling.

"How are things between you two anyway?" I shifted and folded my legs beneath me.

"I've noticed a slight change in his attitude towards me, if that's what you mean."

"I think he's beginning to like you."

From the look on Charlotte's face, I assumed this was not a good thing. Her expression changed from shock to confusion, then outright denial. "No. Not with a human. Not with anyone."

"Charlotte?"

"What if I lost control, Grace? What if I hurt him?"

"You wouldn't. You're good, remember? Besides, Arch can hold his own," I said.

"Not with me he can't."

Well that was news to me. Archer had never fought a vamp he couldn't handle, which was why he was still breathing, but Charlotte was far too serious and it frightened me.

"You forget that I'm different to other vampires. If I wanted to kill Archer, he would have no chance of survival."

"But I've seen you fight."

"It's not about fighting; it's the fact he trusts me now. His guard would be down."

She had a point; I thought she was being too hard on herself, but I wasn't going to push the issue. Things would run their course, and we would all deal with it together. We were a team, whether any of us liked it or not. I got up and headed to the door.

"Well, wish me luck. I think I know already what Arch is going to say."

Charlotte hesitated and I lingered with my hand on the door knob, waiting for her to speak. She sat perfectly still in that familiar way of hers. I was about to leave when she finally said something. "What if I did have an inkling of some feelings for him? How would you feel?"

"If I know one thing about my brother it's that he's very loyal." I stared at Charlotte across the silence. "Of course, his decisions are his, not mine. But please promise you'll try not to hurt him. When it boils down to it he will always come first, and I don't want to be put in that position."

Charlotte replied with a nod and a tight-lipped smile. I pulled the door closed behind me then headed down the stairs out into the fresh air and towards the boys' dorm. Archer had said he'd meet me in the common room. I was getting a little nervous about telling him my news; boy, was I going to be in trouble.

When I got there, Ryan sat on one of the couches, reading a magazine.

"Catching up on the latest celebrity goss, huh?"

"Oh, hey Grace. Gotta love those trashy mags."

"Have you seen Arch anywhere?" I asked.

Before he could answer, I felt two strong hands on my shoulders, and a soft kiss was planted on my cheek. My heart fluttered and I turned to smile at Josh.

"I saw him walking across the yard," Josh said.

"You haven't said anything to him today, have you?" I folded myself into his arms. He shook his head and gently kissed my lips. It made me a little lightheaded and I had to pull back to re-focus. When I saw Archer walking towards the door, I prised myself away from Josh.

"I'm going to take a walk with Arch," I said. "I'll see you in a bit?"

"Don't be too long."

I stepped outside and linked my arm through Archer's, pulling him away from the common room.

"What's with the hugging?" he asked, looking over his shoulder.

"I need to tell you something."

"Okay, Gracie, what have you done?"

"Why do you automatically think I've done something?" I walked to the dorm steps and sat down in a patch of low afternoon sunlight. Archer sat beside me and gave me his big brother, concerned look.

"Because when you start sentences with, 'I need to tell you something', it's never good news."

"Well, that depends what side you're looking from."

"Just out with it, would you?"

I tried to stall for a few seconds, to form the words in my head into a coherent sentence and find a way of saying what I needed to without the risk of a freak-out from Archer. But that would never happen, so I just had to come right out and tell him.

"You showed him your wings?" he shouted.

"Shhh, not so loud." I looked around. Luckily no one was within earshot.

"And then he kissed you?"

"Yes," I said. "He thinks I'm Heaven in the flesh. It was the most perfect first kiss ever."

"You know that's it now—you've probably sealed your fate," he said.

I took a deep breath and blew it out slowly. "You could be a little less angry."

"No, Gracie. I can't!"

When I'd come back from the outcrop, I'd floated through the rest of the day on a cloud of happiness. I hadn't let myself think about the consequences of my actions, even though they would probably be huge. Archer was right; everything would be different now. It was one thing to swear to protect the enemy, but another to commit an angel's ultimate sin. Ever since the great fall, we were strictly forbidden to have any intimate relationship with a human, but I'd gone and done it anyway.

"Please don't burst my bubble."

"I don't think it will be me bursting your bubble, Gracie. You'll have to answer to them." He pointed to the sky.

The sun was setting, turning the clouds blood red. I put my face in my hands and moaned quietly. What had I done?

"But we're in this together, right?" I looked at my brother and saw the anger was gone, replaced by sympathy, or was it pity? I didn't want pity!

"I love you, so yes, we're in this together. I think we established that when we were born, and again when we agreed to protect a vampire."

"Speaking of Charlotte," I said, getting up, "I know how you feel about her."

"Is there anything you don't know?"

"Yes, believe it or not. But you of all people know how it works."

"Definitely hard to have secrets," he said.

"She's never had a human companion before. Give it time."

Archer gave me a brotherly hug. We walked back to the common room where Josh was waiting for me.

"Oh, hey, you guys are back," he said as we walked through the door.

"I'm going to stay here a while," I said.

Archer sighed. "Guess I'll see you later, then."

I caught a quick exchange between him and Josh before he left. In the meantime, Emma and Claudia had turned up. I didn't see Abby anywhere, which was probably a good thing. I said hello to Claudia before she wandered off to play cards with a group in the far corner.

It turned out I was pretty good at playing pool. Emma and I teamed up and we kicked some serious butt, showing the boys how it was done.

"How about some one-on-one this time," I said.

"You're on!" Ryan went to rack the balls again.

"All right everyone, time to get a move on," a strong male voice said. I'd been having so much fun I didn't realise the time. Mr Bruner stood in the doorway with his arms crossed. "Lights out was ten minutes ago, and you," he said, pointing to Ryan and Josh, "both have an early training session in the morning. First one for the year."

"Yes sir, Coach, sir," Ryan said comically, standing to attention and saluting him.

"Don't be smart, Mr Pierce. Five minutes, everyone." Mr Bruner spun on his heels and marched down the hall.

"They start you early," I said

"We're playing Macquarie High first up. There's a bit of competition between us. Coach says we have to be on our game," Josh said.

I'd never been interested in soccer, or any sport that didn't involve killing a vamp for that matter. I didn't really understand the point.

Josh snuggled into my neck and I giggled. "Room twenty-nine," he whispered.

"That tickles, and I don't need to know your room number to find you."

"So you'll come?" He stared hopefully into my eyes.

"Why do you think I've been hanging around all night, silly?" I leaned in, softly putting my lips on his. When Josh kissed me, I no longer felt the dread in the pit of my stomach, and in his arms nothing else mattered. To me he was the sun, moon, and stars, and my entire world was in orbit around him.

"See you in a bit," I said.

I told the others good night and walked slowly back towards the girls' dorm with Emma and Claudia. I needed to give Josh enough time to get to his room and make it look like I was leaving.

"You and Josh, huh?" Emma said, nudging me. "Good on you, Grace. You were driving me crazy."

"Abby won't be very happy." I glanced at Claudia.

"They were together a long time, but we all knew it

was going to end," Claudia said. "She was the only one who couldn't see it."

"So you don't hate me then?"

"Why would I hate you?" Claudia asked.

"You're Abby's friend. I just thought ..."

"No, don't be silly," she said. "Abby will get over it. See you tomorrow."

Emma and I squealed over some juicy details about Josh before parting ways. I stood in the shadow of the Moreton Bay fig and shivered. It looked creepier in the moonlight. I'd decided to make myself wait five minutes, but five minutes seemed to drag out for eternity and I couldn't stand it any longer. I took cover behind the thick trunk of the tree, checked no one was watching then thought of Josh. My light surrounded me, and moments later I was smiling at his awestruck face as I landed in his room.

"It really amazes me how you do that. I still can't believe you're real."

"Some things just can't be explained," I said, curling myself into his arms. "Can I stay all night?"

"I wouldn't let you go even if you tried."

We talked for a while about all sorts of things—his dad, his mum, Charlotte, me. Josh's mum had died in a farming accident when he was ten. I didn't need to ask too many details; it was all there in his head. He liked talking about her; the part he didn't like was how she'd died. He felt responsible, and couldn't understand why it had happened. Everyone knew the story, but no one ever talked about it.

After a while I began to doze. Josh's fingers gently caressed my cheek, and I fell asleep with my head on his chest, listening to the melodic thrum of his heart.

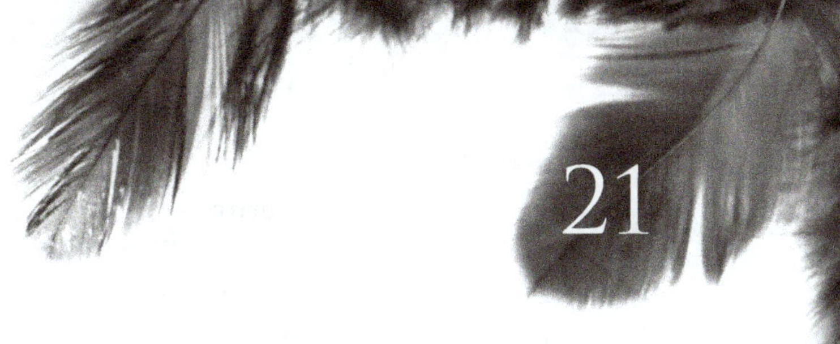

21

GRACE
Late Wednesday night

While I lay in Josh's arms I was summoned before the Council. I was in big trouble, but I was beyond caring. I could handle being exiled if it meant I could be with Josh and save Charlotte. The Council was wrong to ask me to take her soul.

I stood before them in the light, my white dress flapping in the breeze, and the silence closed in on me. I felt like a stranger in my own home.

"You bring me here and yet you're afraid to speak," I said. "What has been asked of me is wrong."

"No, Grace. You have turned your back on us and sworn to protect your enemy," the Council's response echoed around me.

"Archer was right; there are different rules in Heaven. As angels we are supposed to love all God's creatures unconditionally.”

“Charlotte is not God’s creature—”

“Her soul is pure,” I screamed in frustration.

“She is a creature from Lucifer’s army, a creature of the night. Her soul is trapped. It must be freed.”

“Charlotte has never harmed a human She is not evil, and I refuse to let her die.”

“She does not belong in existence. If you do not do it, another angel will.”

“You disgust me. To think you would kill someone so freely. I will fight for her. I will *not* let you do this, even if I have to fight forever.”

“Then let it be so,” the Council said. “There is also the question of your indiscretion. We have been watching this unfold over the past few days.”

“You leave Josh out of this; he has nothing to do with it.” I clenched my hands into fists, and my nails dug into my palms.

“He has everything to do with it, Grace. You have pulled him into this situation, and he is now in grave danger due to your actions. You are a higher being, and yet you bow down to the weakness of mortal life.”

“I can, and I will, protect him. And Charlotte, too, or I will die trying.”

“You have let your human form cloud your judgement. Eventually they will be gone and you will live on, cast out of your home for eternity.”

“If it means saving them, I don’t care,” I said.

“Then go, become one of the fallen and never walk in the heavens again. You have committed the unforgivable sin, turned your back on your God, and we hereby cast you down."

Then everything went black.

I couldn't tell which way was up. I tumbled over and over myself, free falling through the darkness. I curled into a tight ball, pulled my knees to my chest, and squeezed my eyes shut. Icy cold air rushed past me and I shuddered, waiting for it to end. My hair whipped at my face, and my dress tangled in my legs.

The fall took longer than I'd expected. The bitter air began to change, and I was overcome with blazing heat. When I opened my eyes everything around me was black, and the heat was so intense I felt I would burn to ash. I came to an abrupt stop. My stomach rolled over itself and I uncurled from my ball. I hadn't actually hit anything, but my feet were on solid ground.

An orange light crept into my surroundings, and I took a few tentative steps towards it. I emerged from the mouth of a dark cave and stood at the edge of a huge chasm filled with fire. Through the flames I saw the outline of a beautiful iron gate supported by ebony pillars. My jaw dropped; the gate was identical to the one in Heaven, except it was death black. On either side of the gate stood a menacing Moreton Bay fig, leafless and charred with gnarled and grotesque limbs. Now I understood why those trees gave me the creeps.

"Hell's gate," I whispered to myself.

Only a few of Heaven's angels had ever seen it, and as I stood before it, I was scared. When I looked down at my dress I was horrified to see it was no longer white. It was tattered at the edges and as black as the iron on the gate. I turned to look at my wings, and I couldn't stop the tears that coursed down my cheeks. My feathers were no longer bright white with an ethereal glow; instead they were a dirty grey edged in black.

"The mark of the fallen," a voice said from beside me. "Hello, Grace."

Seth was dressed only in tattered black jeans. His bronzed muscular chest was bare, and his wings were completely devoid of colour. They were the colour of death. The tattoo on his left arm was highly noticeable, and for a brief moment I was distracted by its beauty.

"Dare I say, I told you so?" He snickered.

"I am not like you, Seth."

"Then what on earth are you doing here?"

"My reasons are good and solid," I said.

"So were mine."

"I will fight you as long as I walk the earth."

"Well, now that's going to be a long time. It should be fun. Don't stay down here too long; it gets rather hot." Seth left as quickly as he came.

For a while I listened to the crackling fire and the voices of the infinite damned souls it held, screaming in anger and pain. Some of their faces took shape, writhing and twisting over one another. I didn't really know how to get back. I hoped the principle was the same as when I returned from my dreams after seeing the Council, so I closed my eyes and went inside myself. Thinking of Earth and Josh, I willed my essence back to my human body.

When I woke, I was covered in sweat and something was holding me down. I struggled, broke free, and flew across the room.

"Whoa, hold up, it's just me." Josh's kind voice came

from the bed.

"Josh! Did I hurt you?"

"I didn't know you were that strong, but no, I'm okay." He laughed.

"I'm sorry." I leaned against the door.

He frowned. "What's wrong? You've had a very fitful sleep."

"I met with the Council."

That was all I could say before sliding to the floor in a heap. Josh bounded off the bed and pulled me into his arms. He didn't say anything and let me cry it out. When my sobs reduced to sniffles, he took my face in his hands and gently kissed away my tears before softly kissing me. I fell into him and pulled him even closer, twisting my fingers into his soft dark hair. When I finally pulled away, he stared into my eyes.

"Tell me what happened," he said.

"I fell."

"Um … What does that mean? Are you still … an angel?"

"They cast me down from Heaven and …" I looked at my hands and fiddled with my ring. The stone had turned black. "I stood before Hell's gate."

Josh was silent for a while. I sensed his fear, but I couldn't read anything that told me he would run.

"It can't be all bad. You're still here," he finally said.

"I can never go back, Josh. I've become one of the fallen, like Seth."

"Seth's a fallen angel?" He ran a hand through his hair.

I shrank away from him and wrapped my arms around my knees. Josh got to his feet, then reached down and helped me up. I moved away towards the window and turned my back to him, but not without first seeing the pained expression in his eyes.

"Are you okay?" he said.

"No … Everything is different." I glanced in the mirror, and my eyes glistened with fresh tears. "My glow has gone and my wings are black. What will happen when you see the other changes in me?"

"You're still glowing, and I know you're good. I have never known anyone as loyal, and faithful, and pure-hearted as you. Evil is not a part of you, no matter what colour your wings are."

"Will you come with me to the outcrop? I need to show you."

Josh nodded and I walked into his outstretched arms. I rested my head on his chest, held him tight, and sent my thoughts to our destination. But instead of emanating light, thin fingers of blackness reached out and twisted around us, and we disappeared into a dark mist. We set down softly on the rock. I let go of Josh and took a few steps away.

"See? I'm surrounded by darkness now," I said.

"Grace—"

"Are you ready?"

Josh took a deep breath. "As ready as I was the first time you did this."

I clasped my hands together and the dark mist flowed out from the centre of my ring. My wings pushed past the straps of the singlet top I'd borrowed from Charlotte. It felt good to stretch, and I gave my feathers a flutter in the early morning moonlight.

"Hmmm, I see what you mean," Josh said.

I scowled at him and began to pace. Absentmindedly, I fiddled with my ring and rattled off the changes I'd already noticed. "So far, I've lost my glow, I now mist instead of orb, my ring has changed, and my wings are black. What did I miss?" I stopped pacing and gestured for Josh to look at me.

"Grace, I really think you're overreacting. You're worrying about nothing."

"Nothing! I have been exiled from Heaven. My wings are black!"

"Actually, they're a light grey with black edges."

"This isn't funny."

"You're still beautiful, and I think you're forgetting the big picture. Do the names Archer and Charlotte ring any bells?" Josh came to me and took my hand. I relished his familiar warmth and stepped closer to him. "Do you, yourself, feel any different in here?" He placed his finger gently on my forehead. "Or in here?" He moved his hand and placed his palm across my heart.

He was right; I didn't feel different. I knew what I was fighting for. I shook my head, and Josh wrapped his arms around me. He gently caressed my feathers and ran his fingers along the contours of my wings. His touch was soothing, and I began to calm down.

"Then everything will be fine," he said. "You're still a bad-arse Protection Angel, and watch out anyone who tries to get in your way."

22

JOSH

Early Thursday morning

Holding Grace while she slept was an amazing feeling. I was the happiest I'd ever been lying there soaking up her warmth. She hadn't slept well, and I wasn't surprised. Becoming a fallen angel in your dreams did kind of suck—big time.

Grace slept soundly. I imagined she'd be exhausted after her ordeal, but my eyes were like saucers, and Ryan and I had a seven a.m. training session in a few hours. There were so many things running through my mind I had no hope of falling asleep, so I busied myself by getting dressed and attempting to put my thoughts into order. I'd only just come to terms with finding out Grace was an angel, and that vampires existed, then she fell. On the outside it probably looked like I had it together, but it was all very confusing and weird.

Suddenly, Grace flew off the bed.

"We have to go. Now!" She grabbed my arm.

The next moment we were standing in a clearing, the dark morning sky weighing down on us. I didn't feel as sick this time with the whole *Grace travel* thing, but it still rocked me.

In the darkness I could make out the shape of a large shed and a small house.

"Where are we?" I asked. "And what's the matter? You're freaking me out."

She didn't answer, just stood and looked around, turning slowly in a circle. I waved my hand across her line of sight and she ignored me, batting it away.

"Grace?" I planted myself in front of her and grabbed her shoulders, forcing her to look at me. "I can't help if you don't tell me what's going on."

"Charlotte and Arch. I'm trying to find them." Her eyes looked a little crazed, darting here and there, reflecting the moonlight. Okay, this was getting weirder. Standing in the middle of God knew where, watching my girlfriend go crazy.

Girlfriend ... I liked the sound of that.

"Josh." She snapped her fingers at me. "Focus!"

"Well, I would if you'd tell me what's—"

"Found them."

Grace grabbed my arm again and within seconds thick forest surrounded us—yep, definitely getting used to Angel Air. She pulled me down into the bracken fern and held her finger to her lips. My eyes adjusted to the darkness, and the silhouettes of four or five people formed through the gloom, two of them stood close together.

"Can you stay out of sight? I don't want you to get

hurt?" Grace whispered.

Before I could answer, she did her misty thing and disappeared. My heart pounded in my chest so hard I thought it would explode.

Don't get hurt—I could do that.

Grace materialised in the middle of the group and punched one guy in the face. Another went blurry and lunged at her; she took him out with a round-house kick. If I went by what Grace had told me, they were obviously vampires.

The sky was beginning to lighten so sunrise wasn't far off. The two figures standing close together were actually tied to each other at the wrists, back to back. One of them turned, and I looked straight into Archer's eyes. I watched in awe as Grace bent down and drew a knife from his ankle. She flicked it up to cut the rope that bound him to Charlotte.

I leaned against the thick trunk of a tallowwood and attempted to make myself invisible, but I wasn't the one with the superpowers. Seth stood off to one side with a smirk on his face, watching everything unfold. Suddenly, the ground fell away, and I was lifted into the air and shoved against the tree. A pair of deathly black eyes stared at me. They were the ones I'd seen in the cemetery the other night.

From my elevated viewpoint I caught glimpses of Grace and Seth both coming in and out of their mist, while Archer fought off the other guy. I tried kicking out a few times but my attacker was really strong. I thought I could hold my own but it looked like I had no chance. My vision blurred, and a little help would have been very much appreciated.

Charlotte appeared from nowhere and grabbed my attacker. Something snapped, and it echoed into the morning. The vampire screamed then released me, and I fell to the ground as he retreated.

Grace appeared beside Charlotte, and both of them stood over me. Great, I was being protected by two girls. How humiliating.

"The sun is almost up, Seth. Better get what's left of your boys inside before it gets too hot," Grace said.

"This is not over." Seth grabbed both the vamps. The guy who'd attacked me screamed again, and they all turned to mist before us.

"Yeah, I've heard that before." Grace stared at the lingering black cloud. "Everyone okay?" She looked around.

Archer walked over to where I sat in the ferns. "I'd be better if Cain had a stake in his chest," he said.

I stared at Grace. "They were the vampires you told me about?"

"I thought I told you to stay out of sight." She put her hand out to help me up. I gave her a quick kiss and my neck hurt from the movement, but she was worth the pain.

"Why were Arch and Charlotte tied together?" I said.

"They couldn't work on Charlotte without me incapacitated. But we had it under control," Archer said.

"Why didn't they kill you?" I asked.

"I don't know." Archer threw his hands up. "Maybe they like me."

"I want to know what you gooses were doing out here in the first place." Grace frowned.

"Eating."

"Hunting."

Archer and Charlotte spoke at the same time. *Eating.* Gross. What had I gotten myself into? This was all too freaky, not to mention my throat ached from being squashed by Mr Iron Fingers.

"Okay, holdup," I said. "I may not want to go there but, working on Charlotte?"

"Blood siphoning." Grace turned to Charlotte. "Did they get much?"

"A couple of vials, then you showed up." Charlotte rubbed her arm. "Thanks for that, by the way."

I shuddered. "Do I even want to know any of this?" Suddenly, I was very aware of how cold I felt, which was odd as the morning was already quite warm. The sun peeked over the horizon, filtering its early light into the trees and turning the sky a pink orange.

"It's the shock," Grace said.

For a moment I was puzzled, then remembered she could hear my thoughts. I think I went a little numb at that point. The gentle pressure of Grace squeezing my hand brought me back to the present, and I cast the feeling of uncertainty from my mind.

"Um, Archer?" I pointed to his leg. "You're bleeding."

"Grace will fix it," he said, flinging his foot up to rest on her hip.

"Get off me, you oaf." She pushed him away. She took his hand, and we all watched as nothing happened. Grace's eyes darkened, and she furrowed her brow. She didn't look too happy.

"What are we waiting for?" I dared to ask. "You guys hold hands in the bush all the time?"

"Ha, funny." Grace released Archer's hand. "Must be

another thing that's changed."

"You've lost your healing power?" Archer said.

"Looks that way."

Now I remembered the part where she'd told me she could heal people. It was one of the main reasons she'd been assigned as Archer's Protection Angel, to keep him alive for the next Tate family generation. I wondered what was going to happen with that. Grace scowled. I didn't really like the knowing-all-my-thoughts thing, but I didn't protest.

"How did that happen?" Archer asked.

"I fell this morning. Didn't you notice me misting all over the place? A lot of things have changed," she said.

"Sorry, Gracie, I was a bit busy fighting the bad guys. That sucks."

"You have no idea."

Grace and Archer stared at each other for a moment. Archer pursed his lips but didn't say anything else. Charlotte moved to Archer's side. She bared her teeth, and a small hissing sound came from her mouth as her fangs extended. I couldn't help flinching. She pierced the end of her finger with one sharp point, drawing blood. She crouched down and smeared it over Archer's wound. Double gross. I had to look away, but not before I saw the cut on his leg begin to heal.

"Well, thank God I have you now," Grace said to Charlotte. "Fat good I am as a protector if I can't even heal anymore; this blows." She stormed off through the trees.

I went to follow but Archer held me back, shaking his head.

My watch told me I had exactly ten minutes before

training started. Running around an oval twenty times and being subjected to who knew how many push-ups was the last thing I felt like doing.

The three of us headed after Grace and back to the clearing. It looked different in the early morning sunlight—not as creepy.

"Grace is probably in the shed," Archer said as we walked across the dew-covered grass. "She can take you back to school."

"You live here?"

"You sound surprised." Archer stopped by a door in the side of the building.

"It's just, when Grace said you lived in a shed, I didn't think it would be this … big."

Charlotte giggled, and I jumped. She'd been so quiet I'd forgotten she was there.

Grace opened the door and stepped outside, closing it gently behind her. "I'll show you around this afternoon. I think we should come back and figure out a plan."

Grace circled her arms around my waist. I had no time to protest before we were back in my dorm room. I was exhausted, as if I'd travelled from one side of the country and back again all in one night. Grace told me to go to training, to let off some steam and clear my head, and that she'd see me in class in a couple of hours.

The past day or so had sent me on a rollercoaster ride of ups and downs, physically and emotionally, and I was worried about Grace and the others. She assured me we would all be fine during the day. Our main threat was Seth, and Grace said she could handle him.

I hoped she was right.

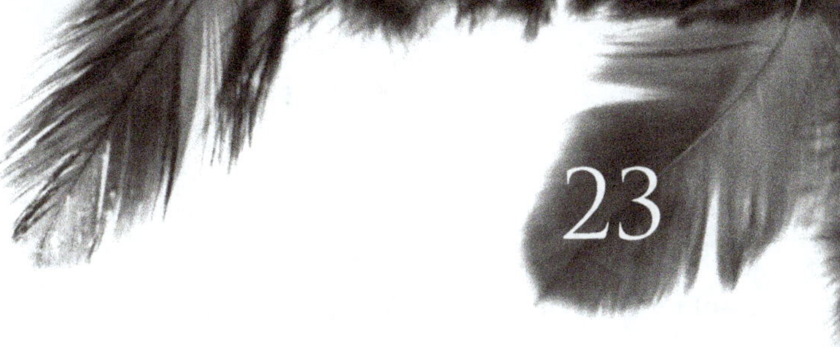

23

GRACE
Thursday morning

Losing my healing power sucked. What use was I as a Protection Angel if I couldn't heal those I needed to protect? Charlotte was fine; she could heal herself, but Archer, and Josh? What had I done?

When I arrived back at the shed I scolded myself for getting not only me, but the others into this mess. Thank goodness Emma had no idea about my double, now pathetic, superhero life.

Archer sat at the Formica table, his chin on his hands, staring at me. I didn't need to be a mind reader to know what he was thinking. He wasn't impressed, but he'd stick by me.

"It'll work out," he said. I sat down across from him. "Our family has survived this long—we'll be fine."

"That's just it, Arch. After all these years of fighting

as a Tate, I'm now the one who has ruined it all. I've betrayed you and the family name."

"Would you snap out of it?" He sat up straight and clenched his fists. "You have not betrayed me. You're fighting for what you believe in, and I admire you for that."

I smiled, but in my emotional state I suddenly felt really tired.

A knocking sound echoed through the shed.

"Are you expecting someone?" Archer asked.

The knock came again. I shook my head and gave Archer a baffled look. Neither of us was in any state to accept company. My jeans were smeared with mud, and I was pretty sure twigs were tangled in my hair and my face was streaked with dirt. Archer's face was dirty, his shirt was torn, and there were traces of blood and muck on his leg.

All I wanted was a hot shower and to get ready for school, but I got up and walked to the door with Archer following.

My next mistake was the result of fatigue and letting my guard down. I should have noticed there were no thoughts coming from outside, and that could only mean one of two things. There was no one there, or it was another angel blocking me.

When I opened the door, I didn't know what had hit me. There was a moment of weightlessness as I flew through the air and landed with a thump on my butt, narrowly missing the coffee table in the centre of the shed. Archer got flung sideways when my arm hit him. We both scrambled back to our feet.

Framed by the doorway and bathed in a soft golden

glow was the most beautiful girl you'd ever seen. I used to glow like that, but she put both Charlotte and me combined to shame. Her eyes were a sparkling washed out blue, and her hair was like golden silk. She was dressed in white linen pants and a flowing white top, playing the part well. Her light blue topaz ring glistened on her right hand. The stone matched her eyes perfectly and was surrounded by a large, intricate wing pattern in two-tone gold.

"Angelica."

"Grace."

"You two know each other?" Archer asked.

"You could say that," I said. "Angelica *was* one of my best friends."

"Angels have best friends?"

Angelica and I ignored him and stared each other down. In my peripheral vision I saw Archer's head moving back and forth, like he was watching a tennis match.

"From the looks of you, we're going to have to do this the hard way," Angelica said. "What happened?"

"I stood up for what I believe in."

"And look where it got you." She shook her head and looked down her perfect nose. "Consider this a warning; we will go after Charlotte—"

"We?" Archer said.

I caught a hint of smugness in Angelica's expression. She made her way across the threshold into the shed, and Annie, our social worker, stepped into view. When Archer realised who it was, he quickly moved to my side. He'd never liked Annie, and now I thought he liked her even less. She took Angelica's place in the doorway, dressed in her crisp cream suit. Something glinted on her hand. She was wearing her ring, no longer hanging from the delicate chain around her neck where it must have been all along. The smooth tiger's eye stone was set in the centre of diamond encrusted wings.

"Why didn't you tell me you were one of us?" I said.

"You never asked. Besides, someone had to protect the protector," Annie said.

"Are you serious? I don't need protecting."

"Maybe not, but you obviously needed guiding. I've been with the Tate family in some way, shape or form for almost as long as you, Grace, whether it was as a family friend, your aunt, or your social worker—even your step-mother on one occasion."

"Get out of my house," I said, "before I make you."

"You're no match for us. You're weaker now you've switched sides," Angelica said.

"She hasn't switched sides." Archer clenched his fists.

"In our eyes she has; she's lucky she was only cast out and not completely stripped of her wings."

That was new; I didn't know the fallen could be stripped. I took a few steps towards Angelica and Annie and threatened them again, but they didn't budge.

"If you're after Charlotte so badly, why are you standing in my shed?"

"It will happen all in good time," Angelica said.

I couldn't get past their mental walls which meant getting any information from them was impossible.

"You really have no idea, do you?" Annie asked.

"About what? That you're a two-faced bi—"

"About Charlotte," she said. "She's not who she seems.

You should be careful who you decide to protect. But you can't say the Council didn't warn you."

"Warn me about what? They want me to kill her!"

"No, release her soul." Angelica smiled sweetly, and I cringed.

"Well, that's not going to happen," I said. "And, like I've already said. Get. Out."

They both stared at me in their perfect angelic way. My temper got the better of me and I drew my hand back ready to strike, knowing it wouldn't harm them much. To my utter shock and dismay, as I extended my arm, a ball of fire sailed across the room. It just missed the orbs of light spinning in the doorway before landing outside on the grass. I watched, speechless, as the fire spread until Archer ran and stomped it out. He looked back through the door with his mouth hanging open. When I thought about it, balls of fire actually made sense. I'd forgotten Seth fought that way, too, and now there was another item I could add to my growing list of changes.

24

JOSH
Thursday afternoon

Training had been a nightmare. Not only was I out of form, but Mr Bruner had grilled me in front of everyone for being late. Ryan knew something was up and had given me sideways glances all session, but he didn't press the issue. The only thing I really wanted was some sleep.

The atmosphere at lunch was kind of weird. Archer gave us the run-down on what had happened after I'd left this morning, and we'd all agreed to keep a better eye on Charlotte.

With so many eyes and ears at Hopetown Valley High, it was difficult to talk about what we were going to do. And not being able to bring Ryan and Emma into the loop was hard, but it was for the best, for their safety and ours. I hated not confiding in Ryan when he knew something was wrong. I also hated knowing Grace knew how scared I was. It was just one more thing she had to worry about.

The rest of my classes passed in a blur. When the last bell finally rang I was glad the day was over, but I wasn't looking forward to the night ahead. The bad guys came out at night, and the ones after Charlotte were pretty mean. The whole situation confused me a little. I would be safe during the day because Grace assured me no angel would harm a human, but Charlotte was now a target from both sides. Things were so messed up, and after not even a week back at school it felt like an eternity since I'd said goodbye to my dad.

The four of us stood at the school gate and went through our plan one more time. It wasn't much of a plan. Grace and Archer would go home as usual, then Grace would come back for me. Charlotte would meet us at the shed since she'd have no trouble sneaking out.

"Fifteen minutes," Grace said. "Will you be ready?"

"Grace, I'm a guy. I can be ready in two."

"What about them? Have you said anything?" Grace glanced towards the dorm stairs.

"Who, Ryan? He's so preoccupied with Emma he won't notice I'm gone," I said.

"And no one cares enough to notice if I'm not here," Charlotte said. "I don't see why I have to leave."

"People won't notice because you're so quiet, not because they don't care, and I think you'll be safer with us." Archer kicked a stone along the ground.

"Let's do this then. See you in a bit," I said.

I gave Grace a peck on the cheek and watched her walk to the car with Archer. When I looked at Charlotte

I couldn't help but feel a bond forming between us. We were in this together, and it was nice to know we had each other's backs.

"I guess we just go and wait for Grace to come get us," I said.

Charlotte nodded, but neither of us moved. It seemed like she had something to say, so I waited. Charlotte was a beautiful girl but I'd never really taken the time to look at her properly—I was always looking at Grace. Charlotte's eyes were black as coal but deep as the ocean. They were filled with anguish, and it made her near perfect face seem tired. When she spoke, her voice quavered.

"You have no idea how sorry I am, Josh."

"Sorry? What for?"

"For getting you into this situation, coming here, and tipping the balance in your life."

"I don't think you can blame yourself for what's happened. Besides, my life was far from balanced."

"Sure I can blame myself. Grace fell because of me, protecting me, and now you're all in danger," she said.

I couldn't help thinking, *you're a vampire; you're supposed to be stronger than me,* but emotionally I didn't think she was.

"I can't handle losing someone I care about, again," she said.

Gently, I squeezed her arm for reassurance and told her that everything would work out. I felt sorry for Charlotte, for what she was, but I'd discovered after my mum died that feeling sorry got you nowhere.

I walked Charlotte to the stairs, then headed to my room. When I passed the common room Emma and Ryan were inside. He gave me a nod; he definitely knew something was up, but I appreciated him not asking. Under normal circumstances, I'd tell him what was wrong eventually, but these were not normal circumstances.

When I reached my room, Grace sat cross-legged on the bed. "What took you so long?" she asked.

"Sorry, Charlotte and I were talking. She feels terrible about our … situation." I pulled a pair of jeans and a fresh T-shirt from the cupboard. "She thinks it's all her fault."

Grace sighed and pulled her knees to her chest. I got changed quickly, not worried about her seeing me in my boxers, although she did raise her eyebrows. *One day, we'd be able to …*

"Josh, not now."

"I'm a guy, Grace. I can't help thinking about you … and me …" I sat beside her and drew her into my arms. "I find it hard to focus when you're around."

"I know. It's just that you've … done *that* before. I've never … and we don't know … and there's so much…"

She stopped when I placed my finger gently on her lips. I didn't need to be able to read her mind to know she was in turmoil, and that the danger we faced was very real. But I didn't care. As long as I had her nothing else mattered. She fit perfectly in my arms, like a key in a lock. Sometimes I didn't like that she knew what I was thinking, but at the same time I was glad. She knew exactly how I felt without me saying a word.

Softly, I brushed her lips with mine. Grace pushed into me and parted my mouth with hers. She tasted so sweet. Her warmth wrapped itself around me, and for a moment we were lost in one another. We fell onto the bed and she kissed me harder, drawing me closer. I pulled away a little and stared at her. Grace's skin glowed softly and I gently stroked her cheek, still unable to believe that she was real.

"You bring out the best in me," she said, pressing her cheek into my palm and closing her eyes. "I wish we could stay like this, but we need to get Charlotte. Arch is probably worrying; I've been away too long."

After one more kiss, I jumped up and pulled her to her feet. "Okay captain, Angel Air is ready for take-off."

Grace giggled, and I hugged her tightly. We grabbed Charlotte on our way to the shed, and Grace was right—Archer had started to worry. He was pacing in the clearing when we misted in.

"Where have you been?" he asked, running to us. "What took so long?"

"Chill out, Arch. We're here now," Grace said, taking my hand and leading me towards the shed.

The inside of Grace and Archer's *house* was nothing like I'd expected. The left wall of the big shed housed a makeshift kitchen with three tables as benches, some plastic tubs underneath them for storage, and an old Kelvinator fridge. There was a tap in the wall with another plastic tub under it for a sink. The kitchen table was an old Formica one—probably from the 60s or 70s—and the four timber chairs around it were mismatched. A gas stove was set up on the bench with a small cupboard sitting next to it. Some chairs lined the rest of that wall, as well as an old church pew with a mirror on it. Three couches sat in the middle of the big space—two lined up next to each other, and one angled off to the right. There was also a coffee table on an old carpet square with three more chairs positioned around it—one a big comfy-looking arm chair.

The right wall had two big roller doors which were probably used when the place was actually a farm shed and not a house. Above us was another floor, like a loft. It took up half the length of the shed. A metal staircase started behind the couches and led up to a landing. A couple of metres back from the railing was a wall with two doors in it. I couldn't see any beds on the bottom floor, so the doors must have led to the bedrooms.

"What's wrong?" I heard Archer ask. I'd been so caught up taking in the shed I hadn't noticed what was going on.

"I think I need an invitation," Charlotte said. "It's your home. You have to invite me in."

"Then please come in, my beautiful fair maiden." Archer bowed deeply and grinned. Grace giggled. Charlotte's pale complexion took on a pink tinge, and she stepped through the door to take his hand.

"Did anyone see you?" Archer asked. "Did Seth …?"

"We won't be missed; we're down for study time, so no one should check on us. As long as we turn up to class tomorrow, we'll be fine," I said.

"School is the least of our worries. I think what Arch meant was, did anyone nasty see us." Grace sat on one of the threadbare couches. "And the answer is no, but Seth will show up eventually. For now I don't think he knows Josh and Charlotte aren't at the school."

"So what do we do?" I asked.

"We wait." Grace shrugged as if to say, *what more can we do?*

I didn't like the idea of waiting; it made me feel like a rat in a maze, not knowing what was around the corner.

"Waiting is the best thing we can do," Grace said. "Let them come to us. We have the advantage."

"What advantage?" Archer said. "They're coming at us from both sides." He sat on one of the other couches next to Charlotte. She was quiet as usual. I worried at the edge of my T-shirt.

"Would you stop that? Come and sit down." Grace waved me over, and I sat beside her. She leaned into me and her closeness was a nice comfort.

"Our advantage is exactly what you just said, Arch. They're coming at us from both sides. They won't be able to not fight each other. We know our constants are Angelica, Annie and Seth, and me. None of us can die. If we can somehow use Angelica and Annie—"

"We can knock out the vamps. Charlotte will at least be safe from them," Archer said. "They want her alive, so we can try and use that against them."

"Who's Annie?" I asked.

"Our social worker," Grace said.

I raised my eyebrows.

Archer chuckled. "It's complicated."

"You don't say."

In theory, it sounded like a good plan. In practise it would probably be a different story. We talked for a while and came to the conclusion that, if given the chance, the angels wouldn't be able to stop themselves from trying to destroy the vamps, and vice versa. Then a small problem we hadn't considered dawned on me.

"Hey guys, what about me?" I asked. "I can't fight."

"Then we'll teach you," Grace said.

"What, in ten minutes? The sun is almost down; the vamps might be here soon. And why hasn't Angelica turned up yet?"

"You're helping in more ways than you know. Angels of the Light can't harm a human; you and Arch are safe from them. If anything, they will protect you."

"I don't want their protection," Archer said.

So Archer and I were safe from the good side, but not the bad. And Charlotte was safer with the bad side, but not the good. Grace would be fine either way, which was great to know, but what a mess we were in. I wondered at that point if I said a prayer whether it would be answered. *Please God, protect my fallen angel girlfriend, her brother, and our friend who happens to be a vampire.* I was leaning towards no. I didn't think it would go down too well.

"Let's do this then." I jumped up from the couch. "Let my crash course in vamp slaying and fighting angels begin."

25

GRACE
Thursday night

My one wish would be to keep Archer and my friends safe. Josh was my biggest concern, and I couldn't help feeling worried watching Archer try to teach him a few things. It wasn't that he was a bad fighter; he just wasn't a hunter, or an angel, or a vampire. I watched as Archer put Josh on his butt for the fifth time in as many minutes. Josh was getting annoyed.

I walked quickly across the clearing and spoke to Archer so no one else could hear. *Arch, let up. This isn't working.*

Yeah, but it's fun. He grinned at me.

Just stop for a minute. I want to try something.

Josh kicked the ground and walked away from us a bit. He clenched his fists and shook his head, staring at his feet. Apart from being utterly embarrassed, he was thinking how useless he was.

"You are not useless." I went over to him and took his hand. "Stand still and close your eyes."

"What—?"

"Please do it. I want to show you something."

He did as I said and I took his other hand, facing him. I channelled my mind to his and blocked everything else out. This was something I suspected I could do but had never actually attempted; I usually kept the mind-talking in the family.

Please don't freak out.

His hands tightened around mine. "You've already done plenty to freak me out, and I'm still here."

You don't need to talk—just think. Think what you want to say to me.

Have I told you, I love you?

Open your eyes and think it again.

Josh blinked and stared at me. *I love you more than I ever thought possible.*

I know.

The look of surprise on his face made me smile.

"How do you do that?"

"It's all part of the package. I've never actually done this with a normal human before, but I think now I've forced you to hear me it will be easier. Arch and I can hold the line open when we want to, so I'm hoping you and I can do the same."

Josh looked a little taken aback, and I couldn't really blame him; there was so much he'd had to deal with in the past few days. When I asked him to close his eyes again, he didn't question me. I let go of his hands and moved around behind him. I motioned for Archer and

Charlotte to move away; a finger to my lips told them not to speak.

Josh, now you have your eyes closed, you should be able to hear and smell better, and be more aware of your surroundings.

What are you getting at, Grace? He shifted slightly on his feet.

Arch and Charlotte are somewhere in the clearing. I'm going to signal them to come closer, and I want you to point to them.

Are you serious? I can't see.

Just try.

The three of us danced around Josh for about half an hour. At first he struggled, but he got the hang of hearing the slightest shift in movement and learned to trust his gut. We stepped up the game and told him to prepare for some physical contact. Josh managed to avoid a few lunges and kicks, but not all of them.

"Ouch! That hurt." Josh was on his butt again, this time because of me.

"Sorry, but do you get it now?" I asked.

"I think so."

"You don't always need to see to fight. You need to use your instinct."

"Now all we have to do is teach you some basic moves and you'll be a better fighter than you were, which isn't hard," Archer said, clapping Josh on the back.

"And it's not only about strength or speed," I said, wrapping my arm around Josh's waist. "It's about wit and cunning, outsmarting your opponent, and using their weaknesses against them."

Something buzzed against my hip, and Josh pulled his phone from his pocket. I guessed it was Ryan before he answered. So much for being too preoccupied.

"With Grace … for the night, yes. Okay, hang on." Josh passed me the phone.

"What on earth are you doing?" Emma yelled down the line. I had to pull the phone away from my ear she was so loud. "Do you know what will happen if he's found out?"

"Emma, it's okay; it's just one night. And so you know, Charlotte is here as well."

"Oh my God, are you guys crazy?"

Maybe. But we had more pressing issues to worry about than school detention. I detected a hint of jealousy in her voice. She wanted to be with us. Our conversation went back and forth for a few minutes, and I told her what felt like a hundred times not to worry. She wasn't convinced.

"We'll see you in the morning. Everything will be fine." I ended the call and handed the phone back to Josh. Emma was such a worry wart.

The four of us kept at it, practising into the night until I was sure Josh could fight at least to save himself. Soft moonlight bathed the clearing and I stopped to take a look around. There was one question weighing on my mind. Why hadn't we been interrupted? If I knew Angelica like I thought I did, she was probably waiting until her chances of getting at Charlotte were better. Angel or not, four against two were pretty bad odds. But the absence of Seth, Matthew, and Cain troubled me. Charlotte seemed to be their highest priority, and with Seth's help they should have been able to track her down. Maybe I was being paranoid, but there was definitely something wrong. I had a feeling I couldn't explain.

"What's the matter, Grace?" Archer came over to where I stood, staring into the trees.

"Nothing, I hope. I think we should get some rest. There are only a few hours before dawn, and I don't think we'll have any visitors tonight."

"I just need to eat." Charlotte stared at a spot on the ground.

"I'll come." Archer grabbed her hand and pulled her towards the trees. He laughed at my expression. "We won't be long. Ten minutes, tops."

Josh walked me back to the shed, his arm around my shoulders. Together we climbed the stairs to the loft. I couldn't shake the feeling that there was something wrong, but I pushed it to the back of my mind. Josh scanned my bookshelf and made a few Shakespeare-related comments before coming to sit with me on the bed. We talked a little, waiting until we heard Archer and Charlotte come back before lying down and getting comfortable.

Josh was having inappropriate thoughts about us again, and I smiled to myself. Boys had one-track minds. But the thought of being that close to him scared me. I was unsure what effect it would have on either of us. The possible outcomes were numerous, and although we both wanted to be close to each other, it was probably not a good time. I snuggled in to Josh and sighed. The feeling of his strong embrace made me immensely happy, and I felt safe. Within moments he was snoring softly.

When I finally fell asleep I plunged headfirst into a dream. Josh and I stood on the rock outcrop where I'd first revealed myself to him. We gazed at the beautiful valley, but something in the air didn't feel right. The sky shifted, changing colour before our eyes, and the clouds raced across the sky. The wind picked up and I turned to Josh, but I was alone. Frantically, I spun in all directions, trying to find him. I heard him call my name. I walked to the edge of the rock and looked down into his scared face. He was falling away from me, and I couldn't reach him.

My wings unfurled and I spread them wide, diving towards him. The air turned cold and the sky went an inky black. The closer I got to Josh, the farther he fell; it felt like we would fall for eternity. When I finally caught him, I grabbed him eagerly and pulled him close, cradling him in my arms. I flew us back to the outcrop, laid him down on the hard rock, and looked at him.

The eyes staring at me were cold and dead, lifeless, but what scared me the most was that it wasn't Josh lying in my arms anymore. An ear-piercing scream stabbed the air and echoed over the valley, it took a few seconds for my brain to register that the scream was mine.

I woke with a start and sat up in bed, gasping for air, feeling like I was suffocating.

Josh rolled towards me. "Grace, what is it? What happened?"

My body shook all over and I burrowed into his chest. He held me, gently stroking my hair, until I calmed down. After I'd relayed the details of my dream, Josh lifted my chin and kissed me softly.

"It was only a dream," he said.

"My dreams are never *only* dreams. I'm scared." Scared that something would happen to him, but worse, that something horrible had *already* happened.

"Hey, we've got this far. We'll be okay," he said.

I really wanted to believe him, but somehow I wasn't completely convinced.

26

GRACE

Friday morning

We decided not to tell Archer and Charlotte about my dream; I didn't want to worry them any more than I had to.

Everyone was quiet as we got ready for school. My morning shower felt like bliss, but did little to calm the feeling of dread in my stomach. At least it was Friday and there was only one more day before the weekend. It was a welcoming thought; after the week we'd had I was looking forward to letting my hair down on Saturday night. You only turned eighteen once in a lifetime—maybe not so much in my case—but Archer still wasn't convinced a party was a good idea.

The short ride to school was quiet, too. Archer drove with Charlotte next to him while I sat in the back with Josh. When we pulled into the gravel driveway, like we had so many times before, something was different. Something was wrong. We passed the gate where almost the entire school's population milled around. Everyone looked lost, and some were crying. Archer parked the car and made a comment I didn't hear, and I jumped out.

There wasn't much conversation going on in the crowd, but the noise in their heads was horrendous. Once I passed through the gate I began to run, trying to find some truth in what I was hearing, in what everyone was thinking. What I saw next confirmed it.

My legs buckled beneath me and I fell to the asphalt. The pain didn't register as the rough ground cut my knees open. My body was wracked with sobs of grief and devastation, and I couldn't get up. An ambulance made its way slowly across the yard with Ryan walking along-side it, his face wet with tears. It was then I knew Emma was dead. For a moment Ryan's eyes met mine, and the pain I saw in them made me want to scream until my voice was gone.

Two sets of strong hands lifted me off the ground and supported my weight. There was no way I could stand on my own. The muffled sound of students talking merged into one big drone. I felt lost, empty. Archer and Josh led me out of the path of the ambulance, and we could do nothing but look as it passed through the gate. Ryan stopped, his shoulders heaving, before turning in our direction.

His face contorted with emotion, and if I'd looked in a mirror my face would have been the same. I screamed Emma's name, over and over again, until my throat was raw.

I let myself be led through the school. I couldn't tell who was there—I was so out of it. Someone, Archer I think, lifted me onto a hard bed that smelled of disinfectant. The pillow rustled under my head, and the weight of a blanket covered me.

"She's in shock," a voice said. "She'll need you more than ever. Best friends, weren't they?"

I didn't know who was talking. My eyes were squeezed tightly shut. I wanted it all to be a dream. Why Emma? Please not Emma. When I opened my eyes my gaze fell on Josh and he jumped up from his chair by the bed. He stroked my hair, his touch tender and comforting. I looked at Archer and Charlotte, and then Ryan. The nightmare was real. His face was harrowed, and I thought he'd cried enough tears for all of us ten times over.

Josh tried to help me up, but I gave him one firm shake of my head. He sat back down and waited. Emotion and grief washed over me, making me dizzy. It was hard to stand, but I did. Slowly, I walked the few steps across the room to Ryan. He rose from his chair and stared into my eyes.

"Why didn't you call me the minute you knew?" I said.

Archer touched my arm. "Go easy, Grace. We're all upset."

"Don't tell me what to do!" I said.

"I'm sorry." Ryan stared at his feet. "The last hour has been a bit of a blur."

"No." I swiped a tear from my cheek. "I'm the one who's sorry. I'm not angry at you. I'm just ... angry." I hugged Ryan tightly, and we stood there holding each other for a long time.

Grace, Archer thought. *We need to find out what happened.*

I pulled away from Ryan. *I don't want to know, Arch. She's dead. Emma is gone, so what does it matter?*

The door to the room squeaked open and Miss Miller, the school nurse, stuck her head through. I was in the school sick room, and suddenly I wanted to be anywhere but there.

"Grace, dear, you're up." She looked at everyone in the room before turning back to me. "I'm terribly sorry about your friend, if you're feeling well enough the school has assembled in the yard, although you are quite welcome to stay here if you like."

Before I could reply, Miss Miller left. The door closed with a soft click. The last thing I felt like doing was facing everyone, but I couldn't stay in that stuffy room either. I bet Seth had something to do with what had happened. The thought of seeing him made me cringe.

I opened the door and walked out, knowing the others would follow. My silence was rude and bitchy, but it was not every day your best friend died. They'd just have to deal with it.

The yard was in complete chaos; those who weren't crying wore worried expressions. The faculty was lined up on the steps, talking amongst itself, and Mr Gerard, Hopetown Valley High's headmaster, appeared to be rather ruffled around the edges.

Josh, Archer, and Charlotte stayed near me, but I paid them no attention as I scanned the crowd for Seth. He leaned against the cafeteria wall, flanked by Ivan and Blake. When I caught his gaze, it took an enormous amount of strength for me not to look away. I angrily swiped at my wet eyes.

Seth's jaw was set; his face stern. I recoiled at the thoughts he assaulted me with. He managed to give me a complete overview of what had happened to Emma in less than five seconds. The next moment I was sitting on the ground, replaying what Seth had forced me to see over and over in my mind.

Emma walked through the gate of the school cemetery towards the graves, and I wanted to scream to her, to tell her to come back, but it was no use. What was she doing there?

With a blur of movement, she was thrown to the ground. Seth must have been somewhere, watching, as his memory showed Matthew standing over Emma. I tried to blink away the image in my head, but I couldn't get rid of it. Matthew leaned down and picked her up; her eyes were wide with fear. She screamed but the sound turned to a gurgle as he clamped a hand over her mouth. His fangs glistened in the moonlight, and he bit her.

I got to my feet and tried to run to save her. The sound of more screams reverberated in my head, and I felt someone's arms around me. The last thing I saw from Seth was Emma's lifeless eyes as she hung limply in Matthew's arms. Everything went dark, and all I wanted to do was run.

"Grace!" Archer said. Then I felt the sting of his palm across my face. I stopped struggling and his features came into focus, the darkness fading away.

"Did you just slap me?"

"You wouldn't stop screaming."

My back was pressed against something cool, and I turned to see Charlotte holding me. Josh kept a safe distance, and I didn't blame him. To everyone else it probably looked like I'd gone crazy, and my little performance had quite an audience. Mr Gerard, along with Mr Bruner, was making his way through the crowd. Miss Miller also appeared and advised Archer to take me home. Seth was nowhere in sight.

"Please, everyone, calm down," Mr Gerard said while Archer put his arm around me. "Parents are in the process of being notified of recent events."

Emma's death had now become an event. My stomach rolled.

"Classes for the day have been cancelled," Mr Gerard continued. "Boarders, please don't stray too far from the dorms. Day students, you may go home."

"The police are looking into the situation," Mr Bruner said. "If anyone has any information we request that you please come forward."

"Mr Tate," a gentle voice said, "I suggest you help your sister to the car." It was Miss Miller. I'd been leaning against Archer and would have fallen over if he wasn't there. With his arm around my waist he led me towards the gate and out to the car. My entire body felt numb.

"Where's Josh?" I asked in a panic.

"I'm right here, Grace." He slipped his arm around me, too. Archer pressed the button on the car key and it beeped as the door lock popped up.

"Ryan! Where is he?" My eyes darted around, and I found him standing with Charlotte under one of the Moreton Bay figs. A shiver ran through me. She had adopted her statuesque pose; he wrung his hands together and stared at the ground.

"We have to tell him," I said to the boys.

They looked at me as if I'd gone completely mad.

"Grace, you can't be serious. You're in shock. You're not thinking straight."

"Do not patronise me, Archer Henry Tate. He has a right to know why she died."

Charlotte slowly nodded. She'd been listening and agreed with me. Archer would find it hard to argue with her. She gently put her hand on Ryan's back and led him over to the car.

"You want me to come to Grace's place?" Ryan stared at Josh, frowning. "But I go home on the weekends, and you're not supposed to leave the school without permission."

"I don't think we'll be missed. If it makes you feel better, I'll talk to your parents and tell them you're with me. I was going to ring Dad anyway." Josh pulled out his phone to make the calls. I leaned against the car, feeling extremely tired, and closed my eyes.

"I'm really sorry, Grace." Charlotte put her cool hand on my arm.

I felt a little better, surrounded by people who loved me, but how was I supposed to survive this? I'd faced death, lost loved ones, and fought the powers of evil, but since leaving Heaven I'd never thought I would again face losing my best friend. I was afraid the memories alone would destroy me. I could live forever, but losing Emma made me feel dead inside.

27

JOSH

My dad's voice was so loud I had to pull the phone away from my ear. "Are you crazy? The answer is no. I'm coming to get you right now."

"Dad, calm down." I'd been trying to convince him I was fine and not in any danger—if only that were true. "She needs me."

"Who, Abby? I thought you two were breaking up?"

"Would you listen? Her name is Grace, and her best friend just died. I need to be here."

"How on earth did she die, Josh? I want you home. I've already lost your mother; I can't lose you, too."

"Dad …" That hit a nerve. So far I'd been as strong as I could, but someone you know dying eventually has an effect on you, especially when it brings back memories of your dead mother. Tears pricked the corners of my eyes. I rubbed my face and paced in front of Grace's car.

"I can't abandon her when she needs me." I stopped and smiled at her.

"When did you start seeing this girl?"

"Would you just say yes already? Her house is ten minutes down the road. We'll be safer there than here." Grace cringed, probably because I was shouting. The silence on the other end of the phone made me nervous. "Dad?"

"Okay, I'll call the school and tell them you have my permission to stay with a friend. But you call me twice a day, Josh. And don't do anything stupid."

"I won't, Dad. Thanks." I ended the call before he could protest any further and put my phone back in my pocket. Next, we needed to get Ryan's parents on side. My best friend looked utterly shattered, and it made me want to cry. He actually looked worse than Grace. But Grace was a tough girl, and I was sure she'd seen things far more terrible in her lifetime.

Ryan had spoken to his parents during the week. He'd told them all about Emma and how they were seeing each other. Because he was a five-day boarder he should have been going home for the weekend, and he was trying to convince his mum to let him spend that time with me.

"Mum, I'll be fine." Ryan gripped his phone until his knuckles turned white.

I put my hand out and wriggled my fingers for him to give me his phone, but he wouldn't. Ryan was getting frustrated, so I grabbed the phone anyway to talk to Mrs Pierce, assuring her Grace's place would be safe.

"Yes, Mrs Pierce ... no one is sure yet how Emma died ... The police are looking into it."

She finally agreed to let Ryan come with me. "Well, I suppose you could do more for him than I could right now," she said. "Stay safe."

"Thanks, Mrs Pierce. Ryan will call you twice a day when I call Dad."

I could understand her apprehension—Ryan was her baby, being the youngest of three boys, and she was just reacting like every other parent would. I gave Ryan back his phone, glad we would all be together. Maybe it would make it easier to tell Ryan the truth. I hoped he would take things as well as I had.

"I'm going to grab us some stuff," I said. "Want me to grab your weekend bag?" I looked at Ryan and he nodded.

"I'll come," Charlotte said, quietly.

Grace stiffened.

"Just some clothes and stuff. We'll only be a minute." I kissed her on the cheek.

We stopped at the bottom of the girls' dorm stairs and Charlotte went to say something, but stopped. Her beautiful face twisted through many different expressions before she let out a frustrated groan. I offered her a sympathetic smile. Most people would think sympathising with a vampire was stupid, but most people didn't believe in vampires or know Charlotte. She was the quietest, sweetest, friendliest person I'd ever met. Sure, she could rip your head off, but just because you could do something didn't mean you would. Over the past five days we'd all grown close, and what she said next nearly shattered me.

"I have to leave."

"What? No, you can't. We need you."

"No, you don't," she said, shaking her head. "I'm the

last thing you need. I'm the reason we're in this mess."

"Have any of us said this is your fault? We made a choice. Grace made a choice that changed the path of her entire existence; you can't walk away."

"You'll be safer without me, and no one will be chasing you. It's me they want."

"Like hell if I'm going to let you do this, Charlotte."

"If only you knew the truth, then all you'd want is for me to go."

"What? No, I'd never—"

"Goodbye, Josh." She gave me a quick kiss on the cheek and ran up the stairs.

How was I going to tell Grace, and Archer? I took the stairs two at a time. When I got to my room, I grabbed my bag and threw in a few T-shirts and some jeans. Then I went to Ryan's room to get the bag he always had ready for weekends at home. Grace would not be happy; I wasn't even sure if she could handle it after losing Emma. On the way back I hoped Charlotte would be waiting for me, but she wasn't there.

When I reached the car, I avoided the questioning looks from my friends. I yanked the door open, threw my bag onto the back seat, and then slammed the door shut.

"Where's Charlotte?" Archer asked, scanning the sea of people still milling around.

"She's not coming."

"What did you say?" Archer's eyes darkened.

"She's not coming," Grace repeated.

"You knew?" I asked. "Of course you knew; you know everything. You seem to be taking it well."

"Not everything," she said.

Archer made to go after Charlotte. I didn't blame him; I wanted to shake some sense into her, too.

"Arch, don't." Grace grabbed his arm. "Charlotte is trying to do the right thing. She'll be back."

"No, I can't let her do this. They'll find her."

"Arch ..." Grace held him firm, and he eventually gave in. He didn't appear to be too happy—I knew I wasn't.

The four of us watched the school for a while, giving Charlotte time to come back, but she didn't. Parents came to collect their kids, and some had a few words to say to the teachers. One mum practically yelled at Mr Gerard. He ended up asking a nearby police officer to escort her back to her car.

Two police cruisers, followed by a forensics truck, came through the gate. The driver of the first car spoke to Mr Gerard before leading the convoy out of the school. I watched more tears silently roll down Grace's cheeks and pulled her close. Now was probably a good time to leave. I opened the passenger door and helped Grace into the car. Once we were all in, Archer made his way out onto the road. He glanced back a few times, probably looking for Charlotte.

The bright afternoon sunlight shone into the clearing, and Archer parked the Defender under the carport. None of us really knew what to say. I felt lost. Where did we go from here? Ryan had never been to the shed, but I think he was too preoccupied to notice anything around him. I hoped the shock of telling him the truth wouldn't tip him over the edge. He seemed to be teetering rather close, and he could go either way. It wasn't every day you woke up to discover your girlfriend was dead, and I could sympathise. I felt like I was balancing on the edge myself. Emma's death brought back memories I didn't particularly want to face, and I wondered whether the truth even mattered now that Charlotte was gone, too.

28

GRACE

Friday afternoon

My best friend was dead, her boyfriend was a mess, and my brother's almost girlfriend, who happened to be a vampire, had just walked away. Gee, life was good. Josh, surprisingly, seemed like the only stable one left.

I'd known about Charlotte's decision to go since we'd first learned of Emma's death. She felt responsible, and I didn't blame her, but I was angry at her for leaving. I was where I was at that exact moment because of her, and I wasn't going to let her get away with it. After everything I'd been through, I refused to let her put herself in danger. I needed to think, so I walked to the mouth of the path that led into the forest. Josh started to follow, but Archer held him back.

Where are you going, Gracie? Archer thought.

Just … I need a little time.

As long as you come back.
You know I will.

With a heavy sigh, I veered off the path and walked west, towards the setting sun. I took out my phone and dialled Emma's home number. After about ten rings it went to the answering machine, so I left a message. The Shroves were probably busy with all sorts of horrible stuff. In a way, I was glad I didn't have to talk to them. It would have been hard not to cry.

I picked my way through the bracken fern and didn't stop until I found what I was searching for. The low sandstone wall, about as high as my knees, was mostly hidden by undergrowth and stained with moss and dirt. Two rows of graves lay in the grounds surrounding the Tate family mausoleum, which looked like a small old sandstone church. It was a place I'd rarely visited until Pa had died. The ruins of the old cemetery would become lost eventually; Archer and I were the last who knew of its existence. Now I was fallen, there'd be no more Tate hunting teams to continue the mission. No one else had a hope in finding it anyway. It was protected by an enchantment. Only those with Tate blood in their veins could find it and bring others with them.

The moment I stepped over the wall, the flood gates to all my earthly memories opened. I was sad because it was the end of the line; I would never protect another Tate. Archer was the last. Even if he married and had children, I would not be reborn as one of them.

The graves were covered by tangled plants and moss. My brothers, my parents, the entire family line was laid out before me. Now I knew why I hardly ever visited, it was way too depressing. The freshest grave in the family plot—and the last in the row—was Pa's. So much had happened since he'd left more than a year ago. How I wished he was still around. Pa always knew how to fix things, even if they didn't need fixing. He'd been like a father to me, and I missed him terribly. I brushed the dirt and debris from his headstone then sat cross-legged on the cool ground. After everything this week had handed me, I felt I needed some guidance.

"What have I done, Pa?" I put my face in my hands. The tears took over for the hundredth time that day.

I wasn't expecting an answer, so I was surprised when the trees rustled and a breeze tickled my neck. With a smile, I watched as leaves danced across the ground. The cool air of dusk warmed as the gentle wind returned to where I sat. Pa stood near his grave, the air now still. He wore his pale blue overalls and checked flannelette shirt, the sleeves rolled up, just how I remembered. His form was transparent, which meant he didn't have much time. Once in Heaven, spirits weren't supposed to return to Earth, and it baffled me how he was there.

"It's good to see you, Grace."

My mouth felt dry, I didn't know what to say or where to start. I wanted to pour my heart out to him, tell him everything and cry until I couldn't cry anymore, but he knew it all already.

"How did you get here?" I asked.

"I had a little help from a friend."

"I've messed up, Pa."

His familiar chuckle sounded like music to my ears and made me smile. Creases formed around his hazel eyes as he smiled. "You did what you thought was right. You are strong, Grace; you do not need a title to be good, and good deeds do not come with bad intentions."

Here I was, the angel from Heaven, and I needed my Pa to point out the obvious. "And bad intentions do not follow good deeds," I said. "I know, Pa, you taught us well."

"It's you who taught Archer and me well. Fallen or not, I know you will do, and have done, what you feel is right."

"Then why do I feel as if I haven't?"

"You cannot control the actions of others, as much as you may want to. Not everything is within your grasp. You do what you can and let others do the rest. And you should never be afraid to ask for help."

The trees above rustled faintly again, and another breeze swirled around me. My heart filled with happiness, and it warmed my soul.

Pa smiled. "There's someone else who wants to see you."

The breeze left and everything became still. A white butterfly flittered past and circled around Pa. It landed at his feet and spread its wings wide. From the centre it grew and Emma appeared, clothed in a simple white dress. Angels called what she was wearing a transition outfit. She walked towards me, and I couldn't get to my feet quick enough. I threw my arms around her, and I never wanted to let go. Pa was here in spirit only, but Emma hadn't completely crossed over. She didn't have much time, or she'd be caught in limbo forever.

Emma's expression was stern as she held me at arm's length. "You know you need to snap out of it and pull yourself together, Grace."

Well, dying hadn't changed her one little bit.

"I miss you, too."

"Now you know I'm okay you can do what you have to do. Go and get Charlotte, and save the world at the same time," she said. "Just be careful; not everything is as it seems."

"What do you mean?"

Emma shook her head and pursed her lips. "You have to work it out for yourself."

"So you're not mad at me?"

"For what? Not telling me about your superhero status? That you can leap buildings in a single bound?" We both laughed. "So where is your invisible plane?"

"Not mad at me then."

"No, Grace, you do what you got to do. Maybe I'll be able to help more, someday."

Emma's hands felt warm inside mine, and my heart was both happy and sad all at once. Happy because she would be okay, sad because I didn't know if I'd see her again.

"I can't believe Seth did this to you," I said.

"He didn't, and he's not as bad as you think."

"You didn't just say that."

"It's true, and I think maybe you need to give him another chance."

"He stood and watched you die. That does not deserve another chance!"

"No," Emma said. "He tried to save me."

I couldn't believe what I was hearing. There was a time when I'd liked Seth, loved him even, but I still wasn't convinced. If anything, I thought the argument leaned heavily in the other direction.

"We have to go, Emma," Pa said. "Follow your heart, Grace, and your path will be true."

"No, wait! You can't go yet. I can't get to Heaven to see you anymore. When … what about Ryan?"

But they were already fading away.

"Follow your heart …" Emma's voice was no more than a whisper.

Follow my heart—that was just great. Didn't my heart get me in this mess in the first place? I needed to vent, to let off some steam. Where was a vampire to stake when I needed one?

On my way back to the shed I tried to think of the best way to tell Ryan everything, including the nice chit-chat with his dead girlfriend. *You see, Ryan,* I'd say, *I'm an angel.* I'd probably leave out the fallen part at first. *And my brother, well, he kills vampires but has the hots for one.* I could see Ryan's reaction, he'd think I was insane, but maybe I wasn't giving him enough credit. Josh had handled it pretty well, although his girlfriend hadn't just died when he'd found out.

Misting home would have been much faster, but I wanted a little more time to myself. As it was, the end of the path arrived too quickly. I walked across the clearing, and the boys were nowhere in sight. The day had disappeared and the stars twinkled above. Crickets chirped in the grass, and a few bats took to the sky. *Well, I better get this over with.* The sooner Ryan knew the better. Protection from the sun wouldn't be back until morning. Night had descended, and with darkness came trouble.

29

JOSH
Friday night

When Grace walked away it was hard. I wanted to be there for her, to help. Archer wouldn't let me follow; he said she'd be back and I hoped he was right.

Ryan wandered to the edge of the clearing, his arms folded, staring into the trees. I took the opportunity to talk to Archer about what we should tell him, or how we should even start to tell him the truth.

"Well, how did Grace tell you?" he asked.

"She didn't really *tell* me, she *showed* me, but I don't know if that would freak Ryan out too much." We stood in silence. Archer stared at the ground; I stared at him.

"I may have an idea." He headed towards the cottage. "Come on."

"Hey, Ryan," I said. "Want to join us?"

Dark circles ringed Ryan's eyes. He offered a simple

nod, then wrapped his arms around himself as if he were cold, and followed. I hadn't been inside the cottage; Grace had said they moved out of it in the 60s, before Archer's time. From the outside it appeared rundown, almost derelict.

We climbed the concrete steps after Archer. He held the crooked door open, and we entered into a small foyer. Everything in the house looked clean and new. Polished floors, white walls—the only thing that was remotely old was the furniture, and even that was in perfect condition. The kitchen and breakfast counter were straight ahead. A large window framed the view of the trees outside. On our right were two closed doors. Ryan glanced around, seeming to show a bit more interest, and he looked a little brighter.

Archer led us to the left through a small open-plan dining room then into a living area.

"This is it," he said, with a grin on his face.

"Um, it's a couch," I said, "and a coffee table with a floor rug." I turned a full circle to take in the room, or what there was of it. The front window framed the shed. Outside, a light breeze tossed some leaves across the clearing. Ryan walked to the far wall and stared at it.

"That's it. Look closely and tell me what you see," Archer said.

"A wall," I said.

"Come on, Josh, look harder."

"It's a false wall," Ryan said, so softly I almost didn't hear him. At first his words didn't register and I stood there, looking like an idiot. When they finally sunk in, I definitely felt like an idiot.

"A false wall," I said.

"Bingo!" Archer pushed gently on a section of the wall and a small panel flipped open, revealing a keypad. His fingers were quick across the keys and a whooshing sound revealed a doorway.

"Welcome to the Tate family arsenal." Archer grinned.

"Arsenal, as in weapons?" Ryan asked.

Archer stepped aside to let us through. "Go in and see for yourselves."

It was nothing short of amazing. A lot of the things in the room I couldn't even name. There were weapons that looked older than my great-grandfather, and then some. Ryan walked slowly down the length of the wall, taking it all in. Knives, swords, axes, a couple of cross bows, and all sorts of other stuff. I'd never seen so many weapons in one place.

Ryan stopped to examine what looked like a tool belt. He reached out and touched the wooden sticks encased in loops of leather. They looked lethal, honed to a sharp point with handles wrapped in twine.

"What are these?" He turned Archer.

"Those are wooden stakes made from Alpine Ash. We get them from down south." Archer smiled again.

Ryan licked his lips. His mouth moved, but he didn't speak. I knew what the stakes were and what their use was, but Ryan couldn't be expected to know.

"They're the best weapon for killing them—the most effective anyway," Archer said.

Archer and I exchanged a glance, and I supposed it was now or never.

"Vampires," I said.

A few moments passed before Ryan replied. "You're kidding, right? Vampires? Like Buffy style?"

I raised my eyebrows and shrugged.

Archer laughed and slapped him on the shoulder before grabbing the stake belt down from the hook. He slid one stake from its loop and handed it to Ryan.

"Exactly like Buffy style."

"Cool." Ryan turned the stake over a few times, feeling the sharp tip with his finger.

The front door opened and footsteps clicked on the timber floor.

"Arch, Josh? Are you in here?" Grace's voice travelled through the cottage. I ran out to the dining room and swept her into my arms. Before she could say anything, I kissed her deeply. I was so glad she was back and hoped she'd dealt with whatever it was she went searching for.

"You scared me," I said. "I was worried."

"I would never leave you." She stood on her toes to kiss me again.

Archer cleared his throat, bringing me back to reality. He and Ryan were in the middle of the living room, Ryan holding the stake in his hand.

"What does he know?" Grace asked, moving to stand beside Archer.

"That we kill vampires," he said.

"And ...?"

"We were getting to that part," I said, sitting on the edge of the couch.

"And what?" Ryan looked around at all of us. "Come on, guys. What are you talking about?"

"Charlotte," I said.

"What does Charlotte have to do with—?"

"You haven't noticed anything weird about her?"

"Weird? Not really. She's a bit odd, as in quiet. She's also a little pale for the country sun, but Grace is pale, too."

"Charlotte is a vampire," Archer said. I raised my eyebrows. "What? Josh, don't look at me like that."

"You could have told him differently," I said.

"Differently? How else do you say it?"

"Why haven't you staked her?" Ryan asked. "If she's a vampire, she's evil. And why the hell are we all so chummy with her?"

"Hey, easy." Grace laid her hand on Ryan's arm. "It's a little complicated. And you're taking the existence of vampires a lot better than I thought you would."

"The world is full of weird crap, right?" Ryan said.

"Like you would not believe."

"We haven't staked her because she's different. In case you haven't noticed," I said, "she walks around in the sun like a normal person."

"She's good," Archer said.

Grace nodded. "Really good. She kills vamps, too."

"Hang on." Ryan's eyes darted between us. "You're telling me one, that vampires are real. And two, there are good vampires? Well, that's a little hard to believe."

We spent some time explaining the entire story, starting with Grace and Archer. It took a while to get through the details, and why Charlotte was in danger. I watched in mild amusement as Ryan's expression changed a number of times. By the end he was sitting on the couch beside me, massaging his temples.

"Okay, let me get this straight," Ryan said. "Charlotte is a special vampire who has super blood that all the other vampires want, and Grace is an angel?"

"Protection Angel," she corrected him. "Hence the reason why we're in this mess."

"And where does Emma fit in?"

"That was a power play," Grace said. "I killed one of Matthew's boys, so he killed the closest person to me that was easily accessible. Only difference is, he doesn't play fair."

"She was killed by a vampire?" Ryan looked like he needed something to punch. "So why aren't we out there staking the crap out of those—"

"Believe me," Grace said, "the one thing I want is dust on my boots, but we have to be careful. I don't want us getting killed. Besides, she's fine. I just spoke to her."

"What?" Ryan and I said at the same time.

Archer smiled smugly. Oh right, twin connection. Grace hadn't connected with me since that first time in the clearing; sometimes I wished she would fill me in a bit more.

"I was sitting in the cemetery—"

"What cemetery?" I asked. Grace ignored me.

"—and I was talking to Pa when a white butterfly appeared. Emma came to tell me she was all right, and to follow my heart."

"Since when has anyone needed to tell you that?" Archer scoffed.

She swatted him on the arm. "The point is, Emma is okay, and we don't need to worry about her."

"So, what now?" I asked.

"Now," Grace said, "we go and get Charlotte and try to fix this mess."

That sounded like a plan, and it sure did beat sitting around feeling sorry for ourselves on a Friday night.

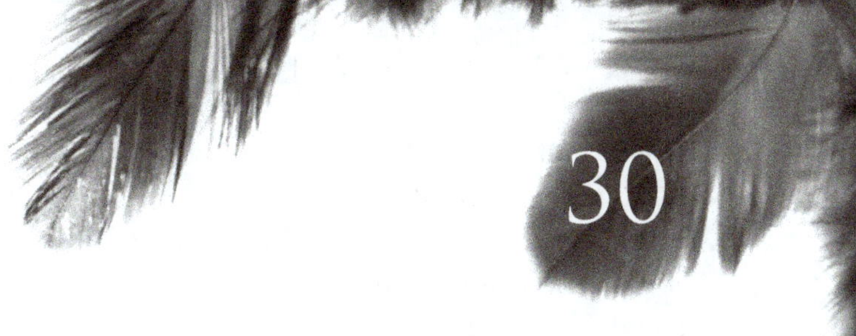

30

GRACE
Saturday morning

The first rays of sun peeked through my loft window; I stretched and turned towards Josh. We'd both flaked fully clothed the night before, and he was snoring softly. I took a moment to gaze at him. His dark hair was tousled, and his fringe flopped over his eyes. I wished we could stay like that, frozen in time, not worrying about anything. It would be better to have him frozen awake though. I chuckled to myself.

Instead of waking him, I lay there and thought about the previous night. Charlotte was proving to be a tough nut to crack; we'd spent hours trying to track her down before giving up. Every time I managed to pinpoint where she was, she'd be off again. She knew how to play me, thinking one thing but doing another. Or I'd finally get within listening distance, and she'd run before I had a chance to stop her. All I wanted was to talk to her; she was making it mighty hard.

"Just as stubborn as you," Archer had said.

I saw the anguish in his eyes each time she slipped through our fingers. She was trying to protect us, but didn't she get it? I'd fallen for her and vowed to protect her. I wasn't going to go away that easily.

We hadn't seen Angelica or Annie either, but they were out there somewhere, watching from their high horse and waiting for the right moment to act. Angels sent to kill the innocent—I never thought I'd see the day. Technically Charlotte wasn't innocent because she was a vampire, but rules were made to be broken. She was innocent in my eyes.

I sat up and threw my legs over the side of the bed. I hoped to find Charlotte today, and to get through another day and night unscathed. Then I remembered. I'd completely forgotten about our birthday party. It wasn't going to be the same without Emma. Maybe Archer was right about it being a bad idea, but perhaps we could use it to our advantage. I was pretty sure Seth knew we were having some people over—actually, I was sure the whole school knew—which meant he wouldn't be able to resist showing up.

"Hey, Grace, what's the matter?" Josh asked in a sleepy voice. I'd been deep in thought, staring at the wall, fiddling with my ring.

"Oh, just the usual." I smiled. "You know, dead best friend, elusive vampire, angels on the warpath." I shrugged. We looked at each other for a few moments, then burst out laughing. I laughed so hard I had tears in my eyes, and it felt good.

Josh stroked my cheek with the back of his hand. "We'll find her." He leaned in to kiss me.

On second thought, that moment in Josh's arms kissing him, was where I would want to be frozen.

"You know, people are going to come here tonight."

"The party." Josh ran a hand through his hair. "I'd forgotten about that. We could tell them it's off, that you're not feeling up to visitors."

"No, I actually think it will work in our favour."

"How so?"

"Charlotte's conscience will get the better of her. She won't be able to stay away knowing innocent people might be in danger."

"Who said anything about putting our friends in danger?" Josh asked.

I shrugged. "The whole school probably knows about the party. Seth will show up with his vamp friends—"

"And this is a good thing?"

"Charlotte is too much like me. After spending your entire existence fighting something, it's not that easy to walk away."

"You're going to use everyone as bait," Josh said.

"And, if I know Angelica," I said, ignoring his last remark, "she will wait for the bad boys to turn up, too. Why waste time looking for something when you know where it will be in twelve hours?"

"Holy crap, Grace. You're using everyone as bait!"

"No ... I'm betting Charlotte thinks she'll need to come. Everyone else will be perfectly safe—I hope."

Josh looked at me with apprehension, and I heard

him yelling *no* in his head. He didn't like the thought of putting our friends in danger, but I had no other ideas. Chasing Charlotte had proven futile. We needed her to come to us.

My phone rang, it's loud trill breaking the silence. I jumped up to take the call from Emma's mum.

"Hi, Mrs Shrove. I'm so sorry—"

"Grace, dear, I wanted to see if you were okay?"

"Me? I should be asking you that."

We talked and shed some tears together. Josh held my hand, squeezing it gently now and then. Emma's dad also hopped on the line to see if I was all right. What was it with them, checking up on me when their daughter was the one who'd died?

"She'll be well looked after, Mrs Shrove; I know it," I said. Josh smiled. "Okay, I'll see you Monday." I ended the call and watched the light on the screen blink off. Josh still held my hand.

"The funeral is Monday morning."

"Your birthday," he said.

"Don't remind me, please."

Josh raised my chin gently with his finger and lightly pressed his lips to mine. I knew what his intensions were; I always knew what his intentions were. He'd been justifying it in his head that he wanted to take my mind off things, and this time I let him.

I wrapped my arms around his neck and we dropped onto the bed. He kissed me deeply, fiercely, and I tasted blood in my mouth but I didn't care. My hands slid down his chest, and I hooked my fingers into the belt loops of his jeans. He kissed my neck, making my spine tingle.

Josh rolled over and pulled me on top of him. I took a deep breath and rested my forehead on his, closing my eyes. His hands were warm against my skin as he lifted my top to caress my back, his fingertips gently tracing the lines where my wings hid.

"Promise you'll never leave me," I said.

"Where would I go, Grace? You have my heart. And my soul if you want it."

In that moment, it didn't matter that Josh was human and I was an angel. It didn't matter that what we were doing was against the rules, and it didn't matter that I would outlive him a thousand lifetimes over. All that mattered was us, and I melted into his kiss.

Then Archer popped into my head and ruined the moment. *Gracie,* he thought.

I ignored him and concentrated on Josh. Whatever my brother wanted could wait.

Gracie, if you don't answer I'll come in.

Sighing, I pulled away from Josh and sat up on the bed.

"Grace, what's wrong?" Josh asked.

"It's Archer. He's outside the door."

We both looked at the closed door of my room.

"Well, are you going to come in?" Josh said, not trying to hide his annoyance. The door opened enough for Archer to stick his head through, an amused smirk on his face. "What is so important you couldn't wait, I don't know, half an hour?"

"Josh." I put my hand gently on his arm. "Angelica is downstairs."

"Bit more important than feeling up my sister, don't you think?" Archer laughed. I threw a pillow at him, and he ducked. "See you two in a minute."

We made ourselves more presentable and less ruffled-looking before leaving the loft. Angelica stood beside one of the couches, her nose in the air.

"Please, have a seat," I said.

"Think I'll pass." She moved towards me.

"Snob."

"Traitor."

"Wouldn't want any dirt on those pristine linen pants, would we?" I said.

"Is that a footprint on your butt, you know, from being kicked out of Heaven?"

"Okay, girls, I'm going to jump in before you start pulling hair and scratching each other's eyes out." Archer stood between us.

Gently, I grabbed his shoulders and moved him out of the way.

What do you want? I stared at Angelica, channelling all my anger at her.

You know what I want.

She isn't here.

I can see that. Where is she?

"What are they doing?" Josh whispered to Archer. To him I was just standing there, staring at Angelica.

"Angelica is leaving." I walked to the door and held it open.

"Actually, I've come to make you a deal."

"I don't make deals with the devil, so to speak."

"Grace, you are closer to the devil than I am." She laughed, and the sound made me cringe. Angelica was supposed to be the epitome of goodness, like I once was, but her halo was hurting my eyes and her purity made me want to vomit.

"No deals," I said.

"Your status fully restored. For Charlotte."

"Seriously? You would do that for me? I'm so touched. Like I said, I don't make deals with the devil."

Josh fidgeted at the table while I stood with one hand on the door, gesturing for Angelica to leave. Archer walked over and I hid a smile, knowing what he was about to do.

"Would you like a footprint on your butt, too? You know, from being kicked out of the Tate family shed." He mimed a kick at Angelica and she flinched, stepping into the doorway.

"Have it your way. We'll be back."

"We're shaking in our boots. Don't let the door bruise your butt on the way out." I slammed it in her face.

"What's going on?" Ryan asked from the top of the stairs, stretching and scratching his head.

"Not much," I said, "just putting out the garbage."

Archer, Josh, and I burst into fits of laughter, and Ryan looked at us as if we'd all lost our minds.

31

GRACE

My stomach felt heavy with worry for Charlotte, but if Angelica didn't know where she was it meant the vampire was probably still alive. I hoped Charlotte knew what she was doing. We decided to keep a low profile after Angelica left and get some things sorted for the party.

We built a small bonfire in the centre of the clearing. The boys were off in the forest doing guy things, while I stared at a pile of sticks, thinking.

The mid-morning sun was warm on my face; I closed my eyes, relishing its touch. My wings felt cramped, and I decided to give them a stretch. No one was around to see so it couldn't hurt. They pushed gently past the straps of my red singlet top until they were fully unfurled. I stretched them wide and gave them a gentle flutter.

I looked at my hands, and a tiny thought entered my mind. I'd worn the ring on my right ring finger for as long as I could remember; it had always been there, from the moment I'd come into creation, and I'd never questioned its existence. My union with God was symbolised by that ring, and for that reason I'd never taken it off. Curious, I fiddled with it for a few seconds, then began to slide it down my finger.

"I wouldn't do that if I were you," Seth said. He came around the bonfire to stand beside me.

"What are you doing here?" I sighed, pushing my ring back into place.

Seth regarded me for a moment. "Trust me," he finally said. "You don't want to take your ring off."

"Give me one good reason why I should trust you? You … you left." He flinched, his expression hardening. "You watched Emma die."

"In all fairness, I did try to stop Matthew, and you still don't want to take off your ring."

"Why? What will happen?" I asked.

"I can't believe after thousands of years as an angel, you've never worked out what your ring is for."

"It's a symbol of my connection with God. Or rather it was before it turned black," I said.

"Mine did the same thing when I fell. If you remember, my stone used to be amber; now it's onyx like yours."

I glanced at Seth's ring—one sweeping angel's wing surrounding a jet black stone. I twirled my ring again, trying to picture what it used to look like when it held the sparkling blue sapphire. A stone as dark as death stared back at me.

"All fallen angels have black onyx in their ring—those who still have rings," Seth said.

For a moment, I let my guard slip. I was confused and wondered why Seth had come. He always had a hidden agenda, but this time something felt different.

"You still haven't worked it out?" he asked. "For someone who's been around as long as you, you're pretty dumb."

"Hey—"

"If you take that ring off, you will lose your wings. They'll be stripped."

"Angelica said I was lucky not to have been stripped after I fell."

"And she's right," he said. "But no doubt she intends to try."

I rolled everything Seth had said over in my mind and stopped on one thing that puzzled me. "Annie wasn't wearing her ring; it was around her neck. So why did she keep her wings?"

"If it was around her neck then technically she was wearing it. I guess the Council made an exception, and Angels of the Light have ways around almost everything. Besides, as far as I know, only another angel can strip you. Unless you're stupid enough to do it yourself."

"Why are you telling me this? Are you helping me?"

Seth's eyes softened. He looked like he actually cared, which frightened me. We'd fought for so many years, and it hurt too much to remember what it was like when we'd been friends. I pushed into his mind and glimpsed the beginning of a thought.

Because I ...

Seth?

Get out, Grace. "If Angelica loses her ring, she also loses her wings," he said. "Think about it. She will be powerless against you, against us.”

“There is no *us*, Seth.”

His expression turned cold. I could feel the wall he’d put back up between us, not even realising how far it had come down in the first place.

“Ivan and Blake, have they been stripped?” I asked.

“My boys got into a little trouble, yes. Their rings are with the Guardian.”

“There’s a Guardian?” I shook my head and rubbed my temples. “Why don’t I know any of this? Has my existence been that sheltered? Am I really that naïve?”

“Don’t beat yourself up too much; I don’t actually know who it is. The Guardian’s identity has been a secret for a very long time. Besides, you’re just a Protection Angel. Need-to-know basis I guess.”

That was true; my status in Heaven had been on the lowest rung, but Seth’s knowledge got under my skin and it looked like I had a few things to learn. While I was thinking and trying to process all the new information, he’d come a little closer. I raised my head and stared up into his eyes. His face was only inches from mine, and his cold expression bore into me.

“Can we be killed if we’ve been stripped?” I asked, my pulse racing.

“Yes, but it’s complicated. Lose your wings and you lose your power. It also makes you weak, hence the reason Ivan and Blake are more bark than bite. They don’t put themselves in dangerous situations anymore. They’re hoping to get their rings back one day.”

Seth reached out and stroked my feathers. I shrank away from his touch, folding my wings as close to my body as possible, but I stood my ground.

Do you remember what it was like before my fall? Seth's stare held mine, and I found I couldn't look away.

Of course I did, but I was used to the way he was now. I'd blocked the other memories. I didn't want to go there.

Seth stroked my cheek with the tips of his fingers and I closed my eyes, shivering at his touch.

Please, Seth, don't.

You know why I fell, don't you?

I didn't answer. I didn't want to, and for some stupid reason, I didn't move.

It's too painful to remember, I thought. *Please ... don't.*

"Why did you really come?" I put up the wall inside my head and stepped back. "Why are you trying to help me defeat Angelica?" And then it dawned on me. A smile spread across Seth's face as he saw my realisation. "You need me. You want her gone, and you can't do it yourself."

"You do always figure things out eventually, Grace."

Angelica wasn't the only reason he was there, though. I could feel it. Memories flooded my thoughts, and this time I didn't stop them. My time in Heaven with Seth played out in my mind. It hurt. I'd worked so hard to keep it locked up. I didn't want to remember. When Seth had left, my world shattered. We'd been in sync for so long that it was like the night losing its stars. Angelica had told me we were better off without him; he wasn't a true servant of God and was where he belonged. I came to Earth not long after. Well, a few hundred years, but that was nothing in the scheme of things for an angel. I'd spent so long trying to block it out, throwing myself into protecting the Tates and fighting evil, but with Seth on my heels everywhere I went, sometimes it was hard.

Finally, it dawned on me why he fell. How could I have been so blind? Angelica and Seth had been my best friends; how did I not see it before?

"You fell because of me," I said.

A lonely tear slipped down my cheek, and Seth reached out as if to catch it in his palm, but instead he brushed it away with his thumb. The memory of catching Seth's tear in my hand flashed across my mind and I stared into his cold eyes. He glared at me in silence.

Finally, Seth said, "You might want to go get Charlotte. Matthew got hold of her early this morning. She's locked in a warehouse out on the highway."

"Seth ...?"

"Just go, Grace. I'm done with Matthew and his crap. Chasing Charlotte was fun, but I want Angelica now. She's the one who convinced you to hate me so much in the first place."

"No, you did a good job of doing that yourself."

He stroked my cheek again, and it made me shiver.

"Angels aren't supposed to fall in love, especially with each other. But for the record, you were worth it."

And then he was gone.

32

GRACE

Saturday afternoon

Seth's touch lingered on my cheek as I retracted my wings. The good news—there was a way to defeat Angelica, or pull her down a few rungs. The bad news—well, I didn't want to think about that.

"Grace?" Josh called across the clearing. "What did *he* want?" He came to my side.

I took a breath and let it out slowly. "To tell me Charlotte is locked in a warehouse on the outskirts of town, amongst other things."

"Charlotte is what? Why are we standing here? Find her!" Archer said.

"You could be a little less rude," I said.

"Oh, we're sorry, Grace, did we interrupt a private moment between you and Seth?" Josh said.

"It wasn't like that."

"I saw the way he touched you."

"You don't know what you're talking about." I shook my head.

"I know what I saw."

"Josh, Seth and I have history. Not even Archer knows about it."

"Well, that's news to me." Archer scowled.

Great, my boyfriend and my brother were angry at me for something that was out of my control. I wouldn't win this one, but I had to try.

Josh, please ...

"Would you stop doing that?" He stormed off towards the shed.

Ryan was silent throughout the entire exchange. He shrugged and followed his best friend. He wasn't angry; he just felt he had a responsibility to Josh.

"Ryan," I said. "We'll be back soon with Charlotte."

He nodded and continued walking.

Archer clenched his fists at his sides. "What the hell ... what were you thinking, Gracie?"

"Arch, it's complicated. I can't explain—"

"Try." My brother stood over me, not about to back down.

The story would take too long to tell, so I opened my memories to Archer and flooded his mind with a snapshot of my life before him, before our family. Archer's eyes widened with every new piece of information.

"Well, that kind of sucks."

"Can we go get Charlotte now?" I held out my hand.

"You don't love him back, do you?"

I glared at Archer and he flinched, then took my outstretched hand without another word. I misted us to the other side of town, and we landed in a laneway between two big warehouses. We walked to the end and out into a car park. Concentrating, I searched for Charlotte, locking in on her thoughts.

"She's over there." I pointed to a dilapidated tin shed a block down the street.

I misted again and we landed inside the warehouse. The shape of some old farm machinery came into focus as my eyes adjusted to the gloom. Apart from the two rundown tractors and a bulldozer, the place was empty. I couldn't see Charlotte anywhere, but I could feel her.

"Charlotte?" I said into the darkness.

"Grace? Upstairs." Her voice echoed off the metal walls.

A staircase in one corner led up to a glass office. Archer and I ran to the bottom and picked our way over the rusting steps. It took a few shoves to open the door at the top, and when we entered the small room we found Charlotte chained to a chair. Or rather, she was under a huge pile of chains that wrapped around her body and her legs. Hercules wouldn't have been able to break free.

"What took you guys so long?"

"You kept running away, remember?" Archer knelt down to pick the padlocks holding Charlotte captive.

"We stopped looking—figured you'd come when you were ready. Seth told us where you were. Looks like we won't have to use bait." I laughed. Archer threw me a look, and Charlotte raised an eyebrow. "Never mind," I said quickly. "Are you coming back? We may have a way to put Angelica in her place, and fight off the blood-crazy vamps."

"This bit you haven't told me," Archer said.

"All in good time. Let's get Charlotte home first."

Archer unravelled the chains. When he was done, Charlotte rubbed her wrists where they'd been bound, then launched at Archer and hugged him. He spun her around a few times to see if she was hurt.

"Archer, I'm fine," Charlotte said. "But I have some bad news. Matthew and Cain drained more of my blood—about another four vials."

"That is bad news," Archer said. "I thought one drop was enough."

Charlotte nodded. "One drop is plenty, but it doesn't last long because their blood cleans it out of their system. But the more they drink, the longer the effect. In theory, if they drink enough the change could be permanent."

We stared at each another in silence as the horror of what was possible hit home.

"You're saying if they drink enough they'll become like you, and be able to walk around during daylight hours forever?" Archer asked.

There's a reason I'm so quiet, Arch; I don't like to draw attention to myself. It's too dangerous."

"You do that just by existing." He smiled.

"Has it ever happened before?" I said. "The permanent change?"

"No." Charlotte shook her head. "Vampires like me have always defeated those who have threatened us. But I think we're okay for now. They haven't had any yet. Matthew mumbled something about not having enough—"

"To create his army." I worried at my lip.

Charlotte nodded.

"That's good to know, but tell me one more thing." Archer sat on the chair and rubbed his face with both hands. "Are you going to run again?"

Charlotte pursed her lips then wiped her face, smearing blood from her tears across her cheek. One shake of her head was all it took, and Archer sighed with relief.

Something didn't quite add up, though. For a split second, I wondered if Charlotte was telling the truth. Of course she was. What reason would she have not to? Still, I peeked inside her head and found the closed box that had been there before. Our eyes met, and I forced myself to smile.

"Is there something you're not telling me, Charlotte?" I asked. *I know you're hiding something.*

She hesitated as if she'd heard me, and then simply shook her head. "I'm just tired."

"Leave her alone, Grace. She's been through a lot," Archer said.

I decided to let it go.

We all held hands and I misted us back to the clearing. My stomach did flip-flops on the walk to the shed, and the reception I received from Josh was less than welcoming. He gave Charlotte a relieved hug; I got a very cold shoulder.

I let out a deep breath and sat at the kitchen table, motioning for Archer and Charlotte to follow. Archer got excited when I gave them the rundown on what Seth had told me about my ring. He saw it as the definitive way to keep us all safe.

"I think we should be more concerned about Matthew and Cain, than Angelica," Charlotte said. "When they show up I'm pretty sure they'll have taken my blood, which means they'll be faster, and stronger, and harder to fight."

Ryan and Josh listened to our conversation but didn't

offer their opinion. They were scared—they'd just never admit it. Josh was also angry, which was overriding his fear. It could work in his favour, but when someone was scared they tended to make mistakes.

We dressed in jeans and loose-fitting T-shirts, then went to the cottage to raid the arsenal. Charlotte was in her element, running her fingers lightly over the weapons as she walked the length of the wall. Archer gave Ryan the bare minimum, one stake for each back pocket, and showed him a few quick moves. I threw a stake belt and a dagger with an ankle strap to Charlotte. She put them on quickly and went back to looking at the rest of the gear.

My stake belt fitted into the small of my back, concealed by my top. I strapped a knife to my upper left arm and another to my ankle. Josh let me fit a stake belt to him but he didn't speak. I could feel his gaze burning into me, and my fingers tingled when they brushed the warm skin on his stomach. When I was done, I met his stare and fought the tears stinging my eyes. I'd shed too many tears lately. Josh leaned down and kissed my forehead, then turned and walked out of the cottage.

"He'll come around," Ryan said. "He's just mad."

"I know." I sighed.

Back in the shed we sat in silence and ate a quick throw-together meal. As I watched Ryan eat his instant pasta, I thought back over the last day or so. We were all having a hard time dealing with everything, especially Emma's death, and I wanted nothing more than to hide from all of it. But giving up wouldn't solve anything. I had to face my problems head on. I wasn't a runner.

I was a fighter.

197

33

JOSH

Archer and I had spent the morning with Ryan, wandering around the forest, bringing him up to speed with the world of angels and vampires, and trying to teach him a few moves. He wasn't very good but he could at least throw a punch.

Now, we stood at the edge of the clearing watching Grace and Seth, and she seemed a little caught up in what he was saying. He reached out and stroked her wings, and my blood ran cold. I remembered the first time I'd touched her wings—how soft they were. She shied away from him, and I had an overwhelming urge to punch his lights out. Then he stroked her cheek as well, which made me even more furious. This time she didn't pull away.

"Those wings are pretty amazing," Ryan said.

I glared at him.

"What is she doing with him?" I didn't really expect an answer, and Seth was already gone. I headed across the clearing, calling her name.

"What did *he* want?" I made no attempt to hide my anger.

Grace tried to tell me something about Charlotte but I wasn't listening. I wasn't even aware of the words flying between us; I was too busy seeing red. Grace tried to talk in my head, which added more fuel to the already raging fire. I needed to walk away.

I stormed off to the shed with Ryan in my wake. Who did she think she was? After all we'd been through this week, to let Seth, of all people, touch her like that. I threw open the door and yelled in frustration, kicking the coffee table before sitting on the couch.

"You don't think maybe you're overreacting?" Ryan asked cautiously, coming to sit beside me.

"She let him touch her wings. That's way too intimate for my liking. I thought it was something we shared. Now she's shared it with *him*."

"They probably have history, Josh. They've been around long enough ..."

I stared at my best friend. "Whose side are you on? And you're taking all this supernatural crap pretty easily."

"I don't like taking sides." Ryan shrugged. "And Emma died yesterday. I never for a second believed something like that could happen. It makes me think that anything is possible."

It dawned on me how much of an idiot I was being, and I put my face in my hands. Grace was still here, but Ryan had lost his girlfriend.

"Listen, I'm sorry, mate. I didn't mean to be so crappy and insensitive."

"Don't worry about it. Grace said Emma's okay, and I believe her."

We sat and waited for Archer and Grace to come back with Charlotte. There wasn't much else we could do. I thought about having a few drinks that night and letting my hair down. A lot of us were underage, but not by much, and it was easier to get away with it when you lived in the country. I wondered who would actually turn up. My guess was not as many as we'd initially thought after what had happened with Emma.

The others came back, and Charlotte was a sight for sore eyes. I didn't think I'd be so happy to see her. She seemed unharmed, and after giving her a welcoming hug I resumed my position on the couch. I tried my best to ignore Grace; I wanted her to know I was mad. From the corner of my eye, I watched as the three of them sat at the kitchen table.

Grace raved about some ring and how it could be our answer to everything. Archer got excited at the prospect of defeating Angelica and keeping Charlotte safe. I was all for the latter, but I was still mad and not in the mood for thinking. All I could see was the way Seth had touched Grace. It wasn't an innocent touch—there'd been something behind it that I didn't like.

"We should get ready for tonight before everyone starts to show up," Grace said, sliding her chair back from the table. "Jeans and loose-fitting T-shirts; we'll need a bit of concealment."

We changed in silence, the girls in Grace's room, and

the boys in Archer's. Grace and I came out of the bedrooms at the same time, and I stopped to look at her—my beautiful Grace. All I wanted was to hold her, pull her into my arms and say sorry for being a total dick. But my pride stood between us, and instead I looked away. She knew what I was thinking anyway—I could feel her.

"Josh," she said.

"Don't, Grace." *Just let me be mad at you, please.*

I heard her release a long deep breath as I walked down the stairs.

In the cottage we armed up, stake belts and daggers all round. I let Grace help me, and our eyes connected again. Hers glistened with tears but she managed to keep them at bay. I gently kissed her forehead before walking out of the cottage.

After a quiet dinner, we all went outside. The sun slipped below the horizon and the sky turned a deep crimson red. Shadows danced into the clearing and the crickets started their song.

"Should we light the bonfire?" Archer said.

Grace held out her hand and a ball of fire appeared in her palm. Ryan drew in a sharp breath, his eyes widening, and a smile touched Grace's lips. She'd told me about the change in her fighting technique, but I was yet to see it. It felt surreal, standing there watching her twirl the ball of fire with her fingers. She drew her arm back and tossed the blazing ball onto the pile of wood. The flames lit up the clearing, flickering back and forth, mesmerising and beautiful.

Archer went to the edge of the clearing and dragged some fallen logs around the fire for seats. It amazed me how strong he was. We scrounged a few more chairs and put the Eskys out along the shed wall, ready for everyone's drinks. Grace set up a camping table with some bowls of chips and finger food. Archer and Charlotte sat on a log while Ryan picked out a plastic garden chair we'd found under the car port. Grace stared into the fire, and I stood staring through the flames at her, waiting for everyone to arrive.

34

JOSH
Saturday night

The fire threw its light around the dim clearing. Kids from school showed up in small groups and chose their seats around the bonfire. I'd tied a balloon to Grace's rickety old letter box to help everyone find the place. Grace stared into the flames, every now and then acknowledging if someone spoke to her. I didn't think anyone there was a close friend of Grace or Archer's; they just wanted to party.

Charlotte and Archer moved over near the shed with Ryan, pulling up prime position next to one of the Eskys. Charlotte wouldn't want to get too close to the fire.

A familiar voice shouted my name. Abby's older brother, Jesse, walked down the driveway. He threw me a can, then shook my hand. Despite the age difference between us, we were good friends, and I hadn't seen him since before Christmas so it was a nice surprise.

"What's this I hear about you and Abs breaking up?" He chuckled.

"You know, mate, it just wasn't working."

"She can be a bit much, I'll admit, but she's still not very impressed with you."

Tell me something I don't know. I took a swig of my drink. I stole a glance at Grace who was still looking into the fire.

"Well, Josh, fancy seeing you here." Abby walked over to us with Claudia at her side.

Claudia offered me a sympathetic look and said hi before wandering off to see who else was around. Abby folded her arms across her chest and switched her dagger-eyed stare between me and her brother. Dressed in a low-cut ice blue singlet top and skinny jeans, she drew my attention for a moment before I glanced at Grace again. She looked at me this time, and I quickly took another sip from my can.

"Don't tell me you're going to fraternise with the enemy, Jesse." Abby scowled.

"Josh didn't break up with me, Abs. We're as good as gold."

"Argh … you suck, Jesse West." And she stomped off after Claudia.

"Suck it up, princess," he said. She turned to glare at him and poked her tongue out. Very mature. I shook my head and had another drink.

The clearing was starting to fill up. When I looked again for Grace, she wasn't there. Jesse saw my gaze flitting around and asked what was up. When I told him I had a new girlfriend and was trying to find her, he punched me on the arm.

"You don't waste any time, stud."

"It's not like that. I hadn't been happy with Abby for a while. Grace is … perfect."

"But?" Jesse prompted me.

"There's this other guy. I'm probably overreacting, but it's complicated."

"Ain't that the truth." Jesse threw back his beer and finished the can before wandering off to get another. He kept them coming, placing a new one in my hand each time he had one. Before long I began to loosen up and feel warmer, until I spotted Grace near the car port talking to Seth.

The way they stood so close together made me stiffen with anger. I couldn't hear what they were saying over the hum in the clearing and the crackling fire, but actions speak louder than words. Even though Grace didn't back away from Seth, she didn't look too impressed—or maybe that was what I wanted to believe.

Jesse followed my line of sight. "That's her I take it."

I took a few steps towards them and froze. What I saw next was enough to shatter my heart into a thousand tiny pieces. I was afraid the pieces would be so small I would never be able to find them to put it back together. Seth slipped one hand behind Grace's back and pulled her close. With his other, he stroked her cheek and she leaned in, closing her eyes. Leaning down, he pressed his forehead against hers. They were close enough to kiss, and I willed her to push him away, to smack him in the face, but she didn't. Finally, she stepped back and Seth walked into the forest.

How could you? I yelled in my mind. Grace was still

for moment. She could hear me, and I waited for her to lift her head. When her eyes met mine they glistened with tears, but I didn't care. I felt numb.

Josh, I … she pushed into my head, but I'd already turned away.

"Somehow, I don't think you're overreacting. Some chicks just aren't worth it," Jesse said.

That was the problem, though—Grace *was* worth it. There had to be a reason why she was getting so close to him, but I was too mad and too drunk to think. The image of her in his arms was burned into my brain.

"I'll be back. Just going to clear my head."

"Want some company?" Jesse asked.

"No … I'll be fine."

I headed down the long driveway with no particular destination in mind. I was angry, and I wanted to get away from the noise, or maybe I needed to distance myself from anything to do with Grace. I kept trying to tell myself there was a reasonable explanation for why she'd let Seth get so close to her, but I was at a complete loss.

I'd made it about three-quarters of the way down the drive when an ear splitting scream sliced into the night, followed by another. I froze, listening. The scream had come from the road, and I wondered if anyone else had heard it. Very unlikely, as the road was a fair way from the clearing. Cautiously, I kept walking.

Jesse's beat up blue ute was parked at the top of the driveway, half in shadow. I briefly wondered, even though he only lived in town, how on earth he would drive home after so many drinks.

The driver's side door was open but the interior light

was off, so I couldn't see inside. I didn't have to. I sensed something was wrong. With each step forward my heart beat faster, and I broke out in a sweat. When I reached the open door I staggered backwards, stifling my own scream, and fell onto the rough bitumen. *No, this isn't happening.* Panic rose inside me.

Claudia slumped in the driver's seat with her legs hanging out the car door. The thick metallic aroma of blood assaulted my nose. It looked like Claudia hadn't had time to put up a fight. She was so still.

The strong urge to be sick rose in my throat, but I suppressed it. All I could do was sit. I didn't want to get up, or look at Abby. She was in the car, too. I pushed myself off the road onto my knees and stood up, staring at Claudia. My courage had run for the hills, but I managed to walk, one step at a time, around the ute. I couldn't see Abby's face through the front windscreen, only her outline in the shadows.

When I opened her door, Abby tumbled out into my arms. I fell back again, and gravel dug into me as I hit the ground. We sat there for what seemed like forever. I cradled Abby in my arms, not wanting to look at her face. When I finally did, she looked peaceful. Her eyes were closed, but she'd put up a decent fight. Her nails were ragged and her clothes were torn. The moonlight shone on her face turning it deathly pale, and that was when I noticed she was still breathing. I held as still as I could and watched her chest to make sure. There was definitely movement.

"Abby!" I shook her, trying to get a response. "Abby?"

She made a funny gurgling sound in her throat. I

gently put her back into the passenger seat. Blood from a jagged wound under her chin covered her neck and chest, and I had to resist the urge to be sick again. She took short, shallow breaths but wasn't conscious.

I guessed Matthew had done this to them. I may not have loved Abby anymore, but she didn't deserve this, and neither did Claudia. I ran back to Claudia's side and moved her more into the car. Her neck was also covered in blood, and she was starting to come around.

"No, don't move," I said, as she raised a hand to her head. "I'm going to get help."

I stepped back and stared at them both, tears sliding down my face; first Emma, and now this. I didn't want to leave Abby and Claudia. They were barely clinging to life, but I needed to go and get Grace; she would know what to do. She needed to know Matthew and Cain were near and that Charlotte wasn't safe. No one was safe.

My body turned back towards the shed, set to autopilot. I called to her in my head, *Grace!* I took one step, then another, and then everything went black.

35

GRACE

People were arriving, but I wasn't paying attention. So many thoughts danced through my head, like the flames dancing in front of me. It was hard to look away from their mesmerising flicker. Josh stood on the other side of the bonfire talking to Abby's brother. I'd never met him, but he seemed nice enough. From what I read he and Josh were good friends.

My earlier encounter with Seth weighed on my mind, as did Josh's reaction. I didn't know where to start, trying to explain it to him. With Archer, it had been easy; once I'd shown him, he'd accepted it. That was what brothers did. Josh was mad at me, and I couldn't blame him. If Abby had approached Josh like that, I would be mad, too.

I was actually angry at myself more than anything. As much as I hated to admit it, I'd liked it when Seth touched me. The more I thought about it, the more I wanted it, but how could I trust him after all the things he'd done? How could I even be thinking about him?

When I glanced up, Abby and Josh were talking. I caught Josh's eye and he quickly looked away.

Grace, we need to talk. Seth stood in the shadows on the edge of the clearing.

I should have ignored him, but I couldn't, and I hated myself for wanting him. Josh was the one I needed to go to, but instead I walked to the car port where Seth came out of the darkness and waited for me. He folded his arms across his chest. The moonlight made his blond hair gleam and his dark eyes sparkle. I hated myself even more, as a hidden desire rose within me.

"What do you want from me, Seth?" I said.

"You know what I want. Now that you're on my side, we can—"

"No. We can't." *Don't touch me.*

I know you feel something for me, Grace.

It doesn't matter. I'm with Josh.

What can he possibly give you?

"What can he give me?" I scoffed. "Everything you can't—love and trust. I could never trust you."

My world was falling apart. I was being pulled from both sides, and I didn't know what to do. Josh was still near the bonfire; I could feel him watching me.

Before I knew what was happening, Seth had hold of me. He wasn't rough, but he wasn't tender either. He stroked my cheek, and I gave in. My eyes closed, and I pushed my face into his hand. The memories of our entire life together flooded through me and engulfed me completely. He leaned down and pressed his forehead to mine.

He wanted to kiss me, and it was taking all his strength to hold back. Surprised, I discovered how badly I wanted him, and my heart told me we were right for each other.

When I pulled away I gasped, wanting more, craving his touch like an addict craves a fix. Seth drifted back into the forest leaving me feeling empty and alone, my face wet with tears. I turned to where Josh stood.

How could you? he thought, before dropping his head and walking away.

Slowly, I backed into the shadows of the forest, and my emotions took over. Through a blurry haze I watched Josh until he'd disappeared down the driveway. Abby's brother went to follow, but Josh waved him away.

Seth's breath was warm on my neck. He tilted my head to the side and caressed my skin with his fingertips. I closed my eyes, attempting to think straight. *What the hell am I doing?* Under his spell, I was unable to resist.

"We need to find Angelica," I finally said, pulling away from him.

Seth's body tensed, and he grabbed my arms. *Looks like she's found us first.* Then he did something I never expected; he pulled me around behind him to protect me. Angelica threw an orb of white light and Seth blocked it with his fire. The balls collided then imploded and fizzled out.

"We *will* have Charlotte by the end of the night," Angelica said.

"Over my dead body." I stepped out from behind Seth. "Oh wait—I can't die."

"She's out there for the taking," Seth said. "Why are you here wasting time with us?"

"Because there are too many innocent people around, aren't there?" I smiled.

Angelica glanced around the forest. "Annie is surveying the scene; it won't be long."

"Listen to yourself," I said. "I can't believe you're scheming to kill someone. That's something Seth would do." He threw me a sideways glance. "Sorry."

"Don't mention it."

"Charlotte isn't *someone*, she's a vampire." Angelica put her hands on her hips.

"A vampire who does more good than you ever have, or will."

"What's happened to you? Don't you remember what it was like in Heaven? Don't you wish you had that back?" Angelica shook her head.

"What happened to me? I stood up for what I believed in. As for wishing for anything, I wish to be anywhere you aren't. I wish you didn't exist."

Seth's smile confirmed what I'd denied all along. It didn't matter that I fought the forces of evil. We were on the same side and had been since the moment I'd fallen. It was us against them—the fallen angels versus the Angels of the Light. I was no longer one of them. As much as I hated to admit it, I was an angel of darkness.

A faint scream sounded into the night, drowned out by the drone of voices in the clearing. I forgot Angelica and instantly searched for my friends. Charlotte, Archer, and Ryan were together and surrounded by other people, but Josh wasn't where I'd expected him to be. When I found him, he was screaming my name. Quickly, I grabbed Seth's hand and misted.

We landed in the mouth of my driveway and I didn't know where to look first. The blur of Matthew's body engulfed Josh and sent him crashing to the ground, knocking him unconscious. Jesse arrived on the scene, panting and out of breath, and Angelica and Annie orbed in next to the blue ute parked on the edge of the shadows.

Archer! Get your butt up to the road, I thought.

Matthew pounced on Josh again, smiling wickedly. Before I could react, he dug his fangs into Josh's neck. Cain stood close by and threw his head back, laughing. My legs felt like lead as I tried to move.

Everything seemed to be happening in slow motion. I turned towards the sound of more screams. Jesse lay on the ground beside the car, cradling Abby in his arms. I hoped to God Angelica and Annie would do something about it.

Help them, Angelica, I thought at her.

Don't tell me what to do, Grace.

Now is not the time to be petty.

Grace! Archer thought as he arrived with Charlotte.

Angelica glanced at Abby then at Charlotte, taking a step in her direction. Then she scowled, and I breathed a sigh of relief when she chose to help the girls instead of chasing the vampire. Seth hauled Matthew off Josh and fought until he got the upper hand. His face was contorted with rage, and he threw ball after ball of fire at Matthew until he fell to the ground in a pile of ash. I watched as Seth kicked it with his boot. Cain turned and ran down the road in a blur; he didn't even look back. I sprang into action and ran to where Josh lay in the road, motionless.

Balls of light whizzed past my head. Fire and light lit up the dark sky as Seth countered the attacks from Angelica and Annie. I hoped they'd seen to the girls properly first.

I didn't see when Ryan had turned up, but he hovered over me, gripping his hair tightly in his fingers. Charlotte's face was the whitest I'd seen it, Archer's gaze darted everywhere, and Josh was barely breathing. I lifted his head and laid it in my lap. Blood oozed from the wound in his neck so I pressed my hand against it, trying to stop the flow.

The ute's engine roared to life and Jesse floored it, tyres screeching on the bitumen. Bits of gravel flung up and hit us as he drove away.

I had to know if the girls were okay. *Angelica, are they ...?* I thought, staring at the back of the ute.

Yes, Grace, we healed them. They're fine and won't remember a thing.

Josh's blood seeped through my fingers and ran down my wrist. *What about Josh?*

No, Grace. Not everyone is meant to be saved.

"Are you serious?" I screamed.

"Grace, what are you doing?" Seth said. "I'm trying to fight here."

We needed to get out of there. Angelica was not going to help Josh, and I couldn't believe she was willing to stand by and let an innocent person die.

"What do I do, Arch?" I said. "I can't heal anymore, and Angelica won't help. He's going to die."

My fingers trembled as I pressed harder against his wound. Archer crouched beside me and rested a reassuring hand on my arm. Ryan paced in front of us, mumbling under his breath and running his hands through his hair. Charlotte hung back, hovering at my shoulder, and that was when I came up with an answer. I turned and stared at her.

She shook her head. "No, Grace, no way. No."

"Charlotte, he's going to die. We don't have much time. I can't lose him."

"Grace, I can't hold them off forever. Get out of here, now!" Seth threw another fire ball.

"Charlotte, please?" I said, begging her to agree.

All it took was one slight nod of her head.

Seth? I'll find you. "Everyone, hold on to me."

"Go!" Seth said.

Annie and Angelica pounded him with their white orbs.

I clutched Josh and made sure Archer, Charlotte, and Ryan had a hand on me, then I took us to the one place I thought we'd be safe. The room we landed in was pitch black, but I knew every nook and cranny like I knew my name was Grace. I traded places with Charlotte then quickly went to a corner and found some matches sitting in a crevice. Once I lit the oil lamps that were set into the sandstone walls, the darkness subsided.

"Where are we?" Ryan asked.

"The mausoleum," I said, "at our family cemetery."

"Where you saw Emma?"

I nodded.

The room housed one solitary resting place. My first father, John William Tate, lay in the centre under a white marble slab, but it wasn't the time to start reminiscing.

"Please," I said to Charlotte. "Do something."

"You know what you're asking of me, don't you?"

"Please ..." I said again.

"What are you expecting her to do? Grace?" I looked at Archer and saw it snap into place in his head. "No, Charlotte, don't." Archer went to her. "You don't have to do this."

With my back against the wall, I sank to the floor, sobbing, whispering please over and over again, and pleading with Charlotte to do something.

"I can't heal him," she said. "He's lost too much blood. It's all or nothing."

"I know. Just do it. Please." I put my hand over my mouth.

Ryan looked on in horror. He sat beside me without taking his eyes off Josh. "What's she going to do? Is he going to die?"

Josh took shallow breaths, and his skin had turned ashen grey. He lay on the cold stone floor, clinging to the last strands of his life while we all watched.

"He will die if she doesn't ... turn him." I wiped my eyes and drew a deep breath. What had I asked her to do?

"What? No!" Ryan said, making to get up.

I pulled him back down, and he didn't struggle, just shook his head as if to say he didn't want to believe it was all happening. I didn't want to, either.

Charlotte cradled Josh's head in her lap, then gently picked up his right hand. She extended her fangs, and they glistened under the light of the oil lamps. She hesitated, before bitting his wrist to drink. Then, using one sharp pointy fang, she slit her own wrist and let her blood run into his mouth.

Streams of blood coursed from Charlotte's eyes, staining her cheeks. The enormity of what I had asked her to do hit me smack in the face. She'd never been a creator before, and she'd never tasted human blood. Charlotte had once told me she swore she would never inflict this life upon anyone, and here she was, breaking her own promise. Uncontrollable sobbing wracked my body. My brother was torn between comforting Charlotte or me. In the end, Archer came to my side and held me tight while Ryan slipped his hand into mine.

Charlotte gently laid Josh's head on the ground. She removed his stake belt and rolled him onto his side, resting his hands near his face. When she was satisfied, she scooted back to the wall, wrapped her arms around herself, and rocked. Across the dim room our eyes met briefly, and again I saw the locked box inside her mind. Whatever it was, she was desperately trying to keep it hidden. She was completely alone with us on one side of the room and her on the other, but Archer would *always* choose me.

Charlotte stared at Josh with sad eyes. "Now, all we can do is wait."

36

GRACE

Early Sunday morning

None of us knew what was happening back at the shed, and I hoped everyone was all right. Josh definitely wasn't. A film of sweat covered his body, and every now and then he cried out in pain. It was heartbreaking to watch. I tried to listen to what he was thinking but there were no coherent thoughts, just blackness.

Charlotte wasn't sure how long the change would take. She couldn't remember most of hers and had never seen one happen. She flinched each time Josh made the slightest movement.

Archer and I hadn't set foot inside the mausoleum for a long time, so everything was coated in a thick film of dirt. Light seeped through the narrow windows, which meant we'd been watching Josh half the night.

"I have to get out of here," I said. My butt was numb

and cold.

"Where are you going?" Archer jumped up. "You can't leave now."

Someone called my name, and I held my hand up to silence Archer. No one had spoken out loud so I strained to listen, hoping it was Josh, but the voice had gone. Frustrated, I rubbed my face and sighed.

"Someone has to find out what's going on. Cain is still out there with Charlotte's blood." I also wanted to know if Seth was okay, and before I could stop the thought, Archer heard it.

His brow furrowed. "I'm coming with you."

The room was silent except for Josh's shallow breathing, if that was what he was still doing.

Archer wasn't going to take no for an answer. "Fine," I said. "Just don't slow me down."

Charlotte and Ryan stayed with Josh. He would need someone when he came round, and I had a feeling he wouldn't want it to be me. If he was angry, Ryan was probably our best chance at calming him down.

Archer followed me out the wooden door and into the cemetery. Walking back to the shed would take too long, so I grabbed Archer's hand and misted us into the dining room of the cottage. I went to the kitchen and splashed some water on my face, wishing I had time for a shower, but there were more pressing issues to deal with.

Dew covered the clearing. It reflected the early morning sunlight, making the grass sparkle like diamonds. It would have been magical if it wasn't littered with cans, rubbish, and overturned chairs. But I liked the eerie silence, and if the knowledge of death, changing vampires, and betrayal weren't hanging over my head, I may have actually enjoyed it.

Archer walked silently beside me to the shed while I tried to figure out what to do next. Seth's wellbeing concerned me because I needed him if we were to have any chance of getting to Angelica. Caught up in my own thoughts, I didn't feel Archer sneak into my head again.

"Why are you so worried about Seth?" Archer asked when we reached the shed door.

"In case you didn't notice, he helped us last night."

"That doesn't mean he will again, and it doesn't erase the past."

"Tell me something I don't know," I said.

"What's going on between you two, Gracie?"

That was a question I couldn't answer. Archer blocked the door and waited for my reply, but I didn't have one. Seth was complicated, the whole damn mess was complicated, and I had to focus on getting Angelica and Annie's rings. Or finding another way to stop them, because I didn't think they would give up in a hurry.

I pushed past my brother, knowing Seth was inside the shed before my hand even touched the door handle. When he got up from the couch, Archer moved in front of me. I could see the hatred dripping off him.

"Would you quit it?" I pushed him out of the way. "And what is it with you two trying to protect me? I can look after myself."

Archer scowled and retreated to the kitchen table, shouldering Seth on the way past.

"Watch it, Tate," Seth said. "I could kill you with a flick of my wrist."

"I'll pretend I didn't hear that." I walked over to Seth and he sat down again. "Are you okay?" I touched a weeping cut near his eye. "They must have got you good if it hasn't healed yet."

"Don't worry—it's nothing." He took my hand and pulled it away from his face. He didn't let it go; instead, he turned it over and traced the lines on my palm. If someone had asked me a few days ago if Seth was capable of doing something so gentle, I would have laughed in his or her face. He raised his eyes to mine. "Are *you* okay, Grace? Is Josh …?"

I drew a deep breath, willing myself not to cry. I'd done enough crying in the past week to last myself a thousand lifetimes.

The weight of Seth's hand around mine suddenly felt awkward and I pulled away, instantly regretting it. Why did it feel wrong when he touched me, but when he didn't it was all I could think about?

"I've been better," I managed to reply. "Josh is …" *changing.* I finished the sentence silently. I couldn't bring myself to say it out loud. Seth's body stiffened and he moved away a little. I knew what he was thinking because we both had our mental guards down. Seth had been comforted by the fact we had forever. He could spend years trying to win me over. Josh should have been dead in seventy years or so if he'd lived out his natural existence, but the bar had just been raised.

"You know, thinking like that is not going to make me like you," I said.

"What will make you like me?" He stood and brushed my cheek with his fingers. I really wished he'd stop doing that; it made my head all cloudy.

Archer cleared his throat and brought me back to the present. "Are we going to sit here discussing your relationship, or are we going after this bitch?"

"Archer!" I said.

He slid his chair back from the table, and it made a horrible squealing sound on the concrete floor.

"I vote for the latter." Seth ran his hands through his hair and stood.

"Do we have a plan then?" Archer said. "Or are you going to keep ogling him until someone else dies?"

"You could try to hide your sarcasm, you know."

"I wouldn't have to if you weren't fraternising with the enemy, Grace."

My mouth dropped open, but I didn't know what to say. The tension hung in the air as the three of us stared each other down.

Archer clenched his fists and leaned on the table. "I know you two have history, but come on ... it's *Seth*. He's—"

"Standing right here, ready to help us," I said.

The boys glared at one another, and I threw my hands up. "Can you stop acting like boys and start behaving like men? Just try to like each other for the next few hours, please. We have two rings we need to figure out how to get."

"One ring." Seth held a thin silver band between his thumb and forefinger. A tiger's eye stone was set in the centre of diamond-encrusted wings.

My mouth dropped open. "Where did you get ... how did you ... Seth?"

Archer tried to hide his shock as he leaned in for a closer look. Seth laid the ring in the palm of my hand, and I tried to ask again how he'd managed to get Annie's ring but I couldn't form the words.

"She was a piece of cake." Seth shrugged. "All I had to do was push her buttons, so to speak, and it was mine for the taking." He laughed at the expression on my face and it made me angry, or was I jealous?

"What do you mean, push her buttons?"

"You've got so much to learn, Grace. I knocked her out." Seth moved towards me until we were almost touching. "There's a spot on our backs, right at the bottom of our wing lines." I froze as he gently slipped his hand under my top and up my back. "Right about here, where they almost join." His touch was soft and surprisingly warm.

"Gracie, what's he …?"

"Arch, it's okay. Isn't it, Seth?" I looked up into his dark, smouldering eyes.

He leaned in and his lips moved against my forehead when he spoke. "One direct hit and you'd be unconscious," he said, before taking his hand away and stepping back.

"Unconscious?" Archer asked.

"An angel's only weakness," Seth said. "Generally, Angels of the Light don't know about it; why would they need to, in their perfectly safe haven of Heaven? Only the Guardian, and a select few, know how to render an angel powerless."

Angels could be knocked unconscious? It had never happened to me, and I didn't think I wanted it to. I was usually the one doing the knocking out. My head was so full of new information I was having trouble putting it into coherent order. I turned Annie's ring over a few times before putting it in my pocket.

Seth looked at me with a devilish, crooked smile, and I couldn't help smiling back. For a moment I wanted to reach out and touch his lips; I wanted to know what they felt like. What was wrong with me? A few days ago, even a few hours ago, I would have been the last person thinking about how much I liked anything about Seth. But the more time I spent with him, the more I didn't want him to leave.

"How do you know all these things?" My voice cracked as I spoke.

"I've been one of the fallen longer than you've been on Earth, Grace. Sometimes you discover things as a matter of survival. Plus, we have access to more knowledge because we've seen both sides of the coin. Angels of the Light are very sheltered, to say the least."

I had so many questions and no time for answers. Where was Annie now she had no wings? Did Angelica know Seth had stripped her?

"Annie is no longer a problem," Seth said, reading my jumbled thoughts. "Angelica, on the other hand, is out there somewhere. She took off as soon as I had the ring in my hand."

"What do you mean, no longer a problem?" Archer asked. "Angels can't die."

"Actually, we can; we just don't publish it in the *How-To of Mystical Creatures* handbook."

"Seth?" I said. "You implied it wasn't easy."

"It's not easy, but it's also not impossible. All you need is the ring, and a drop of the angel's blood, then poof, gone."

Why did everything have to do with blood?

"Now you can add angel killer to your résumé," Archer said.

"Archer, Seth is trying to help us."

"Yeah, remind me again why that is? Oh, that's right. You want to get into my sister's pants."

"Archer!" I could have killed him. My cheeks flamed, and Seth's grin widened.

"What?" Seth asked. "It's true."

Archer stormed out of the shed, and I stared at my feet, unable to meet Seth's gaze. I moved to follow my brother, reaching the door before Seth spoke.

"She's not dead … You have Annie's soul right there in your pocket."

I stopped with my hand on the doorknob, taking the ring out and holding it up to the light. *Her soul?* When I looked closely, a white orb shimmered under the surface of the tiger's eye stone. I looked at Seth with wide, questioning eyes.

"To kill her," he said, "you need to break the ring."

37

JOSH

Sunday morning

Everything was dark. The silence pushed down on me, and all I could hear was a faint ringing in my head, like the sound you hear when you really strain your ears but there's nothing. There had been pain, and I vaguely remembered trying to escape it, to get up and run, but I couldn't. I remembered crying out. There had been muffled voices, but now they were gone.

Also, I felt different. Actually, I didn't feel anything. Several attempts to move and open my eyes proved futile—I was paralysed.

I struggled to remember who I was. I certainly didn't know where I was. The ground was hard, and being surrounded by darkness didn't help. My memories of the past few hours didn't leave me with many clues, only a pain so blinding it blocked everything else.

"I have to get out of here," a voice said. Then another argued with it. The melodic sound of the first triggered something. Grace? *Grace, I'm here. Grace?*

Nothing.

When I strained my ears I heard shallow breathing, and the more I was aware of it, the louder it became, until it thundered inside my head. I tried again and again to scream, but I couldn't move. *This is what hell must feel like.*

Memories of Grace filtered into my mind—the softness of her skin, the sweet sound of her voice, her warmth, her smell. Happiness filled my heart. Then another memory, the one I wished I'd never witnessed, resurfaced, burning itself into the undersides of my eyelids. Seth. Touching her.

I remembered how mad I'd been, storming off down the driveway only to be confronted by more trouble at the other end. I hoped Abby and Claudia were okay, then the pain took over again and all thought of them left my mind.

I was still unable to move. I tried to focus on how to get out of this situation, but my attention was pulled to a burning sensation in my throat. It felt hot, then cold, then hot again. At first it was nice to be able to feel something, and then it grew more intense, spreading to my chest. One second I was on fire, burning from the inside out, and then it was so cold I thought my body would freeze and shatter. The cold and burning slowly spread through the rest of me, and every centimetre it moved the more I tried to call out. What had I done to deserve this?

A shattering scream penetrated the silence. Strong hands pinned my shoulders to the hard ground. I was moving, and for a second I was elated until I realised my body was thrashing and the screaming was coming from my own throat. The loud shallow breathing had turned to panting, and I smelled fear. It was a rancid sweaty smell that didn't belong to whoever was holding me—that smell was like strawberries. Then there was something else—the smell of blood.

My eyes flew open and Charlotte sat on my chest. "Why are you sitting on me?" I calmed a little and gazed at her troubled face.

She jumped up and edged her way to the wall. That was when I noticed Ryan standing in the shadows. I rolled over onto my hands and knees. The fire and ice inside me had subsided, but my throat burned. It took a second to collect myself before I jumped to my feet and scanned the room. It was dark and dank. Soft sunlight filtered through the small window slits, illuminating the dust. I stood beside a sandstone coffin and wasn't sure exactly where I was, so I asked.

"Grace's family cemetery," Ryan said. His eyes shone bright with fear, and he trembled. He looked like he was afraid of me.

"Where's Grace?" Neither of them answered. We stood in silence, Ryan's breathing the only sound in the room. Why could I hear him breathing? "She's with *him,* isn't she?"

"She left with Archer," Charlotte said. "We don't know where they've gone."

Anger rose inside me, and I wanted to break something or someone. Right then, I hated Grace; she'd not only betrayed me, but abandoned me when I'd needed her. If she'd been the one hurt, I would never have left her side.

Everything was different now. I felt different, not myself, but like I was partially removed from my own body. I felt stronger. Charlotte took a tentative step towards me, and I couldn't read her expression. My throat still burned. I rubbed it in an attempt to relieve the pain.

"It won't go away," Charlotte said. "It never goes away."

"What happened to me?"

"The thirst is the hardest part, but you'll learn to live with it."

"Learn to live with it? What do you mean? Tell me what happened!" Before I could stop myself I was on her, surprised at how quickly I'd crossed the room. My hand gripped her neck as I shoved her against the wall.

She didn't whimper or cringe; she simply brought her arms up and knocked my hand away, then punched me in the face, sending me reeling backwards.

"That hurt." I rubbed my jaw.

"Not as much as it would've if you were still human." Charlotte raised her fists, ready to fight.

I couldn't help laughing. "So, what? I'm one of you now? A vampire? Maybe that's why you smell so good." I turned to Ryan.

He took a step away and swallowed. The sound echoed in my ears.

"You want to eat me?" His voice was barely a whisper but I heard him from across the room. It sounded like a novel idea; the thought of tasting his blood made my mouth water.

"Josh, look at me." Charlotte stepped slowly towards me. "You don't want to hurt him; he's your best friend, remember?"

No, I didn't want to hurt him, but I would. Only to get at Ryan, I needed to get through Charlotte. She was a girl so I hoped I was stronger.

Before I could make my decision, her voice resonated around the stone room. "Ryan, *run*."

With Ryan's blood in my sights, I lunged towards him, and I would have made it if I hadn't been knocked off my feet. My back hit the floor and I flipped myself up again, coming face to face with Charlotte. She snarled and bared her fangs, a deep growl rising from her throat. Ryan was nowhere in sight.

"Get out of my way." I tried to push her, but she stood her ground.

"Don't make me hit you again, Joshua Chase."

My fangs extended for the first time, taking me by surprise, and they throbbed like a toothache. I ran my tongue over my teeth, feeling their sharp points, and smiled. Then I took a swing at Charlotte. I'd been taught never to hit a girl, but she was no ordinary girl, and she could take care of herself. She ducked then spun around behind me, but I spun with her. We fought, punch for punch and kick for kick, until I felt my legs go out from under me again. My butt hit the floor, wounding my pride, and I wasn't very happy.

"You're good," I said.

"You have to get past the anger, Josh, and deal."

"Then let me deal in my own way," I said, getting to my feet.

"By killing your friends? No. I will kill you first if I have to."

"There's only one person I want to kill, and he is definitely not my friend."

"I'm your friend." Charlotte lowered her fists, and another drop of blood splashed onto her already smeared cheeks. "I'm sorry for doing this to you, but you were dying. And Grace ..."

"Grace what?" I said. "Cheated on me, then left me here on a hard stone floor to writhe in pain while she flitted off with the enemy?"

"No, she's doing what has to be done. She couldn't bear the thought of losing you. Grace begged me to change you. She didn't want you to die, and Seth helped save you."

"Save me? Is that what you call it? Turning me into a monster is saving me?"

Charlotte tensed. "Is that what you think you are? We're not monsters, Josh," she said.

"What am I then!" I shouldered past her towards the door.

"Please don't go. If they find out you're like me, they'll be after you, too."

She was right and I needed her help, but I was angry. There were things I had to sort through, a certain someone I needed to confront. And how could I know for sure I was like Charlotte? What if I was just your average, everyday vampire? Grace would know by looking at me, but thinking about her hurt too much.

When I walked out into the morning sunshine, its rays made me tingle, like tiny needles dancing on my skin. The sensation wasn't overly pleasant, but one I could get used to. Okay, not an ordinary vampire then. I kicked myself for being so dumb. But if I *was* different like Charlotte, why did I feel so bad? I certainly didn't feel good. All I could think about was revenge and bringing down the one person who'd taken my reason for existing, taken Grace.

My decision to walk away from Charlotte and turn my back on the only person who understood changed everything. Passion and hate blinded me. I ran through the forest, following the sickly scent of fear and the sweet smell of blood. The shadows hid me as I watched my mark and waited.

From that point on, I would spend the rest of my existence washing the blood from my hands.

38

JOSH

The scent of Ryan's blood consumed me, and it was all I could think about as I followed him through the forest. He was just up ahead; the sound of his heart thumped loudly inside my ears.

Becoming a vampire wasn't exactly on my list of New Year's resolutions, and I wasn't sure if I liked being one yet, but I thought I could get used to it. I felt like I was outside my own body, looking down on someone else controlling it. Wanting Ryan's blood was wrong, and I had the power to overcome the urge, but I was having too much fun.

"A little lost, are we?" I said.

He turned, his face plastered with fear. Charlotte was right; I didn't want to hurt him, and if I didn't have her blood running through my veins, Ryan would have already been dead. For the entire half hour I'd been a vampire, I'd understood the meaning of inner turmoil. He was my best friend, but the smell of his blood made my mouth water.

"Were you in on it, too? The idea to make me one of them?" I said.

"You were dying." Ryan took a step away.

"You should have let me die!"

"I didn't make the call—Grace did."

The mere mention of her name made me angry. Who did she think she was, making a decision like that? It wasn't hers to make.

"What do you think of the new look?" I smiled, showing off my nice pointy fangs. Ryan didn't respond. "Let me guess—now you're scared of me?"

"Something like that."

"I bet you're trying to figure out how to get away." I moved closer.

"You're not yourself, Josh."

"Really? I would never have guessed that."

The trees rustled with a faint breeze and a magpie cawed. Ryan stared at me, and I got the impression he was giving up, which annoyed me immensely. Where was the fun in a fight if you were the only one fighting? But then again, Ryan had always been soft. He was never a fighter. Ryan was your typical all-round nice guy. So nice sometimes it made me sick. I'd never have said it to his face, but things had changed. I'd changed.

"Are you going to man up and fight me, or what?"

"I don't want to fight you. You're my best friend," he said.

"Everything's different now."

"Yes, it is, but I know you're still in there. I've always been here for you; why are you taking this out on me?"

My laughter echoed through the trees, and the magpie took flight. That was a good question, but there were so many answers—because he was there, because he was friends with Grace, because I could, because I needed to take it out on *someone,* because all of the above.

"How would you feel after you hurt me?" Ryan asked. "You know I'm not strong enough to fight you."

"I'm guessing I might feel a little better, releasing some anger."

Ryan shook his head. "Who are you? I don't know you anymore." He turned away, taking one step before I raced around in front of him. I grabbed him by the shoulders and shoved him against the nearest tallowwood, a menacing growl rising into my throat.

"You know what? Fine," Ryan said. "Go on, beat me up, eat me, kill me, I don't care. You're a coward; you weren't even brave enough to face the problem, and beating on me doesn't change the fact Grace is probably with Seth right now."

When I heard Seth's name, I lost it. I forgot that Ryan was my best friend, and that I actually had the strength to kill him. All I could see in my mind was the face of the one person who was taking everything from me. Anger flared in the pit of my stomach and rose into my chest. I grabbed Ryan and hit him I don't know how many times.

"Josh, stop!" someone said.

I hesitated, holding Ryan by a fistful of his shirt, and looked at what I'd done. He was barely conscious, his clothes were torn, and blood covered one side of his face. My throat cried out in agony, wanting nothing more than to taste it. The smell that wafted to my nose became the only thing I could think about, but before I could bring my mouth to his neck, I was hit by something strong and very, very angry.

For a moment I was airborne as I flew backwards. My shoulder crashed into a tree. The trunk split, sending a loud crack through the forest. Charlotte stood over me, growling and baring her teeth. This was a side of her I'd never seen, and it wasn't pretty. It made me realise how much she'd been holding back.

"If I were you, I'd run," she said.

I didn't hesitate in taking her advice.

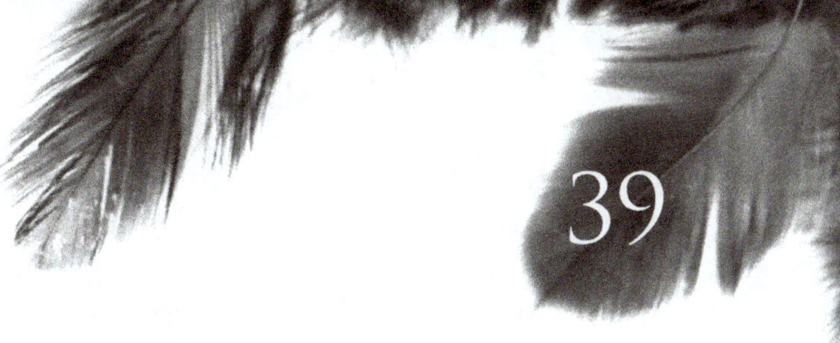

39

GRACE
Sunday afternoon

Archer calmed down from his tantrum, and we spent the morning tidying up the aftermath of the party. It looked like everyone had had a blast in our absence, and the mess was, well, messy. We'd decided looking for Angelica could wait a bit longer. *Let her hang,* were Archer's words, and I was thankful to be doing something normal for once. Cleaning was about as normal as you could get; I wasn't in the mood for any more fighting, physical or otherwise.

My thoughts kept turning to Josh as I stacked chairs and collected the last of the cans. We hadn't heard any news, and I was angry at myself for not staying to help him. The truth was it scared me. What if he woke up and he wasn't Josh anymore? What if he was this terrible, horrible demon instead? I'd stayed away because I didn't want to be there to find out.

I watched Seth rake the ashes from the fire—we now had a nice big dead patch of grass in the clearing. Archer hadn't been too keen on the fallen angel sticking around, but Seth insisted. I didn't know what to think; it was all too complicated. Not that Josh's situation was any less complicated. Boy was I in a pickle.

Movement in the forest caught my attention, and Charlotte burst from the mouth of the path. She slowed as she neared us, carrying someone in her arms. My stomach dropped away to oblivion. It was Ryan. His body was limp, his head lolling about as Charlotte moved.

"He's not dead, but we need to get him inside," she said, without breaking her stride. Blood covered Ryan's face. I took a deep breath and followed them to the shed—so much for normal. Archer was at Charlotte's side throwing angry questions; Seth fell into step with me. What could possibly go wrong next? This totally sucked.

"Yep, I have to agree with you there," Seth said.

We stopped outside the shed door and I looked into his ebony eyes, trying to see if there was any malice behind his words. This time all I saw was sympathy and regret. He went to touch my face but I stepped back, my eyes still locked with his.

"Not now. This is not about us."

"Grace—"

With a shake of my head I silenced him then went through the door to face what was on the other side. Charlotte had put Ryan on the couch. She washed his face with a wet cloth, and the water in the bucket next to her was a murky red. The coppery smell of his blood lingered in the air.

"How do you stand it?" Archer asked, kneeling beside her. "If I can smell it ... All that blood ..."

"You get used to it. After a while, it becomes just another smell."

"Do we know what happened?" I asked.

Charlotte handed the cloth to Archer and got to her feet. "Josh is gone."

The room was silent apart from Ryan's laboured breathing. He'd been unconscious but was coming around, attempting to sit up rather unsuccessfully. Archer helped by propping him up with some cushions, then went to get him a glass of water.

"What do you mean he's gone?" I said. "Gone where?"

"When he woke up, he fought me. He's mad, and I couldn't stop him."

"That doesn't explain why Ryan pretty much needs a hospital. Did Josh do this? Did he ... bite him?"

Charlotte shook her head. "No. Not that I can see. I think I got there in time."

I knelt beside the couch and took Ryan's hand. His eyes fluttered open, and he managed a small smile. He squeezed my fingers, closing his eyes again.

"It's okay, I'm here." I brushed his hair back from his forehead. "Can you tell me what happened?"

Seth made himself comfortable at the kitchen table while Charlotte paced in front of the couch. Any minute, I thought she'd make a hole in the already threadbare rug. Archer perched on the edge of the couch, ready to hear the story.

While Ryan told his version of events I was lucky

enough to be able to see the pictures in his head, although I didn't particularly like what I saw.

"He was really mad, Grace. Charlotte told me to run, so I did. I'm such a loser; I hate confrontation."

"Don't be silly—you had no choice. It was either run or die," I said.

Ryan's memory of Josh and Charlotte arguing scared me, and I didn't recognise the fierce person who'd replaced the kind, caring Josh I knew.

"We fought more after I told Ryan to run. He's strong, and his anger is making him stronger," Charlotte said.

"He tracked me down in the forest. I've never seen him so ..." Ryan said.

I didn't need to be told the rest. I saw it all—the confrontation, the aggressive words, and then nothing. Ryan had said Josh wanted to bite him, and I could see how tortured Josh was. He'd settled for beating up his best friend instead.

"The next thing I remember is waking up here," Ryan said.

"Looks like he's out for my blood," Seth said from the kitchen. He'd been so silent; having him close was something I still wasn't used to.

"Seems that way," I said. "Archer, don't." I got to my feet. I gave him my best dagger eyes before he could put his two bobs' worth in. He snapped his mouth shut as quickly as he'd opened it.

"As much as I would love the opportunity to kick Josh's butt," Seth said, "shouldn't we be more concerned about Angelica? For one, she's still after Charlotte, and for two, she'll be after Josh as well now."

Archer scowled. "Let her have him."

"Archer!" I couldn't believe my brother had said that.

"What? Grace, look what he's done." Archer pointed to Ryan's face.

"He isn't himself right now."

"You can say that again."

"This isn't really Josh's fault," Seth said.

The more Seth opened his mouth, the more I liked what he said. He was thinking straighter than all of us combined, and I couldn't help smiling at him.

"No, it's mine," Charlotte said.

"Okay, everyone, stop! We are not discussing this right now. Seth and I will search for Angelica," I said. "You guys stay with Ryan."

"Who died and made you boss?" Archer raised his eyebrows.

"Hello! Me—fallen angel, you—human."

Archer folded his arms over his chest. "Just use that against me, why don't you?"

I ignored him and turned to Charlotte. "Will your blood help heal Ryan's injuries?"

"Yeah, I'll do what I can."

"I'll be fine, Grace," Ryan said. "He just knocked me out, that's all."

Yeah, and messed your face up a bit.

Under the watchful, glaring eye of my brother, Seth and I crossed the clearing. We had no clue where to look for Angelica, and if she didn't want to be found, then we didn't have much of a chance. Because we were technically on the bad side, it made it that much easier for Angelica and that much harder for us.

"Maybe she's gone back," he said. "I know I would if my friend had ended up like Annie."

My hand moved to my pocket and Annie's ring. It felt odd having someone's soul at my fingertips, knowing I could send them to oblivion so easily. But I didn't want to kill Annie or Angelica. I just wanted them off our backs and for them to see that ending Charlotte's existence wasn't the right thing to do.

"Maybe." I shrugged. "But if I know Angelica like I think I do, she isn't one to give up. She's stubborn."

Seth chuckled. "Sounds like someone else I know."

I followed him into the forest.

40

GRACE
Monday morning

When I lifted my head, my first thought was that I had a horrible taste in my mouth. The second—I wasn't in my own bed. I ran my tongue along my teeth, wishing for toothpaste and a toothbrush.

How was I going to face the day? Emma's funeral was only hours away. The past few days I'd been occupied enough not to think about it, but seeing her parents would be hard, and not having Josh there would be harder. I didn't know if he'd show up, and after what he'd done to Ryan, I wasn't sure if I even wanted him to.

Sadness weighed me down, and I remembered it was my birthday. Turning eighteen should have been a happy occasion, but I felt far from happy. I rubbed the sleep from my eyes, propped myself on my elbow, and looked around the room, accounting for everyone. Archer was curled into a ball at my feet; Seth lay on the floor in front of me; and Charlotte sat at the kitchen table. Ryan was stretched out under a blanket on the other couch. He looked much better, thanks to Charlotte's blood healing most of his wounds. As for the damage done between him and Josh, I wondered if that would ever heal.

Seth and I had searched the forest for hours the night before. Josh had been out there; I'd felt him, and heard him. The anger radiating from him had been toxic, seeping into me like water into a sponge. How could I have thought he would be the same after the change? Every time we got close, he slipped away again. He was playing games, and I was tired of it.

Dim predawn light bathed the room, and I took a moment to take everyone in. So much had happened since the first day back at school—was it really just a week ago? I'd fallen in love, betrayed my home, lost my best friend, hurt Josh, and fallen in love again.

Oh no—was I in love with Seth?

But I also loved Josh, even though I'd never told him.

Could you love two people at the same time?

Seth lay so peacefully on the floor, and I had to resist the urge to touch him. Instead of stabbing a sharp pain through my heart, this time, remembering how things were before he fell brought a smile to my face. Maybe it was supposed to happen this way to bring us together again. Maybe fate had intervened for a reason. Maybe Josh wasn't the one I was supposed to be with.

"Hey," Seth said, and I looked down into his sun-kissed face. "Happy birthday."

"You remembered."

"Of course. There's plenty of room up here"—he tapped his temple—"for useless information." He paused, playing with a loose thread in the carpet. "I'll understand if you don't want me to come today."

"No, it's okay. I think I need all the support I can get." There was a moment of comfortable silence between us before Seth sat up and crossed his legs so his knees touched the front of the couch. Our faces were level, and he leaned in slightly. I waited to see what he would do. He was close enough that I could feel his warm breath on my cheek, and I didn't want him to pull away, but I wasn't sure if I wanted to kiss him either. Now would be a very good time for toothpaste.

You don't have to, if you don't want, he whispered in my head.

I don't know what I want.

He slipped my free hand into his and turned it over, tracing my palm with his finger. Seth's touch was gentle and warm.

Are you trying to seduce me? I thought.

Is it working?

A huge smile spread over his face, and before I had time to react he closed the small gap between us. Never in my existence had I felt something as soft and tender and gentle as that kiss. It surprised me; it was so different to the way Josh had kissed me. It was like we fitted perfectly together, and the moment his lips touched mine it felt right. I found myself wanting more. Eagerly, I slid my hand behind his neck and pulled him closer, twisting my fingers into his short, blond hair. My mind went blank, and all I knew was his touch.

Too soon, Seth pulled away and our lips parted. With our foreheads touching I gasped for breath, my heart racing. He gently raised my chin, then held out his hand and caught my tear in his palm. I hadn't even noticed I'd been crying, and we both watched as the small drop of water turned into a diamond. My tears flowed faster as I remembered catching Seth's tear so long ago.

"I have one of those, too." I smiled.

"You kept it? You know it's said if you catch an angel's tear and it turns into a diamond, the one shedding the tear is your true love."

I turned that over in my mind. "You love me?"

"I have always loved you, Grace."

"So, this is how angels kiss then? I never knew—"

"How good it was?" he asked.

Exactly. My smile widened.

You have no idea how long I've waited for this moment. How long I've waited for you.

I closed my eyes, laid my head on his shoulder, and felt like I was home. I hated myself for feeling that way, for betraying Josh, but I couldn't deny it. You couldn't choose love—it chose you.

Seth's lips brushed my ear, and he whispered, "We have an audience."

When I lifted my head, I faced my brother's ice-cold stare. His hazel eyes darkened as he frowned, looking less than impressed.

"How much did you see, Arch?" I dropped my gaze.

"More than I would've liked. Doesn't he have somewhere else to stay?"

"I have a place in town, but it's not as nice as this."

Seth flashed Archer a grin.

"Whatever." Archer folded his arms over his chest.

Ryan sat up at the sound of Archer's voice and rubbed his eyes. "What's going on?"

The silence hung between us all. Charlotte came to sit beside Archer. Her expression was neutral, and I was grateful she wasn't taking sides.

"To judge others is to judge yourself," she said.

"I can't believe the Council want you gone." I shook my head as I sat up. "The world needs more people like you, Charlotte."

"I wouldn't be so sure about that," she said.

Archer scowled and stood up, heading outside. Seth followed, and I didn't stop him. They could sort out their own differences. I was sick of being mediator.

Happy birthday, big brother, I thought. He didn't reply.

"They'll come good," Ryan said.

"I bet you wish you'd never found out about us and our freaky, supernatural world." I tried to smile.

Ryan sat studying his hands, and I thought he would never answer. Charlotte seemed to be hanging on the edge of her seat, waiting for a response as well.

"I don't know. Emma is gone ... My best friend is ... different. I'm having a pretty tough time dealing right now, but I guess you can't change the past. Would I be better off not knowing? I don't think it would make a difference. She would still be dead, and Josh would still be gone."

Suddenly, I felt very guilty for bringing him into this mess. Losing two people in one week was a lot to take. I was living it as well, but at least my coping mechanisms were a little more advanced.

After breakfast, we took turns in the shower and got ready. At least our grey school uniforms were depressing enough for a funeral. Archer and Seth were both keeping their morning conversation locked away in their heads, which was probably a good thing, and all focus was on Emma and getting through the service in a relatively sane fashion.

It felt weird pulling into the school parking lot; two days away felt like two years. Everyone milling around the main yard looked like strangers to me. They had their funeral faces on, and it made me mad knowing some of them would shed tears for someone they didn't even know or like.

By the sound of the first bell the entire school, along with teachers, parents and family, was crammed into the cathedral. Mr and Mrs Shrove sat in front with Emma's older brothers and their wives. I didn't know them well as they all lived interstate, and I could count on one hand the number of times we'd met. As Emma's friends, Archer, Ryan, Charlotte, and I had the privilege of the second pew. Seth was somewhere with all the others who had to stand. I would have been happier in the back so I could see everyone, but I guessed I had to settle for listening only. After a few minutes it was driving me crazy, and I shut everyone out. There were so many judgemental and bitchy thoughts; I didn't want to know. Josh wasn't around, either; I couldn't sense or hear him. This made me sadder than I'd thought it would. Despite what he'd done, I needed him. I hadn't had a chance to talk to him properly since his rage of jealously started, and I kicked myself again for getting into this mess. I'd have to make a choice, but how did you split your heart in two?

Father Michael's service was short but nice, and Mr Shrove held it together for the eulogy. Before I knew it, Ryan, Archer, Mr Shrove, and Emma's brothers were getting up for the procession, all acting as pallbearers. Everyone filed out the big doors behind them and into the sunshine. Only family and close friends were invited to the graveside part of the ceremony, and it was time to go, but I couldn't. I didn't want to say goodbye. If I stayed right where I was, maybe I wouldn't have to. I'd managed to keep my cheeks dry, but watching Emma being lowered into the ground would open the flood gates. Thinking of her, trying to remember her smile, her laugh, my eyes began to sting. I took a deep breath.

"We'll see you in a bit," Mrs Shrove said, patting my arm on her way past.

I offered her a tight-lipped smile and nodded. Charlotte linked her arm through mine, helping me up. I was glad she was there. We walked the red carpet of the long aisle to the back of the cathedral where Seth stood waiting, leaning against the sandstone wall.

"I'm surprised they still let us in here," he said.

"A house of God is open to all, Seth; you know that."

"Judgement occurs in Heaven." He nodded, pushed the door open, and held it for us. "I haven't forgotten everything."

We walked to the cemetery in silence. The student body had been directed to class for reflection before getting back into the swing of things. "Busy minds don't ponder,"

Mr Gerard had said. How right he was. With my eyes fixed on the ground, I concentrated on putting one foot in front of the other until Charlotte stopped. When I raised my head, I locked eyes with Abby.

"I can't remember if I ever told you how sorry I am about Emma," she said.

I didn't know what to say, so I didn't say anything.

She took this as her cue to keep talking. "Saturday night was fun. Thanks for putting on a great party."

"Did you get home okay?" I asked.

"Yeah, Jesse took us back to the dorm, but I don't really remember leaving." Abby's brow furrowed. "Oh well, again, sorry." She was being genuine, and I was glad to see she was okay.

Emma's casket sat next to a freshly dug grave. We stood in a semi-circle with Father Michael at the head. After saying a few words and waiting for Mr Shrove to nod, he pushed the button to activate the lowering device. The soft whir of the mechanism was the only sound in the quiet cemetery. Even the magpies and cicadas had fallen silent as if out of respect. I watched the box that held my best friend slowly descend into the ground, and that was when the tears started. Staying strong for Emma's family was no longer an option; I couldn't hold it in.

My knees sank into the soft earth at the edge of the grave, and I sobbed uncontrollably. Archer tried to help but I stopped him. I needed to do this alone. After a few moments, I blinked away my tears and looked up at Mrs Shrove. She knew what I wanted to do.

"Go on, Grace," she said. Her cheeks were also wet.

Slowly, I got to my feet and took the few steps to the

mound of dirt at the foot of Emma's grave. I dug my fingers into the soft cold soil and took a fistful, closed my eyes, then threw it onto the casket. I felt a little better, like I could actually let her go. She would be in a safe place. Even if I could never get back there, at least Heaven would look after her.

"Grace," Seth said at my shoulder. "Look."

When I opened my eyes, a beautiful white butterfly fluttered into the sunshine. I held out my hand and it landed lightly on my palm, where it lingered for a moment. Then it took flight, beating its radiant wings against the beautiful azure sky.

41

JOSH

From the shadows of the Moreton Bay fig, I watched Grace walk down the cemetery path, leaning on Charlotte. Seth wasn't far behind, his hands in his pockets and his head down. I stiffened at the sight of him, wanting nothing more than to run down there and pound him into the ground.

They came to a stop beside a freshly dug grave. Ryan and Archer were pallbearers, and I'd watched the casket procession before Grace arrived. I felt a pang of guilt for what I'd done to Ryan, but it didn't last long. I definitely knew one thing—becoming a vampire changed you in ways you never imagined. Sure, you got to run fast and be really strong, but it also hardened your heart.

Grace was on her knees, sobbing over the hole in the ground. Let her cry and suffer. Let her feel pain like I had. At least she'd lost someone to death, but me? I had to watch as she slowly slipped through my fingers. My blood boiled more as Seth stepped close to her and whispered in her ear. I could see the tiny white butterfly as clearly as my own hand. For a moment, I softened when Grace's radiant smile lit up her face. She turned her gaze skyward until the butterfly disappeared.

Grace, being the faithful friend, sat at the edge of the grave for a while longer. Emma's family were already gone, and the others were getting ready to leave. I heard their conversation easily with my new hearing.

"We'll see you back at the shed," Archer said. He gave Grace a quick brotherly kiss then left with Charlotte, passing my mum's grave as they went. Guilt surfaced as I watched Charlotte's hair sway across her shoulders. She had wanted to help me, and I'd pushed her away. Seth said something about searching for Angelica but I blocked his voice and concentrated on Grace. I needed to talk to her by herself, and if I thought her name she'd hear me.

I waited until she was alone before stepping to the edge of the shadows.

Grace.

Slowly, she raised her head. That was when I realised Grace wasn't the one I was angry with. She was beautiful and good, and how could I not love her? Her eyes sparkled with fresh tears, but she didn't move.

Grace, I know you can hear me. Please, I—

Don't, she thought.

We stared at each other.

"I can't do this right now, Josh." Her voice travelled across the cemetery. "I have to go." She dropped her gaze and turned away.

"Grace." I stepped into the sunshine.

"Please, Josh; it's my birthday. Just let me deal."

Her birthday—how could I forget? But how could I remember with everything that had happened?

She took a few steps and I decided I wasn't going to let her go that easily. She always fought for what she believed in, so I was going to fight, too.

I reached her side in seconds, but she didn't stop, so I grabbed her arm to spin her towards me. With one quick movement, Grace hit me and I stumbled backwards, landing heavily. It was good I was a little more resilient after the change, but I couldn't say the same for my pride. I sprang back to my feet and ran to block her path.

"Please, get out of my way," she said.

"Why won't you talk to me?"

Grace looked at her hands and fiddled with her ring. "I can't look at you without hating myself for what I've done."

"You were trying to save me—I get that now."

"But none of this would have happened if I'd never gotten involved with you in the first place."

"What's happened to us? I'm still here; I'm still me."

"No, you're not. Look what you did to Ryan. You're this angry person I don't recognise any more," she said.

"Well, maybe I wouldn't be so angry if the enemy wasn't trying to suck face with my girlfriend!"

"You don't know what you're talking about."

"Yeah, yeah, you and Seth have history, but I'm betting he's already tried one on you, am I right?"

Grace stared at me with wide eyes, and from the look on her face I knew what her answer would be. "Seth kissed me this morning, and I let him."

I bit my tongue and blood welled in my mouth as I fought to contain my anger.

Grace stepped around me and walked to the rusty gate of the cemetery. She paused with her back to me, her hand on the latch, and said, "I don't know how to fix this."

"Just tell me … tell me you love me."

"You know I do, but it's not as simple as that."

"Why, Grace? Why can't it be that simple?"

I was ready to forgive her for everything, for ever letting *him* touch her. All I wanted was to take her in my arms and hold her, for everything to be like it was before Saturday. But she was right; I *was* different.

I took her by the shoulders and turned her towards me. Her eyes looked haunted, and I wished I could get into her head like she could get into mine, but she'd blocked me. I needed to understand why we'd gotten to where we had.

Grace placed her hand on my cheek. I knew she felt cold, hard skin, and not the warmth that used to be there before I was changed. I wondered what she would feel if I kissed her, if it would be different, if I could ever be as tender as I used to be. Maybe now I was a vampire we weren't supposed to be together. I saw how Charlotte looked at Archer, and even though they weren't actually together, it was possible. But Charlotte was an exception. She was like an angel trapped in a demon's body. Could I ever be like that? Could I really give Grace what she wanted? What she needed?

I leaned in to softly brush her lips with mine. For a brief moment, we kissed. Then she misted, and I was left standing in an empty cemetery with no one but the dead for company.

42

GRACE

Early Monday night

By the time I returned to the shed it was almost nightfall. After I saw Josh I'd gone to the outcrop, dropped to my knees, and wept. Through my tears, I'd watched the sun set over the valley, turning the soft white clouds beautiful shades of pink and orange. The thought of spreading my wings and flying away had crossed my mind, but I couldn't do it. I needed to stay for Archer, and Charlotte, if not for myself.

I misted to the middle of the clearing, and my friends came rushing towards me. There were lots of questions. Seth stayed silent, standing back to let the others help me. He knew I'd wanted to be by myself, and I let him in so he could see everything that had happened after he'd left me at the cemetery. He smiled.

"Guys, I'm okay. I just needed thinking time."

"A lot happened while you were *thinking* Gracie." Archer made little speech marks in the air.

"What could possibly have happened? Can't I stop for one minute?"

"Good news first?" Seth asked.

"There's good news?" I scoffed.

"Believe it or not, yes. Angelica has gone home."

That *was* good news, and one less thing to worry about. I could get back to fighting the bad guys and sorting out my life.

"And the bad news?" I looked back and forth between my friends, waiting for someone to continue. "Just spill. If you don't hurry up, I'll come in and take it anyway."

"Josh came looking for you," Charlotte said. "We kicked him out. And, I picked up Cain's scent in the forest. He's been very close to the shed."

Well, fighting vamps was my job. Even if Cain had some of Charlotte's blood, I could still take him. Besides, I hadn't dusted anyone in the last day, so there was something to look forward to. Josh I would have to deal with later.

"There's more." Seth stepped closer. "Angelica has gone, but my sources tell me she's planning to return. You have something she wants."

Oh boy, that *was* bad news. My hand went to my pocket and felt Annie's ring.

"Your sources?" I looked at Seth.

"I know people. Not all Angels of the Light follow the rules. And like I've said before, you have a lot to learn."

I went into the shed to freshen up. After splashing some water on my face and checking my hair, I changed from my uniform into jeans and a black top.

Outside, we armed up before walking the perimeter. I sensed Josh's presence a split second before Seth did, but it still wasn't enough to stop the rock from connecting with Seth's shoulder. The force of the blow spun him sideways, and he thumped into me. I managed to hold his weight and prevent us crashing to the ground.

"Ouch," Seth cried, "that hurt!"

When I looked back along the rock's flight path, I came face to face with Josh. I thought maybe we'd made some progress this morning, even if I had left him hanging. His once beautiful sparkling blue eyes were now a hard, angry black. Hatred for Seth radiated from him, and you didn't need to read his mind to know it. I sensed Archer and the others moving in to protect me. There was no doubt Ryan would do anything to help, I could feel his anger, too, and at that point he loathed Josh more than he'd ever thought possible.

"Do you condemn me by casting the first stone?" Seth stepped forward. "You forget, Joshua—I'm still an angel, and angels don't throw stones." Seth spread his fingers and flicked his wrist. "We throw fire."

I lunged and knocked Seth's aim off-course, sending the flames hurtling towards a tree instead. It went up easily, and Archer ran for the hose at the end of the shed. Josh snarled and bared his fangs then went for Seth, but I placed myself between them.

"Way to go, Grace. You ruined my punchline." Seth scowled.

I put my hand on his chest and pushed him back a few metres. "We're on the same side, remember?" I wanted to say something along the lines of, *grow up and quit being a baby,* but by then the boys' fighting became insignificant.

Cain stood at the edge of the clearing.

Suddenly, all I cared about was Josh, but my feet were frozen in place.

"Josh, behind you!" I said.

He spun then crouched as Cain sprung towards him. Josh grabbed him below the knees, picked him up and threw him over his shoulder. Cain landed with a thud at my feet. I looked down into his evil black eyes.

"I've been waiting for you to show up," I said.

Cain jumped to his feet and grinned wickedly, parading his own set of sharp, glistening fangs. He threw his head back and laughed. I couldn't see what was so funny; then I looked around and understood the enormity of the situation. There were at least twenty figures standing in the shadows of the forest. The sun hadn't set, so I presumed they were high on Charlotte's blood.

"Josh, if you want to live, I suggest you get behind me," I said. "Now!"

Josh glanced over his shoulder, then his figure blurred as he ran to stand with the rest of us.

"Are they on what I think they're on?" Archer asked.

"Looks like it," I said.

"Be careful, everyone," Charlotte said. "They'll be stronger than you think."

The six of us formed a line and edged backwards to the centre of the clearing. Six against twenty wasn't very good odds, but I had faith.

"Back to back when they circle us. And Charlotte,

please keep Ryan alive," I said.

The sound of twenty vampires letting out their war cries was deafening, and I was glad our neighbours weren't close. We all had weapons except Josh, so I threw him a stake.

"Try to stay away from the pointy end; it's bad for your health."

"Thanks for the tip, Grace." Josh smiled, and his fangs extended. He looked just as mean and nasty as Cain, but at least he was making jokes with me—one small step in the right direction.

The vampires charged. Arms and legs, stakes and fangs, flew everywhere. Within minutes we'd knocked off a third of the pack.

"Where did you get these guys from, Cain? They're not too bright," I said as I roundhouse kicked a pretty brunette vamp in the face. A quick stab to her chest and she was dust on my boots. I really loved my job.

"Seth," I called out to him, "let up on the fire balls. You'll burn the shed down."

"Not in my nature to let up on anything, Grace."

Archer and Seth fought side by side; if I'd had the time to stop, I would have taken a photo or two as proof. Josh was taking his anger out on a rather large vamp with big arms and lots of tattoos, and Charlotte kept Ryan out of trouble.

A warm wind rushed through the clearing. I looked up to see Seth in all his glory, wings spread wide, raining fire down on two vamps. He was magnificent. His black feathers rippled under the light of the rising moon, and his tanned skin glowed with the reflection of his own fire. I didn't want him to have all the fun, so I unfurled my wings, joining him in the air.

Everyone stopped fighting and stared up at us. A few of Cain's so-called followers took the opportunity to make tracks into the forest. That left five against five. Cain stood in the middle of what was left of his troop, and he didn't look very pleased.

"Nothing like a fair fight, is there, Cain?" I said.

He glowered up at me. "I'm going to—"

"What? Kill me?" I laughed. "I've heard that before. What's your beef anyway?"

"You killed Tyler and Matthew, and I want her blood." He pointed to Charlotte.

"Actually, just Tyler. Seth killed Matthew, and you can't have her blood."

With the flick of my wrist, I formed another ball of fire in my palm and twirled it with my fingers. Cain looked at each of us in turn, sizing us up.

"It's one on one now, isn't it?" I said. "I guess you need to ask yourself, do you want to die tonight?"

"Can we quit with the nice chit-chat and finish them off?" Seth landed in front of a slender vamp with black hair. She was a little like me if you looked at her from the side, only with fangs. "Boo!" he said, and she jumped. I could hear her tossing up between running and fighting. Seth staked her before she could make a decision.

Cain roared, and we all jumped into the fray. Charlotte took Ryan away to a safe distance. Seth was left with nothing to do after about a minute. Archer had to work a little harder, but he was done quickly, too. That left Josh and me still fighting. Cain was really giving me a run for my money, but I loved every minute of it. I should have finished him off, but after the week I'd had, it felt good to let it all out.

Seth was getting a little antsy with nothing to do, so he strolled over and staked Josh's opponent in the back.

"Hey, I almost had him," Josh said.

"We haven't got all night. I thought you could use some help."

It was probably a good time to get Cain under control, so I dropped to a crouch and kicked his legs out from under him. Then I sat on him. His attitude changed once I had the upper hand.

"Please, don't kill me," Cain said. "I'll tell you anything you want."

"I can read your mind. You don't need to tell me anything." The one thing I hated more than evil vamps were evil vamps that grovelled. "This," I said, driving my stake into his left shoulder and giving it a twist, making him scream, "is for Charlotte." He writhed under me, grabbing at the piece of wood.

Seth came over and stood at Cain's head. "Do you always play with them like this?"

"Yep, she does," Archer said.

I ripped the stake from Cain's shoulder. He screamed again, and I laughed. Maybe I was having a little too much fun.

"And this." I aimed for his heart.

"Is for what?" Cain grabbed my wrist in a sudden burst of strength and squeezed it until I dropped the stake. He threw me, and I landed with a thud. He was gone in a blur, and I was very pissed off.

"Is for being a bad boy," I said, getting up and brushing the grass off me. "Well, that was fun."

Archer raised his eyebrows, and the others looked on in silence.

"What? Why are you all looking at me like that?"

"Did you not notice Cain running away?" Archer threw his hands up.

"I don't see any of you chasing him!" I said.

"You should've put the stake in the right place the first time you stabbed him."

"I wanted him to suffer a little bit first."

"Okay, can you two stop arguing?" Seth said.

Archer glared at him.

I rubbed my wrist where Cain had grabbed it. A faint bruise formed but it was nothing that wouldn't heal quickly. Seth took my hand, inspecting the damage. I had cuts and bruises everywhere, we all did, but it was nothing to worry about. He brushed some grass from my hair and without thinking, I leaned into him. Seth put his arm around me, and Josh made a deep growling sound, baring his fangs. Oh great—we were right back where we'd started.

Josh was about to take a swing at Seth, so I moved out of the way. They fought punch for punch for a few minutes. They could both hold their own in a fight, but then I started to worry. Seth had the upper hand—Josh was strong but inexperienced—and it was getting rough.

"Okay, stop!" I pushed between them. "I will hit you both if I have to."

"There you go. Are you happy?" Josh said, making me flinch. "I killed a few vampires and helped you save the world, but you're still with *him*."

"Leave her alone." Ryan came to my side, never taking his eyes off Josh. "I think it's time for you to leave."

Archer and Charlotte moved closer, too, and it looked like all of us against Josh. I didn't want it to be that way, I wanted the old Josh back, but he was gone and the new Josh scared me. He was someone I didn't know. Maybe it was my fault, and maybe there was something I could have done differently, but I'd had to do what was best for everyone.

Ryan is right, Josh, I pushed into his mind. *Maybe you should go.*

His brow furrowed. He wiped a trickle of blood from the corner of his mouth with the back of his hand.

"Josh ..." I moved towards him.

"No. Stay away from me. I can't do this anymore. It was always going to be him or me. Looks like you got what you wanted."

I couldn't respond. I didn't know what I wanted. I certainly didn't want him to leave, but he couldn't stay either. I stood in the clearing where so much had happened, where for a little while Josh and Seth weren't enemies but had fought side by side, and even though I was sur-rounded by my friends, I felt completely alone. All I could do was watch the person who should have been the love of my life walk away until he was swallowed by the night.

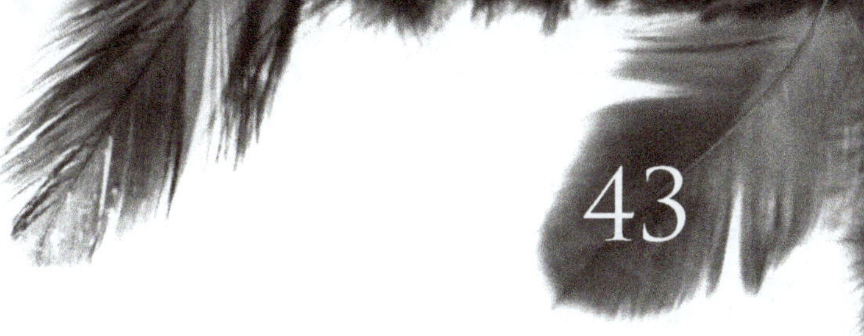

43

GRACE
Monday night

My body felt completely numb. There was no other way to describe it. So numb that all I could do was stand and stare at the place where Josh had disappeared, hoping he would come back.

I retracted my wings and concentrated on breathing. I couldn't believe Josh was gone. Shame washed over me. We'd deserted him at his greatest time of need. He'd never asked to be changed. We'd all played a part in what Josh had become; we were all guilty of betrayal.

"What have we done?" I said.

Seth wandered off to put out a small grass fire near the cottage, and Archer retrieved the weapons that were scattered across the clearing. No one spoke, and I didn't move.

I thought I'd been tough through everything that had happened, but I didn't feel whole anymore. It was like I was cracking down the middle, waiting to fall apart. Why did I have to be the strong one? I was tired of being strong.

Seth stood in front of me so I had no choice but to look at him. He tucked a lock of hair behind my ear then took my face in both his hands. He leaned down and softly kissed me. It wasn't a passionate kiss, but a comforting one, and it warmed my heart. It reminded me of how he used to be before he fell. I rested my head on his chest, and he circled me with his arms. Seth's touch no longer made me feel cold; his embrace was tender and warm, and safe.

"What now?" Ryan asked.

I didn't want to know; I just wanted to stand there listening to Seth's heartbeat. No more running or fighting, no more dying, just peace. But that would be asking too much. It was like having a really great dream and not wanting to wake up—all I wanted was to keep my eyes closed and stay asleep.

Seth's arms tightened around me, and I instantly knew something was wrong.

Angelica landed in the middle of the clearing. Her white wings sparkled like the stars. *So much for peace.*

"I believe you have something I want," she said. "The easy way or the hard way, Grace?"

"I think the easy way will do." I turned to face her. "In case you haven't noticed, you're outnumbered."

"Nothing I can't handle."

Grace, Seth thought. *Block her out and follow my move. Great. Here we go again.*

Seth waited, one arm still around me, sizing Angelica up. He blocked her then showed me his plan. It seemed like a good idea. There was just enough time to warn Archer before Seth let go of me and misted, landing behind Angelica. Archer grabbed Ryan and Charlotte, and they took cover beside the cottage.

With both hands stretched out before me, I conjured my fire. Seth did the same, and we hurtled our attack towards Angelica in perfect unison. But she was quick, and she orbed a second before the balls collided; they exploded and rained fire into the clearing.

"Nice try," Angelica said.

I spun to avoid her light as it raced towards me. It caught me on the shoulder and knocked me off balance, and I landed heavily on the grass. Seth walked towards Angelica, throwing his fire balls with every step, one after the other, but Angelica counter-attacked and knocked each fiery sphere down with her orbs.

I unfurled my wings for the second time that night and took to the sky. Before I could swoop down and make another move, Angelica orbed and materialised above me. There were two of us against her, but it was taking too long.

Take it easy, Grace. No mistakes, Seth thought.

Just nail her already, would you?

I ducked and let Seth's fire rush over my head. Angelica deflected it again with ease. Archer stepped away from the cottage, but I made it clear for him to stay with Charlotte and Ryan. There was nothing they could do while Angelica was in the air.

I landed beside Seth and together we looked up at Angelica. The fact she found fighting so enjoyable made me sick. I loved a good battle that ended with dust on my boots, but I would never hurt an innocent, and I fought for a purpose. That was why her next move shocked me beyond belief.

Angelica cast an orb in the direction of the cottage. It didn't hit anyone, but it pulverised the corner of the small house and sent Archer and the others flying—so much for Angels of the Light protecting the innocent. Ryan copped the brunt. I misted to where he lay on the grass. He was unconscious but still alive.

Archer and Charlotte readied themselves to fight, but by the time I'd accounted for everyone and made sure there were no life-threatening injuries or missing limbs, Angelica had hit Seth. He lay still at her feet. His magnificent ebony wings sprawled out behind him on the grass.

"Fighting dirty, Angelica," I said. "So much for being righteous and holy—harming innocent people."

"You forget, I'm the good guy. You think I'm bad because you're on *that* side of the fence." She knelt beside Seth and slipped his ring from his right hand.

No, I wanted to scream. Something inside me broke the second Seth was stripped of his wings. It was like having the wind knocked out of me, and I scrambled for my next breath. The beautiful feathery forms that flowed so elegantly from his back disintegrated and turned to mist. Angelica smiled.

"You have no idea how long I've been waiting to do that," she said.

Angelica grasped Seth's hand and flattened his palm, then formed a tiny orb on her fingertip. She used it to slice his skin and blood welled from the cut. My heart lurched when I understood what she intended to do.

"Please, stop!" Charlotte said. Her shape was a blur across the clearing, and she came to a halt in front of Angelica. "Take me; I'm the one you want."

Archer went to move but I held him back. Part of me wanted Angelica to take Charlotte and end it, but part of me knew it was already too late for Seth.

"That is noble of you," Angelica said in her sweet voice, "but I think I'd prefer this one, I can always come back for you. It might give you a bit of time to actually tell Grace the truth."

"Truth?" I looked at Charlotte, and in a single blinding moment I saw everything in her eyes. The box inside her head cracked open, and the revelation froze me in place. What I learned in those few seconds was enough for me to doubt and question everything I knew about myself, and enough for me to realise I couldn't trust anyone. I was so shocked I felt completely empty.

Angelica laughed, and the sound brought my attention back to Seth. I misted to try and save him, but I wasn't fast enough. Angelica smeared the stone in Seth's ring with his blood, then rose to her feet and held it out before her.

I took in the colour of Seth's hair, like straw, the shape of his face, the perfect curve of his chin—he looked so peaceful, and I shook my head in denial. This wasn't happening; I'd lost too much already. I could barely see the shape of his body as a cloud of his own essence engulfed it. The blackness swirled around itself, up into the air and into the onyx in his ring. Angelica's arm shook as the mist flooded into the stone, sucked in until there was nothing left. The ring's silver band glinted brightly in the moonlight, and the beautiful dark onyx surrounded by one sweeping angel's wing reflected Seth's imprisoned soul.

The moment Angelica left, I collapsed to the ground. The others came running to my side, and I glared up into Charlotte's dark eyes.

"How could you do something like this? How could you let a filthy creature violate you like that? An angel's soul is the purest that can be. I don't understand ..."

"What are you talking about, Grace?" Archer asked.

"Charlotte isn't what or who she says she is. She's been lying all this time. I was just too stupid to see it."

"I never wanted to hurt any of you," Charlotte said.

"Well, it's too late for that. I gave up everything to protect you. How could you let me do that knowing what I am and what I'd be losing?"

"Because I lost it, too."

"By choice! You didn't give me a choice!

"We all have choices—"

"You made me believe I had none." I got to my feet. "How many more have you created like Josh? What is he, anyway?"

"I don't know. That part I didn't lie about. He was the first human I've turned."

"I think you should leave," I said.

"Grace, no!" Archer said. "She can't leave."

"She has to; she's betrayed us and kept the truth from me." I shook my head. "How an angel can behave like this is beyond me."

"Angel? What do you mean angel? Grace, have you gone mad?"

"Lucas didn't seek out an innocent girl and change her, Arch. Charlotte made all of it up. She made him bite her. Charlotte was an angel, and now she's a vampire with a white soul."

Archer folded his arms over his chest and moved a little closer to me. He was smart enough to know I'd never lie.

"I'm sorry," Charlotte said. "But I needed your protection. Once the angels were after me, you were the only ones who could keep me safe."

"So you lied?" Archer asked. "You know Grace would have helped you anyway, if you'd just told us the truth."

I looked deep into Charlotte's eyes and found the box again. There was something she wasn't telling me.

"Did you let the vamps take your blood on purpose?" I asked.

"No, I would never do that. Grace, you have to believe that my reasons for becoming what I am were good—"

Archer coughed and mumbled some rude words under his breath.

"Right now I don't believe anything you say," I said.

"Lucas knew what my blood could do," Charlotte said. "He discovered its power after he turned me. Word got out, and the rest is history."

"He's still alive, isn't he?"

Charlotte didn't reply. She didn't have to. Her mind opened again, and she showed me more of what she'd been hiding. I relayed everything to Archer, and I could feel the anger growing inside him.

"Who are you? Just … go." He turned his back and walked towards the shed.

A crimson tear slid down Charlotte's cheek. Then she ran, leaving nothing but the bitter taste of betrayal behind.

44

GRACE
Two weeks later

The afternoon summer sun dipped below the horizon, turning the sky a beautiful peachy pink. I sat in my favourite place with my knees drawn up to my chest.

There had been no sign of Josh since the night of my birthday almost two weeks ago. I'd been coming to the outcrop at Hopetown Valley High every day in the hope that he might come, too, and that we could fix things. How would we fix things? There were so many questions, and each and every answer eluded me.

A gentle breeze danced around me, and my hair tickled my face. I tucked a strand behind my ear and remembered how Josh did that so many times in the week we were together. Was it really just a week? I felt as if we'd belonged to one another for an eternity. The past two weeks had been my living hell. Nothing compared to a broken heart.

I crossed my legs and put my hands in my lap, gazing out across the valley. I loved the peacefulness. A magpie cawed and took to the sky, silhouetted against the sunset, and I smiled. I knew the feeling of freedom that came with flight.

With a deep breath, I unclenched my right fist. My nails left little moon shapes on my skin. Gently, I moved the ring that lay on my palm until the tiger's eye stone faced me. The little white cloud that was Annie's soul moved slowly around inside it. I wasn't sure if she could hear me, but I'd been talking to her on my visits to the outcrop. Maybe she did know what I was saying and if so, at least I'd had a chance to tell someone my side of the story.

Archer thought my coming to the outcrop was a waste of time. He chose to wallow back at the shed. We hadn't seen Charlotte either since we'd told her to leave.

I thought we were all responsible for everything that had happened, but I couldn't help shouldering the blame. Ryan said he didn't care, but I knew otherwise. It was a front for his anger.

With a sigh, I picked up the little red velvet pouch that sat on the rock beside me and got to my feet. After popping Annie's ring inside, I pulled the strings tight and shoved it deep into the pocket of my denim shorts.

I sensed him standing behind me before I turned around, but at first I thought I was imagining it. When I did turn to face Josh, he took a step towards me. I needed to pinch myself, to wake up from my dream—it seemed impossible that what I'd been waiting for had finally come. He was real, and being in our place where we'd first kissed, where I'd showed him my true self—it was like we were back where we'd started. Only this time it was all wrong. I longed for that familiar pull between us, like two magnets drawing each other together, but it wasn't there.

He stood at the mouth of the trail and stared, his expression stony. The breeze whipped his dark hair across his forehead, and I drank him in—his face, his dark eyes, and the way his black T-shirt accentuated his broad chest. I forgot he was a vampire; for a moment he was just my Josh, and things were how they'd been before that terrible night.

The silence stretched out between us and we stayed like that long enough for our shadows to disappear with the sun. The near full moon rose in the sky, and Josh's pale skin glowed in its light. I'd almost forgotten how beautiful he was.

He took another step, but didn't speak. I longed to go to him, to wrap myself in his arms and drown myself with his kisses, but it wouldn't change anything. I knew Josh saw the hesitation in my eyes, but he came closer until we were near enough to touch.

"Do you remember what I asked you," Josh said, "when we came here after you fell?"

I nodded. "After my change you asked me if I felt any different up here ..." I brushed the hair back from his forehead. "Or in here ..." I gently laid my palm across his heart. I couldn't feel it beating but it was in there. Josh stared deep into my eyes. "And I said no. Then you told me everything would be all right."

Josh covered my hand with his. On his middle finger

was a simple silver band I couldn't remember seeing before. The familiar sparks prickled my skin when we touched, and although his skin was cool I could still feel the warmth of the love we'd had between us. With his other hand, he tucked my hair behind my ear and brushed a tear from my cheek with his thumb. Ever so slowly he leaned in and kissed me, forcing my mouth open with his tongue. I ran my hands up his neck and twisted my fingers into his hair. He pressed his palms into my back, and it was like neither of us could get enough. When Josh finally pulled away I tasted blood in my mouth.

Josh's fangs extended, and he looked crazed. He held me tightly, but I didn't flinch; protecting myself was not a problem.

"Grace, I'm sorry," he said. "You know I'd never hurt you."

"I know."

"I never had the chance to wish you a happy birthday." He reached into his pocket.

With one arm still around me, he handed me a small black box. I already knew what lay inside—an image of a delicate blue sapphire ring had come to the front of Josh's mind. He wore the ring's partner on his left hand.

"You didn't have to get me anything," I said, opening the box and staring at the sapphire.

"I got it before, you know, that night. I even had it engraved. Your name is on mine so you're with me always. You don't have to wear it but I hope you do."

"Thank you." I closed the box and pushed it into my pocket on top of the little red pouch.

"I love you," Josh said.

"I know that, too."

"Then why have you never said it back?"

I didn't know what to say. How could I tell him everything I was feeling in that moment? How could I say that it wasn't about him anymore, and there were so many other things I needed to worry about?

"Maybe we rushed into it," I said.

"Yeah, maybe we did."

"There is so much I wish I could undo."

Josh didn't reply. He simply held me and stared at the valley. I laid my head on his chest and listened to the silence of his heart.

Finally, I asked, "What are you going to do about your dad? Have you seen him since …?"

"No. I've been home, but I haven't let him see me. I'm not really sure what to do about that part of my situation. I've spoken to him like I usually do so he doesn't suspect anything is wrong."

"Hasn't the school called him?"

"It's amazing what I can do with my glamour," he said with a cheeky smile.

I wanted to ask him about Charlotte, if he'd seen or spoken to her, but I couldn't bring myself to say her name. Her lies made me so angry, and at that point I thought it better that I didn't know where she was.

Instead, I asked, "Do you feel any different? You know, after your change?" I closed my eyes and waited for his answer.

"I don't know, Grace," he said. "Yes and no. I'm not proud of what I did to Ryan. I was angry, and that anger really scared me. I do know the one thing that's constant is you."

I gently pulled away and untangled myself from his embrace, then walked a few steps to the edge of the rock. I wrapped my arms around myself. It wasn't cold, but I felt a chill run through me nonetheless.

"I can't tell you if everything will be all right, because I don't know that it will be," I said. "I have given up so much to protect the people I love. I've been betrayed, I've lost Emma, and …" I paused, not wanting to say Seth's name; it was too painful. "I thought I'd lost you. So please tell me how everything will be okay, because I don't have the answers."

"It's Seth, isn't it?"

My body stiffened at the sound of his name, and it hung between us like lead. I turned to Josh. His eyes were ice cold. I'd known it would come to this, but I'd been denying it. From the moment Josh had turned up, the subject of Seth was on the agenda.

"I have to go after him. I can't leave him trapped."

"Why, Grace? Why not?"

I couldn't believe he'd asked me that question. If Josh knew me as well as he thought he did, he wouldn't have needed to ask.

"Because no matter how much you hate him, he helped us. There is an eternity of history between Seth and me. I don't abandon my friends. And because he would do the same for me."

"Would he?" Josh said. "It seems he did a pretty good job of abandoning you all those years ago, when he fell."

"You don't know—"

"You love him," he said.

My words caught in my throat, and I couldn't go on.

I shook my head and pleaded, "Please don't do this."

I went to Josh and took his hand, entwining my fingers with his. I wished I could fly us away, I didn't care to what location, and anywhere would do. I wanted him, and I wanted us to be together, but that could never happen with Seth hanging over our heads.

"I know you won't give up until you find him. And I can't be here helping you. I can't stand beside you and watch as you search for your ex-lover," Josh said.

"Seth was never my—"

"It doesn't matter." He yanked his hand from mine. "I can't."

Suddenly, I felt cold, and all I wanted was Josh's arms around me, but he was angry and I couldn't blame him. I'd betrayed him once, and he wasn't sure if I'd do it again. It hurt, standing there being able to read him like an open book. If only I'd let him read me, too, he'd know things I could never possibly explain, but I wasn't ready to show him my past.

"Please hold me." I looked up into his dark eyes. He was thinking he would come here and end things quickly like he had with Abby; he wanted to rip the Band-Aid off and toss it over his shoulder and never look back. If only it were that simple. I moved closer and rested my head on his chest. For too long he stood there, arms by his side. When he finally did reach around and embrace me I sobbed, and he squeezed gently.

Josh lifted my chin and brushed my lips with his. "I'm leaving, Grace."

Those were words I didn't want to hear, and I shook my head in denial. Josh held me close to him and stroked my hair, trying to calm me. My body shook as the truth of what he'd said sunk in. He'd just come back; I didn't want him to leave.

"Where will you go?" I said.

"It doesn't matter. Maybe I'll follow Charlotte. I just know I can't be here with you."

For a few minutes I grappled with my thoughts, trying to find a way to make this work, but it couldn't. As long as I was looking for Seth, Josh couldn't be here, and giving up on Seth was not something I was prepared to do.

"How does the saying go?" Josh rested his forehead against mine. "If you love someone, set them free."

He let go and stepped back. My world suddenly felt smaller, colder, and less bearable outside his embrace. I wanted to scream, to close the gap between us that was quickly turning into a chasm, but I couldn't move.

"I'm setting you free," he said. "Go and find Seth, and when you're done, come back."

"I promise I will."

"Don't make promises you can't keep."

"Josh ..." I said, but I couldn't get the rest of the sentence out, and before I had the chance to take a step towards him, he was gone.

For what seemed like forever I stared at the mouth of the path, hoping he would return. After a while I took the small black box from my pocket and flipped it open. The ring inside was so beautiful. Carefully, I pulled it out. A flawless sapphire sat in the centre with a sparkling diamond on either side. I held it up to the moonlight, and the inscription on the inside of the delicate silver band simply read *Josh*. I turned it over in my fingers a few times then spotted something white sticking out of the box. Tucked under the black velvet cushion was a note, and I couldn't get it out fast enough to read it.

Dear Grace,
The past two weeks without you have been the hardest of my life. When I found you, I thought I'd found the one thing that made me whole, the missing piece to fill the space in my heart. Now, I am lost, and it's like the pieces don't fit together properly. I'm not walking away because I want to, but because I have to. We both have things we need to deal with, and it's something we can't do together. Hopefully when we reach the other side, our pieces will be re-worked and our broken hearts will fit back together. No matter what happens, I will always love you.
Josh x

I wasn't quick enough to catch the tear before it fell from my cheek and stained the piece of paper. Gently, I folded Josh's note along the creases, tucked it inside the box and pushed it into my pocket. I stared at the ring in the palm of my hand, trying to decide what to do. The moonlight made the silver shine and the sapphire twinkle. If I put it on I would be making a promise, and I needed to be sure I could keep it.

Tears stung my eyes as I slipped the ring onto my left hand, up and over the knuckle of my middle finger, until it sat perfectly in place.

"And I will always love you, Josh," I said.

If there was one thing I was good at, it was keeping my promises.

FIND OUT WHAT HAPPENS IN

FIGHT FOR ME

THE NEXT INSTALMENT IN
THE TATE CHRONICLES

READ ON FOR
A PREVIEW

1

SETH
The In-Between

I tumbled through the darkness, fighting something I couldn't see. When I tried to unfurl my wings, the scars on my back burned with the painful reminder of what I'd lost. My body twisted, enduring the relentless torture. I stopped. For a moment I was suspended in time, not moving with it or through it. Then everything moved around me, forming a powerful vortex that sucked me further into blackness.

When I came out the other side, thin tendrils of blue celestial fire bound my wrists and ankles. My feet pressed against a solid sheet of black, and millions of tiny lights filled the sky.

A beautiful angelic face—one I'd come to loathe—split the darkness. Her laughter echoed around us before falling away into nothing. Angelica stood before me,

dressed in her impractical white linen. She emanated light and glory.

"I'm going to have *so* much fun with you," she said, a sweet smile touching her lips.

I didn't answer. I didn't want to give her the satisfaction. Instead, I held her pale blue gaze for a moment, before turning away and staring at the floating lights.

"Pretty, aren't they?" Angelica said.

"Where are we?" I asked, attempting to hide the fear in my voice. For the first time since I'd renounced my god and fallen from Heaven, I was scared. Not of Angelica, but of what she could do to me, and to those I loved.

"I think you know where we are. In a place you should have been a long time ago ... Be thankful you're not still in here." She held up my creation ring—an angel's wing swept around the black onyx stone at the centre. A trace of blood marred the silver band.

"Why did you strip me?"

Angelica sniggered, and closed her fist around the ring. "You got in my way," she said. "And you stripped one of my closest friends."

"Then why didn't you bind me and send me into oblivion with the others?" I concentrated on the lights bobbing in the darkness.

"Oh, don't worry, I did bind you. But now I need you to do something for me."

"You're letting me go?"

"Not exactly. Everything comes with a price; you should know that by now."

I clenched my fists in an attempt to control my anger. I'd almost forgotten how infuriating Angelica could be.

Even when we were on the same side, when we'd been friends so long ago, she'd still annoyed me.

"What. Do. You. Want?" I struggled against my restraints.

Angelica walked towards me and didn't stop until our noses almost touched. "I want you to get me that ring. You're the only one who can free her."

"No chance," I said.

"Then your friends will pay."

Angelica conjured an orb of white light. She balanced it on her fingertips, twirled it until it got bigger and flattened out. With both hands, she moulded it roughly into a square, and with a flick of her wrist the makeshift screen stuck itself to the blackness, like a magnet. The kitchen of a terrace house came into focus. The place was a mess. Upturned chairs littered the floor. The table had been split, and the lounge slashed. Blood stained the walls. Angelica twirled her finger again, and the picture rewound, like an old VHS tape. I leant forward, staring at the moving image.

Charlotte and Josh battled with Angelica and some other angels I'd never met.

Angelica won.

Charlotte managed to flee, but Josh lay crumpled in a heap at Angelica's feet. If it had have been anyone else, maybe I'd feel sorry for him, but Josh was one of my least favourite people.

"Is he dead?" I asked.

"Not yet," Angelica said, smiling.

She clicked her fingers and Josh appeared beside me, like she'd shone a stage light on him. Celestial fire also bound his wrists and ankles.

He glowered at me.

The feeling was mutual.

Before we had time to verbally rip shreds off each other, Angelica conjured another orb. She hurled it at Josh and it landed in his chest, penetrating his body until it filled him with light. When the light went out, Josh was gone.

"What have you done to him?" I searched the darkness, but all I saw were the floating lights of fallen souls.

"Watch." Angelica pointed to the screen.

Josh lay on the side of a busy highway. A familiar huge steel bridge loomed over him. It had been a while since I'd stepped foot in Wide Island City.

Angelica clicked her fingers again and the screen fell away, breaking into glass-like shards before disappearing into the darkness.

"What did you do?" I gritted my teeth.

Angelica shrugged. "He no longer has any memory of anything that occurred in the past. Only his future is waiting for him. And think of the destruction he can cause, now he doesn't know who he is."

"You are unbelievable," I said. "You're supposed to be one of the good guys."

She laughed. "The time will come when I'll need you to unlock Annie's ring. Then, and only then, will I restore Josh's memory. You'll be staying here until then."

"What if I couldn't care less if he remembers anything?" I said.

"Then I will spend the rest of my existence making Grace's existence a living hell."

I was beginning to understand where all this was

coming from, but I wanted Angelica to admit it. I took a deep breath and stood perfectly still, levelling my stare with hers. Then I attempted to get inside her head, and discover what was really going on. Her block was strong. She walked back to me and smiled her sickly sweet smile.

"What do you really want?" I asked. There had to be more to it than unlocking Annie's ring. She needed me for something else, the desperation in her eyes proved it.

"I want you to suffer," she whispered.

"Why?" I yelled, making her flinch and step back. "Because I protected her? Because we almost defeated you?"

Angelica threw her head back and laughed. Her shoulders shook and she spread her arms wide. "Do not be fooled into thinking you could ever defeat me."

"Then why?" I asked again.

We stared each other down, neither of us wanting to be the first to look away. This time, I shoved my way inside her head, but she pushed me out with enough force to rock me on my feet.

"It's Grace, isn't it?" I finally asked. "Why do you despise her so much? What did she ever do to you?"

Angelica smiled. "It's actually your fault, really. I hate her because you love her."

2

JOSH
Four months later, early Thursday morning

Lilith found me in a ditch on the side of the highway, covered in filth and soaked with rain. I should've been dead. Actually, I was dead, just not in the conventional way.

I don't remember becoming a vampire, and I can't recall anything before Lilith. She seems to think I have amnesia by choice, but why would anyone *want* to forget who they are? When your memories are screwed, what do you live for? How do you go on when you don't know if there's anyone out there looking for you?

The driver's licence in my pocket told me my name was Joshua David Chase. My eighteenth birthday was a little over a month away, so I was forever frozen at seventeen. I came from the small country town of Flats End near Hopetown Valley, but what I was doing so far from home was a mystery. The only other things I'd had, apart from

288

the clothes on my back, were my phone and a silver ring. On the inside of the band was an inscription, one word: *Grace.* I couldn't remember anyone called Grace. I couldn't remember anyone at all.

I've called Wide Island City home for about four months, and I was glad to have Lilith show me the ropes. She'd taught me everything I knew about my kind. Who would've thought there would be so many rules when it came to being a vampire? She knows where to go, who to talk to and who to eat. When your food source walks around on two legs you kind of have to keep a low profile.

Vampires are killers, and I know that's what we're designed to do—it's how we survive—but each time I take a life it's like I lose a piece of myself. Lilith thinks that's crazy; we're made to drink human blood. We're creatures of the night, your worst nightmare, like Freddy Krueger only prettier.

Lilith gets a kick out of tormenting her subjects, but watching her do it makes me feel sick. The taste and smell of human blood is undeniably enticing, and when the frenzy takes over nothing else matters. You're in the moment, thinking it's so good you can't possibly get enough, but when you come out the other side, the blood leaves a foul aftertaste in your mouth—the taste of death.

From my seat on an alcove step halfway down a deserted lane, I watched as Lilith's long raven hair fell over her face. She had one thick, crimson streak in her fringe, as red as fresh blood. If I didn't have vampire eyes, the rest of her would have been hard to see in the dim light. Dressed entirely in black, she blended into the night.

Lilith knelt beside her latest victim, a pretty blonde

girl, probably about sixteen, and lowered her lips to the bare skin of her neck. The girl's eyes glittered under the moonlight, awash with terror. For a second I was excited, perched on the edge of the step, mesmerised by the scene before me. The girl screamed, splitting the night air and tearing me out of my trance.

Disgust engulfed me.

No one would come to help, even if they did hear her. In the city so many people surround you, but you're in fact completely alone.

Lilith laughed. Blood so dark it was almost black stained her lips, and I shuddered as it trickled down her chin. In that moment I hated her, and myself. I hated that she was all I had, and that she was all that I could remember.

"How does this not bother you?" I jumped up from the step.

"Josh, honey, don't get so worked up. What does it matter now, anyway? She's dead." Lilith stood and dropped the girl, whose head hit the asphalt with a thud.

I cringed and said, "Someone somewhere is going to miss her."

"Come on, baby, don't start with that again."

Lilith reached out and took my hand. She twirled herself in front of me and spun into my chest. We danced a few steps, face to face, down the lane. Lilith was tall; her long hair fell past her shoulders and her skin was pale, almost white. Her eyes were dark and haunted, accentuated by the eyeliner she applied every day. A small diamond stud twinkled in her nose, and a simple black velvet choker with a tear-shaped ruby hanging from the centre adorned her neck. A pink flush crept into her cheeks.

"Don't you get it?" she said. "We can do whatever we like. We are more powerful than any of them out there."

Lilith used to make the rules—not that everyone followed them—and she had been the leader of the city vamps for a long time. But I soon learnt that I'd stumbled into some sort of war. There was one vamp in particular I couldn't quite get my head around. He'd had a good shot at killing me once, but Lilith had gotten in his way.

Lucas was another of the city leaders. He and Lilith had some sort of history, but she never let on what it was. She never told me much of anything, really. Sometimes she was too secretive.

Lilith pressed her body against me then pulled back and ran her hands up my chest and over my shoulders. Unable to resist her, I nipped her on the neck and pulled her to me. She moaned as I ran my tongue over her smooth skin, finding her mouth. Her kisses were always intense, and I licked the points of her fangs. With vampire speed I pushed her up against the wall of the building, and she giggled. Lilith liked to play rough.

Amidst the passion and the heat, there hung a sadness I couldn't shake. Right then, Lilith was everything to me, but there had to be more to my existence than killing the homeless and the runaways. There had to be more to life than hiding out in abandoned buildings by day, and roaming the city streets by night.

"We should move on." I pulled away. She leant against the wall and sucked her bottom lip, her hair awry and her mouth smeared with blood. "If we stay still too long, they'll find us." Other vampires were not the only things we had to contend with.

The buildings around us muffled Lilith's laugh. "They don't scare me, Josh. They make it more interesting."

The angels and the hunters we were running from—although Lilith wouldn't call it running; more like avoiding—had been on us most of the time we'd been together. I wished they would leave us alone.

I watched Lilith for a moment as she headed down the lane, away from the city noise. I didn't know how old she was, but she looked around nineteen.

With one last glance at the dead girl on the ground, I followed Lilith up a rickety fire escape and onto the roof of an abandoned warehouse. When I looked over my shoulder, I caught a quick glimpse of something in the lane below—a flash of white.

The girl had been following us for a while, but no matter how hard I tried I could never catch sight of her face. I paused to stare at the spot where I thought I'd seen her, and willed her to come back into view.

"What's the matter, baby?" Lilith came to my side and peered over the edge of the building.

"It's nothing." I took her hand and led her across the roof.

The arch of the steel city bridge loomed in the distance, and the night darkened as the moon tucked itself behind a cloud. We were in the bad part of town where everything was either rusty, broken or beginning to fall down. It was the way we liked it, though—so many places to hide with no chance of being discovered.

"We need to get you something to eat," Lilith said. "Sorry I didn't leave you any. She tasted too good."

I leapt over the next laneway onto the opposite roof, watching as Lilith did the same. She soared gracefully through the air and landed beside me.

My phone vibrated in my pocket, and I pulled it out. The name 'Dad' flashed on the illuminated screen. I couldn't even remember my own father. The first few times he'd called after Lilith found me, I'd answered in the hope it would spark a memory. I'd gotten nothing. The sound of his voice was like any other human's. I'd pretended I was okay so he would leave me alone. After a while, I stopped answering. Our conversations never amounted to anything, so I didn't see the point. I hit *end* and shoved the phone into my pocket.

"Your father again?" Lilith asked. "And you still don't remember?"

I moved away from her and ran the length of the roof then dropped to the ground. I wasn't in the mood for the you-must-remember-something lecture. A tall chain-wire fence stood across the small city back street, and I climbed up and over it with ease. Lilith fell into step beside me.

Wind buffeted us as a passenger train rattled past; the lights inside turned the windows yellow against the grey metal carriages. I hunched over, stuffing my hands into the pockets of my dark jeans, and walked the path of the train tracks. The gravel crunched under the weight of my boots.

Being a vampire was something Lilith didn't think I was very good at. *You think too much,* she'd said to me once. Apparently I need to follow my instincts, but sometimes my instincts tell me this is all wrong.

293

Another train whooshed past, and the wind made my shirt billow out behind me. Lilith was right; I needed to eat. There was only so much of the burning in my throat I could handle. I stopped, tilted my head to one side and listened. Lilith's glistening eyes locked with mine and she smiled.

"Go on," she said.

The sound of long, deep breaths came from behind the bushes that lined the railway fence. Slowly, I walked over and pulled a branch back. The leaves rustled. Snores came from the pile of dirty rags and newspapers that lay at my feet. It wasn't the most appetising meal, but it would have to do.

As I sank my teeth into the homeless man's neck, I wondered if this was where I was meant to be.

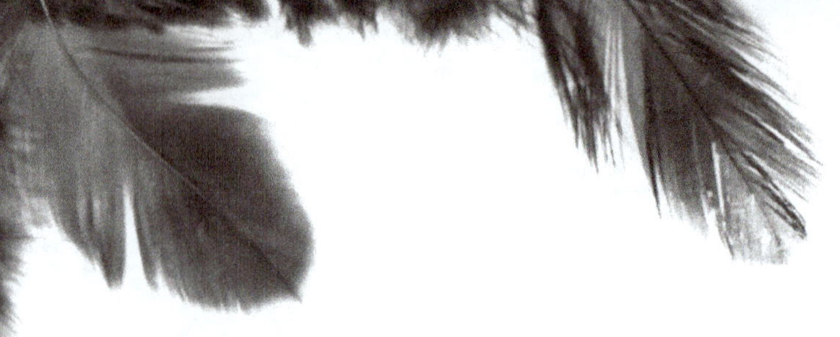

ACKNOWLEDGEMENTS

Writing is something I've always wanted to do, and when I discovered how much I enjoyed pounding the keys on my laptop, everything else seemed to take a back seat, including eating and sleeping.

I'd like to thank my wonderful husband, Brendon, and my two children, for their support and encouragement. Without them I would not have persevered when things weren't working out the way I'd seen them in my head. Their understanding is second to none, especially when I'm off in my make-believe world. Bren, you are my rock, and I love how you encourage me no matter what crazy thing it is I'm trying to do.

Thank you to my wonderful parents, to my brother, Paul, and sister-in-law, Kylie, and the rest of my family. Your on-going support is greatly appreciated. Sometimes a simple word of encouragement is all it takes to get the ideas flowing again.

My network of Facebook friends, thank you for enduring countless happy dances, left-field quotes, weird vampire addictions, cover proof questions, and crazy comments about my great and not-so-great moments on the road to publishing this novel.

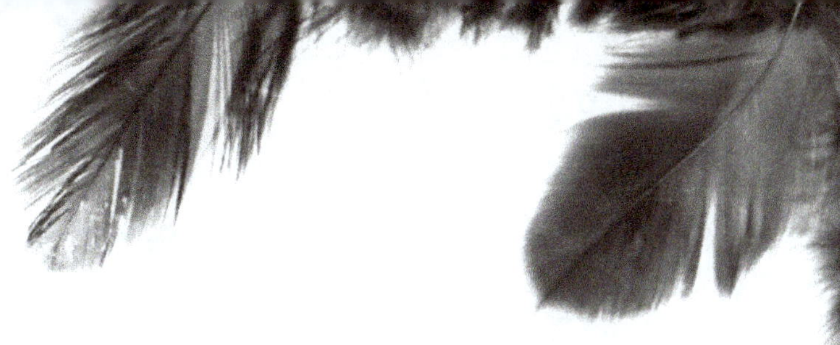

Thank you to the wonderful girls in my book club: Katrina, Lisa, Fiona, Jen, Meredith, and Caroline. Thanks to you I have read so many great books over the past few years that I would never have otherwise picked up.

Huge thanks to the team at NaNoWriMo for setting up a fantastic way of unleashing my creativity. The result at the end of the month may not be a literary masterpiece, but the challenge is all consuming, and the support network is fantastic.

Thank you to Anne for being one of the first to read *Fall For Me* in its early stages. I treasure our friendship, your unwavering belief in me, and your brutal honesty. Sometimes it takes another eye to see where you've gone wrong and put you back on the right path.

Thank you to Kylie for letting me chew your ear off about so many things. I love our long conversations over steaming hot cups of tea.

To my editor, Lauren McKellar, for revisiting this book and helping me fix all the things.

And lastly, a huge thanks from the bottom of my heart to Katrina: my beta reader, proofreader, and closest friend. Thank you for putting up with the seemingly endless versions of this novel, and never once complaining about reading it. Thank you for your honesty, loyalty and unfaltering encouragement. And thank you for being there right from the start.

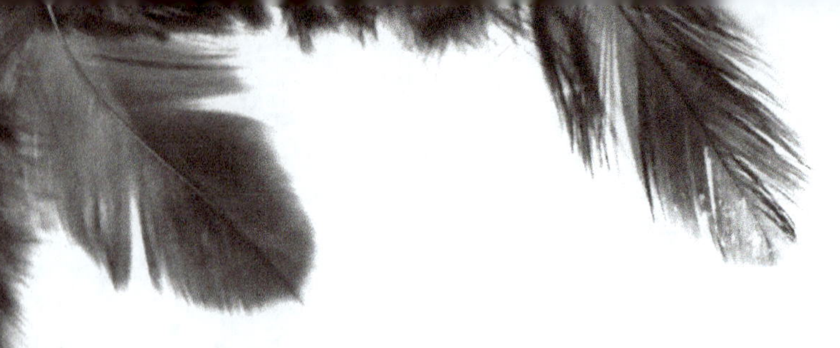

ABOUT THE AUTHOR

K. A. Last was born in Subiaco, Western Australia, and moved to Sydney when she was eight. Artistic and creative by nature, she studied Graphic Design and graduated with an Advanced Diploma. After marrying her high school sweetheart, she concentrated on her career before settling into family life. Blessed with a vivid imagination, K. A. Last began writing to let off creative steam, and fell in love with it. She has a Bachelor of Arts Degree from Charles Sturt University, with a major in English, and minors in Children's Literature, Art History, and Visual Culture. She now resides in the NSW countryside with her family and a menagerie of animals.

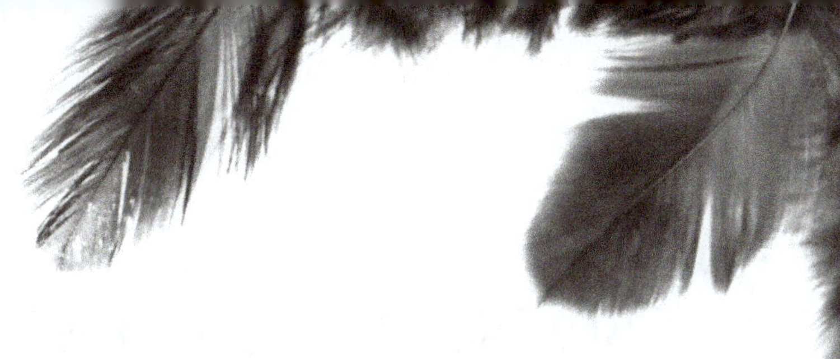

CONNECT WITH
K. A. LAST

**Scan the code to subscribe
to K. A. Last's newsletter.**

Website www.kalastbooks.com.au
Facebook www.facebook.com/KALastBooks
Instagram www.instagram.com/kalastbooks
Pinterest www.pinterest.com/kalast
Goodreads www.goodreads.com/KALast
Twitter www.twitter.com/KALastBooks

BOOKS BY K. A. LAST

YA Fantasy Fiction
Sacrifice – A Fall For Me Prequel
Fall For Me (The Tate Chronicles, #1)
Fight For Me (The Tate Chronicles, #2)
Die For Me (The Tate Chronicles, #3)
Immagica
The Lovely Dark
Ella and Ash (Happily Ever After, #1)
Chasing Neve (Happily Ever After, #2)
False Princess (Happily Ever After, #3)
Dance of Wishes (Happily Ever After, #4)
Winter Flame (Happily Ever After, #5)

YA Contemporary Fiction
Something (All the Things: part one)
Nothing (All the Things: part two)
Everything (All the Things: part three)
The Other Side of Me (All the Things: part four)

Non-fiction
A Novel Idea! Colouring Journal for Writers
A Novel Idea Workbook for Writers